SOPHISTRIES
OF
SUMMER DAYS

SOPHISTRIES
OF
SUMMER DAYS

JENNY LOFTERS

ISBN: 9780578403014

CHAPTER 1

The hurricanes came early to the island the year that the red-haired foreigner came to Naggo Head. The entire village echoed the news about the pretty young lady who arrived at Cross Road in an off-duty milk truck in the breaking dawn of a holy Sunday. It was said that the milk truck pulled up at Cross Road with the empty milk cans clanking in the back. A young, pale lady with hair as red as the setting sun climbed down from among the milk cans carrying a small, brick-colored tote bag, a small, greasy brown paper bag, and a straw hat with a purple ribbon wrapped around it. They said she walked up Naggo Head Road to the Rutherfords' abandoned pink mansion that was perched on top of Pill Hill.

Anyone who saw the stranger took great pride in telling the story. The storyteller with the sighting would take up station around twilight time at the customary gathering in the only grocery shop in Naggo Head.

Miss Zeppa, one of Naggo Head's two widows, extracted her money bag from her bosom, ordered a half pound of salt fish, and recounted that she had seen the foreigner in the seaside market, four miles away in Blue Bay. The foreigner wore dark glasses with golden trim on the round lenses, and the straw hat with the purple ribbon covered her head. She sauntered among the clothing stalls, lingering at Miss Mavis's stall the longest, and with painted fingernails on pale hands she kept touching a green, flared-skirted, sleeveless dress. The postmistress, Miss King, who had come in to buy a pound of flour mixed with cornmeal, and who was so dainty that she barely disturbed the air around her when she moved, dipped in a half curtsy, fingered the high lace collar at her throat, and whispered that the pretty stranger's name on the document she had shown at the post office was Maria White.

Someone else saw the stranger wearing a white night-gown and talking to herself on a bench in the moonlight in the Rutherfords' front yard late at night. Another caused a stir when she insisted that she had seen her that very same night and that she had been singing, not talking. Bro' Man took on the judgment and dismissed it at the top of his voice as "Inconsequential! Inadmissible!" since none of the storytellers could repeat a word of what the stranger said or sang. Bro' Man lived at the top of his voice.

They all agreed on one thing: the stranger spoke upside down, like all foreigners did.

The only place of retail and source of entertainment in Naggo Head was the grocery shop at the entrance to Mongoose Run. It was managed by Mr. and Mistress Ferguson, who had a penchant for serving and the burden to provide entertainment. The few hard-top wooden stools and benches were shifted around the shop by the regulars and customers on an almost hourly basis, their placement opposing the angle at which the brilliant sunlight hit the front of the shop. These stools served as thrones for the person with the current gossip or for the best storytellers. Someone would silence the gathering by saying aloud, "Let de story be tole." Bro' Man was the crowned king of storytelling.

⚓

I saw the foreigner for the first time on the bank of the Sweet River where it curved and narrowed behind Nanna's house. It was the day after my fourteenth birthday. I was just about to lie down in my favorite spot under the coconut tree in the afternoon shade when I saw her under the banyan tree a few yards farther down on the riverbank.

The faded, lavender, floral, short-sleeved dress she wore had a tightly fitted bodice, as if it were made for a smaller woman. Her curly, long hair was the color of the flaming sun setting behind the bamboo trees in Bamboo Walk. Her wide skirt was spread out around her on the grass as if she had taken the time to arrange it. Round, dark glasses with golden rims covered her eyes. One arm was thrown across her waist, and the other rested on a wide-brimmed straw hat at her side. The sunshine that filtered through the leaves of the banyan tree suffused her beautiful upturned face.

A frog warming itself in the sun on a rock near her leaped suddenly into the underbrush, disturbing the dried leaves and a nearby bird. The bird flapped its wings and maneuvered itself through the tree toward the sky, brushing the leaves. Startled, the foreigner raised herself up on her elbows, craning her neck and looking cautiously around her. I ducked out of sight and low into the fever grass and the fairy flowers, knowing then that she was a city person unused to the countryside, with its dense green bushes and small brown animals.

Satisfied that she was safe, the foreigner settled back onto the ground. She raised both arms above her head, crossing them slightly at the wrists, and then stretched her legs and torso languidly. She yawned sleepily and shifted her body to settle it further and more comfortably in the ground. A light breeze lifted one corner of her gauzy skirt. She had walked a long way, and there were two half-moon sweat spots under her small breasts, and large circles at the raised armpits. Immediately I imagined that she wore white cotton panties and that the crotch had a sweat spot. I rose quietly and sneaked away, carrying the shameful thought that had jumped from out of nowhere into my head.

With the faint lingering scent of the fairy flowers on my hands and thistle burrs on my dress, I left the riverbank, bemoaning the invasion of my bubble on the riverbank. I was thankful that the flowers were all dried on their stalks or lying on the ground, for it was said that if a child wandered alone into the woods and picked a fairy flower, that child would never be seen again.

But how had she happened to find the finest spot on the riverbank? I worried that I might never again lie in shaded solitude on the riverbank with an open book on my chest, sucking the sweet juice from a piece of sugarcane; that I might never again in privacy lift my skirt and tuck its hem in the waist of my underwear and then wander barefoot down to the water's edge to lift rocks and peer at a delicately sheer crawfish that had tucked itself away fearfully in the crevice only to flit away in an instant, leaving mud in its wake; that I might never again sit undisturbed under a broad-leafed tree for shelter from the fresh rain pouring from the skies, breathing the odor of dry earth turning to mud and listening to the stiff grass drinking itself full and plush.

I crept home to Nanna. Around this time in my life, I crept around a lot.

Nanna, my mother, and I lived on Mill Yard, near the grocery shop that was at the corner of Mongoose Run. Mill Yard was the only piece of level land on Naggo Head Road. Our four-room house was set far from the road on the very flat, circular piece of land. The land was flat and circular because at one time it had housed a large sugarcane mill with grinders that were propelled manually. My grandfather Papa Doc built the house from the ground up with weathered, unpainted boards from blue mahoe trees. It sat on hand-hewn log stilts that left a foot of air space and hard-packed ground underneath at the front of the house and expanded to two feet at the back end. The corrugated tin roof had not leaked once through all the hurricanes and storms. Smooth, naturally white stepping stones led in from the gateway up to six broad, solid, stone-slab steps that led up to the L-shaped veranda that ran along the front and the entire length of one side of the house.

I loved our home. Hibiscus, wild bluebells, and ferns hedged the circular front yard, where dark green, tightly curled grass covered the ground like a low carpet. A vegetable garden grew parallel to the long sides of the veranda: okras, pumpkins, sugarcane patches, avocado trees, banana trees, breadfruit trees, and eggplants. A footpath led through these trees down to the chicken coop and farther down to the bottomland to the banks of the Sweet River. The latrine and the roofless bathhouse were off on the other side of the house.

We lived close to the earth in Naggo Head. The majority of the residents earned their living off the land, with their hands and their backs. All mechanizations were man or animal powered. The light sources were the sun, the moon, firewood, and kerosene lamps. The firewood, water buckets, mules and carts, mortars and pestles, water wells, and oil lamps provided us with as much comfort as fuel, faucets, and electrical energy did for others.

It was said that Nanna was a descendant of the island's native Indians. There were two kinds of Indians: the gentle, peace-loving, farming and fishing kind, and the warlike kind with the most feared warriors. Nanna belonged to the second kind.

I never knew Nanna's age; I never asked. All I knew was that she was on her third set of teeth and that my mother, who was the only survivor of two siblings, had been a late child. From over-hearing bits and pieces of adult conversations, I had learned that she was the second-oldest citizen in Naggo Head behind the post-mistress's husband, and he was eighty-six. Nanna became a widow when I was eight years old. One day my grandfather Papa Doc was wearing his favorite old straw hat to shade his head from the sun as he went around his vegetable garden picking gungo peas and putting them in the straw basket he carried over his shoulder, and the next day the sunlight went out and he was stretched out on a table in the sitting room with his toes pointing up, a block of ice on his stomach and pennies on his closed eyelids. His nostrils were vast and dark, and I wondered if they had made a mistake in thinking that he was no longer breathing the air.

Nanna's grieving for her husband took the form of preparation for her own passing. No one was really sure when she did it, but my mother and I discovered that she had written our names on pieces of paper and placed them under her cherished cups and saucers, ceramics, and vases. She placed the names in the few books that she owned; she pinned the names to her best linens. She washed and ironed the dress she wanted to wear to her grave and placed it in a drawer with a pair of stockings, shoes, a hat, and a pair of white gloves. The navy-blue shoes were polished and buffed.

My mother and I often sneaked around the house looking at our inheritance—namely, whose name was pinned to what or was under what—without having a sense of the inevitable loss. This was a game to us. Papa Doc had been ill, but I had never heard Nanna complain of a headache or of exhaustion. Perhaps this was why I had never thought of her leaving us or passing away to some other place.

By no stretch of the imagination could we think of waking up to a new day without Nanna's sweet face and patient voice giving direction, steering, guiding, and teaching.

Chapter 2

A few days later, Teacher Vance took center stage in the grocery shop around twilight and proudly professed that the contents of the greasy paper bag the foreigner was carrying when she had arrived at Cross Road had been a coco bread and a beef patty. The driver of the truck had a sister who lived over in Pidgin Cove and who sold spices in the Blue Bay market at the stall next to Pootus, who lived in Naggo Head. The milk truck collected fresh milk from farmers at the western end of the island and transported it back to the dairy factory in the capital town of St. Ann's Town, which most of us called just plain Town.

At this revelation, Bro' Man took center stage.

"A small tote bag, a greasy brown paper bag, and a straw hat? Never get too involved with or do any long-term business with anyone who does not have many material possessions, no matter how little they cost. Stay far from them; it is unnatural. It is the nature of humans to gather stuff around them. A man without things seems always on the verge of committing suicide because he does not have enough to anchor him to life. It is possessions, not people or money, that most often keep man from taking his life. Look at the homeless people who linger around the Queen Victoria statue in Town. In any big city, they walk around by the hundreds hauling bundles of stuff. How many of them do you hear of killing themselves? None."

Bro' Man ought to know, because he was considered by all in Naggo Head to be good at speechmaking and book learning. It was widely believed that he had traveled abroad several times by sea, had been a soldier in an army overseas, and had worked as a special constable in the police force in the capital town of our island. Some believed that he had been involved in all kinds of strange activities overseas, some of them punishable by law. Others believed that he had once been a barrister, but no one questioned him or investigated it. This information was not important to the folks in Naggo Head. It was never about how someone earned his living.

Bro' Man was tall, well over six feet, and thin; he walked with toes pointed outward and with a slight favoring of the right foot. He had a face and head that were scraped clean of hair except for two rambling patches of eyebrows over shockingly baby-round, jet-black eyes set close to his nose. He was always dressed in a tailored pinstripe vest over white cotton shirt and sharply creased khaki pants, with the chain of a pocket watch attached to a front button. The walking stick that he wielded jauntily had a highly decorated head, was a compulsory accessory to his wardrobe, and was a wealthy source of conversational topics for him while he sat on a bench in the grocery shop and drank from the cap of a thermos that everyone knew did not hold coffee or tea. The more filled up Bro' Man became with the drink from his thermos, the more erect his vertebrae got until his chest was the foremost part of his body. He was never seen falling-down drunk; no matter how much he drank from the thermos, he was only near drunk.

I never figured out whether *Bro' Man* was short for *Brother Man* or *Brown Man*. At the time, that information was not important to me. It was also rumored that he had a tattoo of either a pirate's head or a half-naked woman on his back. No one was sure which, and no one had the courage or the inclination to ask.

He was married to a beautiful and real Indian lady. We knew she was a real Indian because she spoke upside down, unlike the other Indians we knew. They were a childless couple, and most of the adults in Naggo Head had their own opinion why. Bro' Man, in one of his near-drunken states, had once declared among the group of men that Miss Priyanka was a genius by day and a beauty by night. "When I met her, she was as pale as the lotus blossom," he had boasted. "The lotus blossom blooms only at night."

And when one of the men in the group had said Miss Priyanka looked like an angel, Bro' Man had suddenly grown quiet. He had mulled this over for a while and then stated solemnly, "The trouble with angels, my friend, is that they are better off in heaven than here on earth. One gets the feeling that soon they will spread their wings and fly away. To keep an angel from flying away, one must be prepared to rip her wings off."

When people said Bro' Man had the most brains in Naggo Head, I would imagine his head full of curly gray brains, with all others having mostly vacant space. Then my vacant space would begin to fill up mysteriously with thoughts and ideas.

⋏

That Sunday afternoon, Naggo Head's midwife, Sister Lady, visited with Nanna. Sunday afternoons were visiting time. The adults took turns walking to one or two neighbors' homes and staying for a while. The children at the visited house showed respect by huddling to one side and were seen but not heard.

My beloved nanna once told me that my mother had been fourteen years old when Sister Lady, on one of her regular evening visits, had told her she was "dumb loud." My mother had picked up Sister Lady's walking stick, which was resting on the veranda rails, and had used it to put a knot on the side of Sister Lady's head. My mother had never said much after that, not even when she had been five months pregnant with me and Nanna had wept with shame and asked her who had done this terrible thing to her.

She had given birth to me at exactly two minutes after midnight on a Wednesday and had shocked Sister Lady, the midwife, three times: first by not making a cry of pain during her long labor, then with my skin complexion, and then when with gasping breath she had said, "Mi naming har Cherrimina."

Nanna had said Sister Lady had rolled her eyes upward and then sideways before she had cried out, "Lawd 'ave mercy *h*upon dis pickney soul! She *h*ah mulatt*ah*! Cherrimina? What kind *h*of name *h*is dat? Sound like bird food." Besides the seaside town three parishes over, at the southern point of the island where the Germans had settled when they had arrived years before, the name "Cherrimina" and my skin complexion were nonexistent in Naggo Head and at that end of the island.

In one of our warm and precious talks, Nanna had told me that she had never complained about my name because she had named my mother Mary for her Christian name and Mary for her middle name. She had said that the first Mary had been from the Bible, and the second Mary had been for her second baby, who had died in infancy. Everyone in Naggo Head knew my mother as Mary Mary, but I am sure they all thought it was just a pet name or an endearment. However, I was the only one who knew that "Mary, Mary, Quite Contrary" was Nanna's favorite nursery rhyme.

I heard it said many times that I had not gotten many of my mother's traits but that I had gotten her silent stillness. No one except Nanna knew of the multitude of thoughts and ideas that I carried around in my head. I often imagined someone taking off the top of my head and all of my stored-up thoughts and ideas flying out in abundance as if they had wings. I felt smartest and brightest whenever I was lying alone under the coconut tree on the riverbank reading a book.

The knot that my mother had put in Sister Lady's head many years before would swell up occasionally, so Sister Lady claimed, and my mother's punishment was to massage it for her. The knot was swollen that Sunday, and my mother was massaging it. The newspaper on Nanna's lap on top of her Bible had a photograph of the royal family under the headline "George VI and Elizabeth Crowned in Abbey."

"Mi see sign *h*of 'ow different de two princess dem is," Sister Lady bellowed. I had always secretly thought she was hard of hearing because of how loudly she spoke and how she cocked her head to one side as if trying to eavesdrop on someone's digestive system.

She laughed heartily. "Princess *H*elizabeth sit prim *h*an' pay *h*attention while Princess Margaret Rose yawn *h*an' squirm. *S*he *h*even yawn right *h*at de *h*archbishop *h*of Cantabury?"

"Keep in min' dat Elizabeth is eleven years old an' Margaret Rose is six an' a half," Nanna said.

"Dey get outta bed seven t'irty dat mahning," my mother threw in.

Nanna and my mother went to pour glasses of lemonade and left Sister Lady and I on the veranda. She picked up the newspaper from the chair, spun it around in several directions, ended with it upside down, and then slapped it back down on the chair.

"'Ow *h*is school, Cherriminah?" Sister Lady asked after a few more minutes weighted down by silence.

"School fine, Sistah Lady, ma'am," I whispered.

She slid a thumb and forefinger of one hand down the corners of her mouth and wiped away froth.

After a few more minutes, she sucked her breath in through her teeth, stomped her feet, turned down the corner of her mouth, and muttered into the silence, "Spokesman fi de dead." And I noticed that she grabbed a firmer hold on her walking stick immediately after the words left her lips. I got up and walked away because I thought more kindly of people when I was away from them.

She called after me, "Where yu going, gurl?"

"Mi have somet'ing to do, Sistah Lady, ma'am," I replied.

"Wha' could yu 'ave to do? Plait sand *h*an' stone breeze?"

I did not reply; she muttered, and I caught only the last part: "walk like a disable' nanny goat."

It was at the exact moment that I realized how powerful my silence was. My silence had the power to take people out of their comfortable and familiar sphere and render them insecure and anxious. My silence had a language of its own. It was a weapon. What I did not say had the potential to be more powerful than what I did say.

I told no one about my sighting of the foreigner on the riverbank.

Chapter 3

The annual summer-holidays shindig was held that Saturday afternoon in the primary school yard at Cross Road. I sat on benches piled in tiers of two in a corner of the school yard and watched the colorful merrymaking with, but apart from, the other youngsters.

Cross Road was named above its status. It was not a place where two roads crossed; it was really just a T-junction where the stony Naggo Head Road met the paved main road that led into the large seaside town of Blue Bay, the capital of our parish. At Cross Road, the Baptist church, the primary school, the bakery attached to a grocery shop, a small clinic, a small library, and the postal agency served several surrounding villages. On Saturday evenings enterprising men and women from Naggo Head and surrounding villages set up stalls along the main paved road.

It was one of the main milk-truck stops every weekday morning on its daily round. Men would get out of bed before dawn to milk their cows and carry the foaming, warm milk in cans to wait in line at Cross Road and sell their milk to the truck. The truck with its huge clanking milk cans in the back would signal the start of the day with the only hustle and bustle heard in the area besides the Saturday evening shindigs and Sunday morning Baptist church bells.

Bulla, the tallest and most handsome man in several surrounding villages, strutted around like a rooster, in a clean white shirt. He wiped the beads of perspiration from his face with a white handkerchief. Other men wiped the perspiration from their foreheads with a thumb, which worked like a car's windscreen wiper on a rainy day.

It was at this dance that I saw the foreigner for the second time. The leaf-green sleeveless dress she wore, set against her red hair, seemed to light up the school yard. She swung a little green handbag carelessly, smiled at everyone, and swayed off time to the calypso beat. No one seemed to want to take time out of their merrymaking to stare at her today. Then I saw Bulla approach her and whisper in her ear, and they moved to the edge of the boogying crowd. A few minutes later, they were lost among the gyrating bodies.

I had my first taste of jealousy, and it was bitter. Bulla was the first man I had absolutely adored with all the energy and blood in my teenage body. His was the name that echoed in my head several times during the day, and he was the first one to turn my shyness to crippling shyness. The sight of him sitting in the back pew at church was enough to make me unable to say my name. Bulla was a preacher's child gone bad, and in Naggo Head that was on par with the Antichrist.

Bulla had not yet gone completely bad, but most people could tell that the devil already had him by the shirttail. It was he whom I thought of late at night before I fell asleep—not shameful thoughts but thoughts of smiles I would give him, of sly peeks that I would take of him that Sunday in church, of me walking up to him after church service and voicing my intelligence. Oh, why was I incapable of light, breezy conversation? Why? Why? When would a man pull me toward him and whisper in my ear? Would I ever have what it took? If yes, when? When? If no, why?

Bulla and the foreigner appeared again, bobbing up and down among the dancers. Bulla drew her close to him, and she went into him easily. It was at that moment I knew that any man who wanted to lay claim on my heart and body must walk with a swagger, be daring and aggressive, and be able to pull me boldly toward him.

About an hour later, Bulla walked past the pavilion, sucking fiercely on a dewy bottle of cola. He had a big wet patch of bright green at the stomach area of his white shirt. Just then the pavilion seat jerked, and someone with fierce body heat sat next to me. It was the foreigner. She fanned herself languidly with her green handbag.

"I saw you on the bank of the stream," she said to me. Her voice was slow and breathy. There was a wet, dark patch at the stomach area of her green dress.

I did not speak.

She continued to speak in the tone of voice of someone who was being ignored and did not mind—perhaps of someone who was used to being ignored.

"You walked away quietly before I could say hello to you. Why?…Do you live in the house on the stream where I saw you?…How can anyone not want to move to this music?…Don't you want to dance?…Can you dance?"

By this time, I could not have answered her even if I wanted to. I was stunned by her eyes. They were gray—so gray they looked like slow-moving smoke—slow-moving and sad eyes, with long-lashed, hooded lids that would slam shut just before she looked away. I had never seen eyes so sad and gray. And so I began to talk. I could always talk around sadness. It was excessive delight and unprovoked malice that rendered me soundless. Or perhaps my spanking-new and untarnished jealousy had given my voice its credentials.

"Dey seh yu from 'Merica."

"They say that? What do you say?"

"Mi say de same."

"I'm from the state of Virginia, USA."

"Dey say yu get snow in 'Merica."

"Some places."

"Dey say 'Mericans live in tall buildings on top of one another."

"Some places."

"Can you ice-skate?"

"No."

"Sweet River."

"What?"

"De stream is called Sweet River."

"Oh."

"Dey say Sweet River is de only river on the island dat run from east to west."

"Oh."

"Why did you come here?"

"What else do they say?

"Dey say you either a fugitive running away from de law or jus' plain crazy in de head."

"What do you say?"

I did not reply. I had not yet decided.

"Be careful of 'They say.' Douglas Malloch says he's the biggest liar in the world."

"Douglas Mahlack? Who he?"

"A poet."

"I say you jus' want some peace an' quiet."

She did not reply immediately. Instead she slammed her eyelids shut in slow motion, turned her head, and looked far off into the horizon before she spoke again.

"My name is Dove. What's yours?"

"Cherrimina."

"Very pretty name."

"Sistah Lady say it sound like bird food."

"Sounds like a red, juicy berry far up in the treetop that all the birds fly down out of the sky just to take a closer look at. I shall call you Cherry."

Just then Bulla swaggered up to the pavilions. He paused, smiled, nodded at her, ignored me, turned, and walked away. The dye on his white shirt was now dry but still green.

Dove rose from her seat and started down the rows of seats after him.

"See you by the Sweet River, Cherry."

"Cherrimina," I called after her.

My grandmother told me many things when we were alone.

"Always tell people yu name is Cherrimina. Yu hear mi, chile?"

"Because why, Nanna?"

"Because Cherry is common, an' you special," she said. "Always remembah dat."

She said to tell her if Sister Lady called me any names that I did not like. I did not tell her many things about Sister Lady because there are some things people who love you just do not want to hear, or should not hear. I did not tell her that Sister Lady had mumbled something about "dripping vanity" the day she saw me sitting on the front steps brushing and drying my hair in the sunshine—not even about the time she had asked me if I were stricken with galloping dumbness.

The few times I had told Nanna of Sister Lady's comments, she had told me to try harder to make friends with her—to try to think of something nice to say to her. Don't just sit there with your hands in your lap; think of something you both have in common, and make a light comment. Nanna had said that I should reach out to Sister Lady because some people are bound so tightly within themselves that everything outside of that wrapping is considered foreign. She had said that they are afraid of anything or anyone that is too different from them.

Sister Lady lived alone on Bird Mountain, about a hundred yards up the road from Nanna. She was the only midwife in the entire surrounding western villages. She traveled on her bicycle with a black leather bag strapped to the carrier at the back.

She was younger than Nanna and still possessed a few signs of a good-looking, voluptuous young woman. Her full bosom had now settled into a comfortable relationship with her waistline, and I was unsure if the waistbands of the skirts she wore were meant to hold the garment on her body or to keep her bosom from falling below her waist. The cotton headscarves with the edges unraveled, which she wore low on her brows, seemed to be the only bit of style or color she had in her scant wardrobe.

Bro' Man told a story several times about him and Sister Lady that one half of me doubted was true and the other half hoped was true. As a boy, Bro' Man had spent summer holidays in Naggo Head with friends of his grandmother. They were next-door neighbors and children playing when one day Bro' Man, whose government name was Harold, had accidentally tapped Sister Lady on the head with a hammer. She had run crying to her mother.

"Mama," she had wailed. "'Arry take de 'ammer an' 'it mi *h*on mi 'ead." Her mother had yelled back at her, "*H*emphasize yu *h*'s, yu *h*idiot *h*offspring."

Bro' Man said that Sister Lady had a bedpan view of the world. I never figured out what that meant, but I wrote it in my notebook. I was never unkind to her, nor was I kind. Mainly I just thought that her unprovoked malice sprung from her seeing life forcing its way through too many naked private parts. I made a vow then that, to keep her from seeing mine, I would never have a baby.

⋏

When it is dark, silence sits very awkwardly in itself. Darkness amplifies noise, and sometimes this noise attacks darkness, rendering it tumefied and terrified, and then swallows it whole.

All of Naggo Head knew that something peculiar was about to happen. Mother Woman took another one of her middle-of-the night excursions up and down Naggo Head Road, bestowing prophesies that resonated throughout. It was widely believed that she could see into the future; that she was a fortune-teller, a seer, a prophet; and that she could sense when Death would snatch someone with his three-pronged pitchfork and when the stork would swoop down on Naggo Head. Some believed all of that, but Bro' Man said she was the Antichrist.

She was rarely seen during these dark hours of excursions because no one dared, or wanted, to look out the window at her, but it was rumored that she was dressed always in white: a white dress, a white turban with pencils stuck in it, and a white pipe gripped between her teeth. The younger residents of Naggo Head believed that she floated above the ground during these trips because no one had ever heard the gravel on Naggo Head Road shifting under her feet. She was a big-boned woman, with a powerful baritone voice that she dragged like a dagger hidden under a dark, wet cloak over us from one end of Naggo Head to the other end, muting all other night sounds and staining the darkness. I had always imagined that everyone lay quivering with breaths held, hoping and praying that the omens were meant for someone else.

"Mark dese words! Yu going to hell in a han'basket!" Mother Woman hollered into the night as if her words were a lance and the darkness a coat of mail.

Because darkness and sleep can confound one's sense of direction, I could not tell if she was coming up from the Cross Road or coming down from the top of Naggo Head.

"Foreignahs! Infidels! No one can escape it. Turn yu roll! Turn yu roll! Turn yu roll! Repent! Repent! Yu can run, but yu can't hide. If yu run like lightning, yu will crash like t'under! July people ah savages. Cut dere veins, an' yu will find ice watah instead of blood. As dey get oldah, dey get coldah."

It was widely believed that those who suspected that the premonitions were about them would get out of bed and turn around three times as she had commanded. The elders in our village must have discussed Mother Woman's warnings, but I never heard them. And while these recurring nighttime episodes were eerie, I did not worry about them.

Chapter 4

We had only one thief in Naggo Head, and for months, he was a mystery. No one knew who he was. All anyone knew was that his skill for climbing trees in the dark was extraordinary, and so was his penchant for other residents' prized fruits or produce. He had picked and eaten the Fergusons' large and juicy Bombay mangoes and piled the peels and seeds under the tree. Miss Ferguson kept the pile under the tree for weeks and would call down from her hilltop home to every passerby she saw on the street to come up and look at the pile and at the tree that had been molested. He had climbed another neighbor's sweetsop tree, picked and eaten the fruit, and left the seeds and some unripe sweetsops in a pile under the tree.

This mystery thief had terrorized the whole of Naggo Head until the night he went to Dadda Brooks's Old Stump property to steal his jelly coconuts. No one, and certainly not the thief, knew that Dadda Brooks had been waging all-night watches for weeks in support of his jelly coconuts. His watching paid off when the shadowy thief crawled over the fence one dark night and quickly jumped on to the tallest coconut tree and skittered up its side on all fours.

Dadda Brooks sneaked up, thrust his machete point, sharpened edge upward, into the coconut tree, and called out: "Get you t'ieving a-double-s outta mi coconut tree." The thief began to shimmy down the tree at lighting speed. Suddenly the moon slid from behind a cloud, and the machete's edge glistened in the moonlight and caught his eye just in time for him to come to a dead stop about two inches from the sharpened steel edge.

The next day the elders in Naggo Head gathered around the thief in the back room of the grocery shop, and they all said they knew how to fix him. A group of curious children had gathered in front of the shop, joyful that it was someone else in trouble with the elders and not them. I was at my favorite listening spot at the backside of the shop, but this time I had climbed the tree to try to get a better view through the missing slat in the tiny window.

Sister Lady blamed the Fergusons for corrupting the thief by putting him into long trousers too soon. She offered to cut the legs off the trousers that they had passed down to him. Old Man Egypt offered to whip him with a wet rope, which caused Mistress Ferguson to lift the hem of her apron and bawl into it. Nanna advised everyone to be kind, and she quoted a scripture from the Bible. Old Man Egypt tried to be kind and suggested they tie the thief down in the graveyard for one night instead—everyone knew that Bull's tombstone was just barely holding him down in his grave.

Hurry Hurry fed the thief mugs of rainwater from the wooden bucket outside and kept asking him why he did it. Hurry Hurry spoke fast, walked fast, and breathed fast. No one could talk to him with eye-to-eye contact because of his rapid-fire movements and speech. It was rumored that he ate his Sunday morning breakfast on Saturday night so he could be first in church on Sunday morning. He sang in the choir and was always the first to finish the hymns. He was an impatient man, and when he had to slow the pace of his thought process to match others', he became excited or frustrated.

"Wha…make…yu…do it…bwoy?" he asked the thief, beating his right fist in his left palm to coincide with each word, the usual action that accompanied his frustration.

Mr. Mackie persuaded the others to take pity on the boy, since coming so close to having his buttocks split up the middle and then soiling his pants were enough punishment. After this was agreed upon by all, Mr. Mackie wrote it down in the lined, dog-eared notebook that he carried around with him, in which he made note of all his good deeds, which he was sure would be in his ledger when he arrived in heaven.

Finally, Bro' Man spoke. "Ugh!" he snorted. "Short pants, no. Wet rope, no. He's becoming a man. His nature is rising. He is having urges, manly urges." He had barely finished speaking before the women started to run through the tiny curtained doorway of the back room toward the front.

Bro' Man turned toward the men and said, "Gentlemen, let's have a talk with this boy about the birds and the bees." The sudden scuttling of the men's feet joined those of the women's scrambling on the wooden floor toward the front of the shop. Sensing danger in this furious scurry, and spurred by instinct, I shimmied down the tree from my listening post and sprinted through the trees toward home.

The thief's name had been Alphanso before this incident, but when Bro' Man declared that Alphanso had come from the Barabbas stock, the name Barabbas stuck. A few days later, a small article in the newspaper read "Fruit Thief Mystery Solved—No Jail." His close encounter with the sharp edge of a machete had put an end to this thieving.

Barabbas was an orphan taken in by Mr. and Mistress Ferguson, the shopkeepers, when he had been sixteen years old and a long way from clean. It was said that his ancestors were the Maroons that had settled in the mountainous regions in the middle of the island, and he had arrived wearing only a pair of patched trousers about two sizes too small and supporting a three-foot tapeworm that he had passed after Mistress Ferguson had purged him with her herbal medicine. He slept in a small room at the back of their grocery shop, worked in the capacity of a watchman, and did odd jobs around the shop and the village during the days. The narrow space at the back of the shop had a small bed covered with a mud-colored bedsheet and partitioned off from the front of the shop by a cotton curtain panel the dun color of a rat bat.

After the machete incident, Barabbas became humbled and spent his spare time running errands and doing chores around the village, especially for the victims of his debauchery. On Friday nights, he rode his bicycle the four miles into Blue Bay to the movie house, and early Saturday mornings whoever's kitchen he visited would hear the entire movie, word for word, as he ate with the family.

He always made a small contribution of food to the family's breakfast menu the evening before. He would stop by their kitchen on his way home from the fields, and from the crocus bag slung over his shoulder, he would pull out perhaps a bundle of lush, leafy callaloo or a handful of young, green bananas, a few pods of ackee, a few ounces of handmade coconut oil in a small earthenware jug, and sometimes even a few chopped-up stalks of the juiciest, softest sugarcane on the western end of the island.

If I had to choose one word to describe Barabbas in a physical sense, it would be *taut*. Not tense, not jittery, just taut. From laboring in the fields under the blazing sun, his stomach muscles were tight, his bicep muscles wiry. His lips were always stretched tautly over his teeth, making it difficult for one to notice his expression changing from smiling to annoyance—that is, if it ever changed. His clothes were skintight, always about a size and a half too small. Even his hair was tight; it was curled tightly and low on his head, and I don't think it was ever necessary for him to get a haircut. The effort that he put into everything he did, combined with the boiling sun, frequently left him with his shirt sopping wet. When I was younger, I thought that his shirt was constantly wet because he kept falling into Sweet River.

In another sense, he was self-contained without a lock and key, bandaged yet not broken, controlled without the harness and bit. He was airtight and watertight. From the minute Barabbas met a stranger, he took charge of getting to know and liking that stranger and getting the stranger to know and like him. And at this he usually succeeded because he truly was an agreeable fellow, and there was never a chance in his mind of anyone's not liking him or of his not liking anyone.

Chapter 5

This Saturday morning, Barabbas was sitting on a bench in our kitchen, telling a story between sips of steaming coffee from a tin cup, mouthfuls of hot cornmeal porridge with cinnamon, and bites of moist fried flour dumplings.

The kitchen was always warm and cozy at meal times. Narrow wooden steps from the pantry at the back of the house led down to the detached kitchen, which had a wood-burning fireplace built in one corner. Cuts of meat or freshly caught fish would hang stiff and brown from twines in the ceiling above the fire. Two small, low wooden benches lined one side of the walls; hanging woven baskets used as storage lined another.

Barabbas's favorite movies were Westerns with Indians and cowboys, but this day he was telling about an Asian horror movie that he had seen at the movie house owned by an Asian family in Blue Bay. I had heard that the movie house had long wooden benches like the pews of a church and that only half of the building had a roof. The covered half had a more expensive ticket price, and the uncovered half was closer to the screen, cheaper, and called the "fowl roost." Barabbas rode the four miles on a bicycle and always had only enough money for the fowl roost.

"Dis is a movie from ancient Jahpan or someplace over dat side of de worl'," he began, "'bout a man name Floda."

"Floda?" my mother asked.

"Yes, Mary Mary," Barabbas replied. "Wha' kinda name is dat? It soun' inside out."

Nanna, as usual, munched her breakfast and listened to his story with a stoic face. Going to the movie house was not Christian-like, but she liked a good story, especially with her morning coffee. I, in awe of anyone who could travel all the way to Blue Bay and anyone who had seen a movie, hung on to his every word.

"It start wit' a ole man crawling on his belly t'rough the dark woods. Not a star in de sky…" And so, alternating between half man and half eating machine and half eating machine and half storyteller, he entertained us.

It went like this: one cold, windy night, a sickly thin man crawled on his belly to a small house in a remote village in the countryside. He scratched weakly on the front door. His long beard and hair were matted. When he spoke, he sounded foreign. The husband and wife of the house took him in, wrapped him in blankets, fed him, and put him to sleep on rags in front of the fireplace.

The next morning all the villagers came with food, clothing, and medications to see the stranger—all except one man, Floda. He was a small man with the face of a bulldog. He lived with dogs, not humans. Although he was the smallest man in the whole village, he was the most powerful in strength and status; his money purse was the heaviest. His spirit was the meanest. Each time his dogs gave birth, Floda would kill the runt of the litter. However, he had never been given reasons to display his callous nature to the people of the village. Floda was the only one who dealt with business outside the village. Anyone with external trade or who needed external services went through him.

The second morning the stranger woke up still sick, and his hair and beard had turned a shocking white overnight. This happening reached Floda's ears.

The third morning the stranger woke up, he had grown white feathered wings from his shoulder blades. This time, Floda went to the house and told the husband and wife to get rid of this ill, white-haired stranger who spoke a different language and had wings growing from his shoulders. He might have a contagious disease, and the whole village would catch it and die out. But the compassionate couple refused to put a sick man out of their house and into the cold.

Floda staged a rally, stood on boxes, and spoke energetically to the people about the dangers of having such a man in their village. Floda and those loyal to him and his beliefs planned to raid the house and take the stranger in his wagon and place him along the main road five miles away, where passersby might take him. Those loyal to the sick stranger and his caregivers rushed to the house to stand guard against the invaders. For the first time, the villagers were split in their actions and beliefs.

However, before they could carry out the raid, a messenger arrived with urgent news about Floda's external dealings. Floda told his supporters to hold off the invasion for one day until he came back. A few minutes after he had set out with his horse and wagon, a windstorm began. The winds whipped the bamboo trees around and blew limbs from trees, knocking Floda unconscious from his horse. Miraculously, two brothers from the nearby village found him and took him home. They fed him, wrapped him in blankets, and put him to rest on rugs in front of the fireplace.

Dawn broke in Floda's village and brought with it a raucous roar. All the villagers who were Floda's supporters had woken up with black wings on their shoulders. The winged mob, armed with machetes and sticks, rushed to the house where the stranger was being sheltered but found that he had died during the night and his allies were putting the last shovels of earth on his grave in the forest behind the house.

Meanwhile, Floda slept through that entire day. He woke in the middle of the night and felt a hardness and stiffness under his back other than the floor. He raised a hand and felt his back. Large black wings had sprouted on his shoulders. His scream was nightmarish.

He heard the heavy feet of men running through the house toward him. He stumbled to the door, intending to scurry away, but the large black wings rustled eerily as they unfurled and spread their full breadth wide across the room.

The two brothers quickly dragged him out of the house, threw him and the blankets into their wagon, and drove him to the edge of the forest. Floda quickly realized that he was not too far from his village. As he crept home, hidden by the bushes along the roadside, he saw a group of men assembled in the forest.

They had been his friends, and they, too, had black wings. But he had the biggest wings. He joined the group and heard their stories. He recounted his story. He got the men to vote him as their leader because he had the biggest wings. He then went home tired and hungry but now pleased with his large wings because of his new control over the men. He opened his front door, and the dogs, which he had maltreated and left unfed for four days, sprang at the winged stranger and ate him alive. All that was left of him were some black feathers.

"De end," said Barabbas, and we all sat in awe-enclosed silence.

"It could have been a better story," Nanna said eventually.

"Better how, Nanna?" Barabbas asked.

"Did any of dose wit' wings try to fly?" Nanna asked.

Barabbas seemed nonplussed. "Fly?" he asked as if he had never heard the word before, as if Nanna were speaking a foreign language.

"Did any of dem flap de wings an' try to get up off de groun'?"

"No, ma'am, Nanna," Barabbas replied.

"You mean to tell me dat dese men had wings and none of dem try to fly?"

"Yes, ma'am, Nanna."

"Not even Floda?"

"Not even Floda, Nanna, ma'am."

"It would have been a bettah story if somebody did try to fly," Nanna remarked. "Floda seem bigger dan his britches; he would be de one to fly. Let him meet his maker trying to fly. Or somet'ing like dat."

"And dey should have called him Lucifer instead of Floda," my mother suggested.

Barabbas sat with his mouth filled with food and open. His story was being challenged. He swallowed hard and made one last effort to rescue it.

"Perhaps some poo' people, beaten-down people jus' can't t'ink about getting up off de groun'," he said. "Perhaps dem on the ground so long dat dey feel safer down dere. Perhaps not everybody wit' wings know what wings can do. Perhaps…"

"Perhaps," Nanna said.

Chapter 6

I was fourteen years old and had a secret shame. I had begun typing. Not on an actual typewriter but on a phantom one in my head. It began about a year earlier, the first time my mother took me with her to Blue Bay on her Saturday shopping trip. We walked the one mile to the Cross Road and rode the Blue Danube transport into the seaside market four miles away.

The wide, restless blue sea seemed too ominous to be so close to humans and alternated between a threatening rumble to joyful slapping and splashing at the platform, planks, and posts of the pier, and a chill ran up my spine when it splashed the white church socks that Nanna had allowed me to wear to market. Women with colorful scarves on their heads, flip-flops on their feet, and patches on their aprons sat on small, low benches among their produce, fruits, and spices and called attention to the yams, ackee pods, ripe mangoes, green bananas, Scotch bonnet peppers, plantains, pawpaws, nutmegs, and scallions laid out on crocus bags on the earth.

After shopping, we waited for the Mayflower transport on the sidewalk outside the public library on Great George Street. I wandered inside the building out of curiosity. There was a woman in an office at the back click-clacking away on a typewriter. She looked like a brown-skinned Betty Boop in decent clothes. Her fingers flew lightly over the keys. I watched her quietly, and she turned and gave me the sweetest smile I had ever seen. I realized sometime later that I had not smiled back. I was too busy checking the letters on each key to see if they were just as those on the picture of the typewriter that I had seen in the advertisement page of the newspaper, and which I had spent many hours memorizing.

On the way home on the transport, I listened to the passengers' conversations and typed most of what they said on a phantom typewriter in my head. They spoke a patois, and though it was not a conscious decision, I typed in English—at least, what I thought was proper English. I have no memory of struggling with punctuation or grammar; my main concerns had been finding and hitting the correct keys and getting the words down as fast as possible. I was so busy typing that I left behind on the bus the brand-new umbrella that my mother had bought me. My mother forgave me. She was very forgiving. She forgave me when I broke her blue vase. She forgave me when I accidentally spilled soursop juice on her customer's finished dress. However, she had never been able to forgive me for catching her smoking a cigarette behind our kitchen.

Our kitchen was detached from the house, and its back side was the perfect place to do forbidden things, since it was toward the bushes and the riverbank. It was at the back of the kitchen that I saw my baby-faced mother leaning against the kitchen with smoke swirling from her nostrils and her half-open, curled lips like a chimney or a smoke-puffing dragon. The fingers of the hand that gripped the cigarette were positioned in a way I had never seen before. They were not the same fingers that kneaded the flour for dumplings or steered fabric under a sewing machine needle. These fingers bordered on vulgar. They coiled around the cigarette like a cobra making love.

One of her legs was raised and pressing the boards behind her, with the other hand akimbo, just like the picture of the woman in red shoes on a poster on the front of the rum bar in Blue Bay. Nanna deemed cigarette smoking to be a sin, and Sister Lady once said that women who smoked cigarettes did not wear underwear.

My mother did not have to warn me not to tell my grandmother. She knew that my mind was like a trap—anything that went in could not get out ever again—but somehow I knew that she had never forgiven me. All she said to me was, "Button yu lip," an expression I heard several times each day because my lower lip had a tendency to come unbuttoned from the top and hang open, and I had to be reminded to close it.

Saturdays were cleaning days, and as I changed Nanna's bed-sheets that Saturday, I wondered what else I did not know about my mother. I made a decision to search her bedroom the next chance I got.

Nanna refused to sleep on a store-bought coir or inner-spring mattress. Instead, she made her own mattress and pillows from banana leaves that were first washed and then hung on the clothesline for weeks to dry. Then the soft areas were ripped from the hard stalks and veins and torn into narrow, straw-like strips. These were then stuffed into a heavy calico sack the size of her bed. Making her bed each morning meant fluffing and squishing the leaves. Hers was the only bed that did not need a mosquito net, and I chalked it up to a natural repellent in the banana leaves.

The memory of sleeping next to Nanna as a child is still moving to my senses. It is one filled with reverberation, fragrance, and cadence. I can still remember nestling into the mattress beside her as the yielding leaves settled lilting and rustling around my body; resting my nose on the warm, supple flesh at the back of her upper arm; and smelling the carbolic soap she used. The feeling of security was immeasurable. It was the kind of security that only comes once or twice in one's lifetime.

The chance to search my mother's room came later that same day. In a cloth pouch in a small wooden trunk behind the headboard, I found a pair of fine-quality high-heeled pumps. They had a black-and-tan, beautifully curved pattern that started at the throat of the shoe and spread out toward the sole like a sunburst. The Mary Jane strap across the top was fastened with a tiny gold button on the side. This was not a shoe to be worn in Naggo Head or on Naggo Head Road.

For days I carried around the image of those shoes in my head, and the thought of when and where she had worn them. I burned with curiosity.

CHAPTER 7

I asked Dove which month she was born.

"July."

We were lying under the banyan tree on the bank of Sweet River.

"Mother Woman said July people are savages." I was speaking mostly proper English by this time. I was mimicking Dove, and I was a good mimic.

"Whoever Mother Woman is, she can go suck on her thumb," she said, and I was surprised when a handbasket did not drop out of nowhere and carry her off to hell. No one had ever dared to speak badly of Mother Woman.

"Shh-hh," I rebuked her. "She will send you to h-e-two-sticks in a handbasket."

Dove laughed uncontrollably.

"How did you get from de east end to Naggo Head at de west end?" I asked Dove.

"In the back of milk trucks."

"Did you hide behin' de milk cans?"

"No. They have a few planks of wood that stretch from one side of the truck to the other for seats. They carry a few passengers like a regular bus."

"Oh? But how did you know de milk truck would come to Naggo Head?"

"I told the first driver of the truck where I wanted to go, and he told me how to connect with each truck."

"Oh."

The surprise at this stupendous feat must have reverberated in my voice, because she continued. "One summer my mother and I hitchhiked from New York City to Florida and back when I was twelve years old, so it was nothing new to me. I know all about finding a house in a new neighborhood."

"Oh," I said again. Traveling from Naggo Head to the seaside town of Blue Bay was a big adventure for everyone I knew. It meant bathing, putting on one's best (including shoes), walking two miles, taking the bus, and getting off into a throng of hustling, bustling people. It meant learning to traverse wide streets at crosswalks and peddlers' while pickpockets and con men played hide-and-seek with patrolling policemen with batons.

"How did you know de milk trucks would connect to each other?"

"Walking up from the pier where the ship docked among the business places and factories, I saw a dairy factory. Later that day I bought a newspaper to see what kind of country this was. In the advertisement columns, I saw the same dairy factory advertising for a truck driver to the western end of the island to collect milk. I walked back to the factory and asked a few questions about the trucks and their routes. The gateman was very kind and explained it all. It was thirteen parishes to the other end of the island. Each truck went two parishes and collected the milk from the next milk truck. It took two days to get to the western end of the island. That night I slept at a cheap hotel on an unprocessed coir mattress. Early the next morning, I waited across the street for the first truck leaving for this end of the island. He was a new driver. He was kind. He allowed me to ride in the front of the truck with him and his side man. The next driver was not as nice. He insisted I ride in the back like any other passenger. I didn't mind. A lady offered me some of her sardine-and-egg lunch as milk pans clattered around us.

"Another woman offered me a bed at her home when it got late evening and the truck route ended for the day until early the next morning. I went home with her, and she cooked; we ate. They were kind people. The husband came home so tired that he fell asleep over his food. He woke up later and scratched his mosquito-bitten back on a doorpost. They offered me their only bed; they would sleep on the floor. I declined gently and slept in the truck. I hardly closed my eyes once all night. I slept in the next truck all day. I heard nothing...I was that tired. I arrived in Naggo Head early that morning. I found my way easily to the Rutherfords' house. I had heard it described as the pink house on the hill."

"How did you get your mother to let you come all the way to the West Indies by yourself?"

"She didn't."

"What yu mean?"

"My mother died a few months ago," she said matter-of-factly. "I woke up one morning and was told by our next-door neighbor that she had run away and left me. It was then that I knew for sure that I needed help."

To my fourteen-year-old mind, anyone without a mother needed help.

I had gone down to the riverbank with a book but decided to wade across the water to pick sugar plums on the other side. Dove appeared on the other side of the river where I had left my shoes, and I was gracious and waved hello. She wanted to pick sugar plums too, and asked me if I knew how to get over to my side of the river without wading across the water. I directed her to walk back up to the road, and just as she crossed the Congo Bridge, she would see a large cottonwood tree; she should cross under the wooden fence at the tree and follow the footpath.

"But a rolling calf live under de cottonwood tree," I finished, trepidation rendering me limp.

"A calf? A baby cow lives under the tree?" she asked with amusement before she sped off.

I waited, nibbling on my fingernails, not because of the rolling calf, since it was daytime, but because of Congo Bridge. Congo Bridge was crammed in a narrow passage on Naggo Head Road between two of the highest mountains in the village. A dense overgrowth of plant life blocked the sunlight, causing a chill in the air. One could see only a few feet deep into the overgrowth, out of which a thin stream of water oozed and the slivers of sunlight that managed to break through the tree limbs created strange patterns on the road. To further create trepidation, acoustic waves reflected off the huge interlacing trees and large leafy greens, causing a reverberation of every shifting stone and every rustle of every leaf in the darkened area.

I was very surprised when Dove finally appeared on my side of the riverbank. She saw my jitteriness and asked why I was nervous. I told her the story of the rolling calf.

It was said by the older inhabitants of Naggo Head and believed by the younger ones that a rolling calf lived under the cottonwood tree at Congo Bridge. It was huge and had red eyes that could spit fire. A heavy chain was attached to its neck, and late at night it would lie in the middle of the road at Congo Bridge, and when it heard someone approaching, it would roll toward him, spitting red-hot coals and fire from its eyes, the heavy chain jangling loudly. The only way to stop it was to lash it with a tarred whip held in the left hand.

She laughed, holding her sides until she began to spit up.

We were now sitting in the shade of the banyan tree on the banks of Sweet River. I had decided by then that she was not just pretty—she was striking. But today her face was hidden under sunglasses and a wide-brimmed straw hat.

"Why didn't you take de Blue Danube transport?" I asked. "It come straight to Cross Road from town."

She did not reply immediately. I waited and made an impressive effort to keep my lips from becoming unbuttoned.

"How old are you, Cherry?"

"Cherrimina."

"How old are you?"

"Fourteen."

"When you get to be twenty like me, you will learn that there is no such thing as a straight road from one place to the other. And even if there is a straight road, sometimes it is not the best road to take. I took the milk trucks because it was more difficult for anyone to track my whereabouts."

"You wanted to get away from someone?"

"Yes."

"Who?"

"A man."

"I know it's a man, but which man?"

She was surprised. "How could you know I wanted to get away from a man?"

It had to be a man, I thought, because the only lady I could think of who wanted to run away from another lady so badly that she would hide away in several milk trucks from one end of an island to the other end was Snow White, and that was only a fairy tale.

I told her this, and she threw her head back and laughed long and loud only with her voice and not with her eyes.

"Cherry, your eyes are so pure and clean that sometimes they frighten me."

"Cherrimina."

"I shall call you *Mina*."

"Who is de man yu running away from?"

Her eyelids slammed shut over her gray eyes as she turned her head and looked away.

I waited. We were still and silent. Dove rose abruptly. "It's time I get back," she said. "Looks like rain. Will you be here tomorrow, Mina?"

I nodded, and she walked away.

I liked my new name. Mina. I lay back in the safe shade of my silence and stillness—so still and silent that all sounds around me slowed, separated, and magnified. The two-man saw sang a chorus as the men over in Dadda Brooks's fields pulled it back and forth through the blue mahoe tree next to the cashew tree. I heard the slipping of a motorcar's tires over each stone as it shuddered far up the incline of Naggo Head Road, but I did not hear the motor. The ladies sitting on banks of broken stones farther down the road wielded their sledgehammers, but I did not hear the hammers hitting the rocks; instead I heard the rocks splitting. The water hurtled over the pebbles on the bottom of the river, and I heard its rise, not its fall. The iguana climbing the side of the breadfruit tree scratched the bark with its front left claw and its back right claw. A leaf fell from a tree, and I heard the letting go of its stem but not when it struck the ground. I heard my brain pulsing and not my heartbeat. I began to type to its rhythm on the phantom typewriter in my head. *She ran away from the man whom she saw murder someone. She ran away from a man who tried to murder her. She ran away from the man from whom she stole money. She ran away from the man who touched her private parts. She ran away from her husband who beat her. She ran away from the man who…*

"Cher-rri-minaaah. Cher-rri-minaaah." My grandmother sang my name in alto from up the house. Twice in alto was not urgent. She just wanted to know where I was or for me to do something simple like go to the grocery shop. Three times in near bass was urgent.

I let her call once more and then sang back, "Com-iiiing, Naaan-naaa."

Walking from the other side of the river took longer than walking from our side. I counted aloud the six front steps as I hopped up to the veranda.

"Where yu was?" Nanna asked.

"Picking sugar plum over on Dadda Brooks's lan'," I lied, planning to ask the Lord for his forgiveness at bedtime.

"Come here."

I moved closer, and she pulled down one of my lower eyelids, then the other.

"You need purging, chile," she announced. And the purging process began. That night she woke me up and gave me a soft green gel-like pill. The next morning for breakfast, she gave me only a hot, smelly herbal tea, which I kept from coming back up with superhuman effort. For lunch I was given chicken broth. My trips to the latrine were monitored. That was the last time I lied to my grandmother that I was picking and eating unripe fruits from which one could get intestinal worms.

Because of the purging, I was not allowed to leave the house for a day. On the second day, I lay in bed recovering from the purging and heard a familiar voice calling my name from far out at the gate.

"Hello! Mina! Does Mina live here?"

"Cherrimina, de foreignah calling yu," my mother whispered in awe as she peered out the veranda window.

I went out to the veranda.

"Push de gate an' come up," I called to Dove.

She was not wearing her sunshades, and she raised a hand to her brow to keep the sun from her eyes.

"Hello. Good afternoon." She nodded to my grandmother and mother. "Mina, I went to the river two days and did not see you. I thought you were ill, so I decided to call on you."

All three of us stared down at her from the veranda without speaking.

"Hope you don't mind," she continued doubtfully.

"Mina?" my mother wondered aloud.

"Mi like Mina," I whispered.

"Introduce de lady, Cherrimina," my grandmother interjected.

Making introductions deserved proper speech, and I tried. "Dove, dis is Nanna, mi gran'modder, and dis is mi modder."

She walked up the steps, shook their hands, and moved to kiss their cheeks but changed her mind when they both pulled back awkwardly.

"Welcome to Naggo Head, Miss Dove," Nanna said. "Take a seat. Mary, pour some lemonade. Cherrimina, button your lips, child, and go put on your slippers." I hurried away.

"How you managing wit' our bright sunshine, Miss Dove?"

"It took a little getting used to, but I am doing fine. I like it, in fact."

"Yu should get yuself a umbrella. Lemonade quench yu t'irst bettah dan watah, Miss Dove," Nanna said. "Mus' be somet'ing in de lime, mi t'ink. We make lemonade wit' lime."

"I have an umbrella. The lemonade is delicious, Nanna."

"May God bless de souls of dose people who die when dat German airship crash an' burn in yu country. Miss Dove, tell me, did yu get a look at it?" Nanna asked.

"The *Hindenburg*? It crashed in New Jersey. I live in Virginia, hundreds and hundreds of miles south of New Jersey."

Nanna told her that she did not speak like a Southerner and that the Rutherfords were from Virginia and they had a different accent.

"I was not raised in Virginia, Nanna."

"Oh!" I heard Nanna say. This was followed by a long pause, broken only by glasses rattling as my mother served the lemonade.

"Drink up," Nanna said.

"We so glad de ice truck come today," Nanna said between tinklings of the pieces of ice in the glass. "There's nothing like a glass of cool lemonade."

"De rain set up fi a heavy shower later," Nanna said.

"So what did de people of Virginia have to say 'bout it?" Nanna asked.

"About what, Miss Nanna?"

"'Bout de airship dat crash an' burn."

I went back out to the veranda and stood quietly aside. Children were to be seen and not heard when adults were conversing.

"Oh, here you are," Dove said and jumped from her seat. She said her thank-you and goodbye, and I hurried her down the broad steps.

"Remember to keep yu foot dem dry, an' keep yu shoes on. Yu mus' allow de purging to take," Nanna called as we went through the banana trees, past the cocoa trees, and down to the riverbank.

"What happened to you for two days?" Dove asked.

"I had purging."

"Had what?

"Purging."

"What is purging?"

I explained that it was medicine to prevent the intestinal worms I could get from eating half-ripe fruits and walking around barefoot.

"Goodness! Did it hurt?"

"No," I replied. And when I learned that she had never had purging, I told her that her gut was probably full of wriggly worms.

We were lying head to head under the coconut tree on the riverbank.

"Strange customs you have on your beautiful island, Mina. People are uncomfortable greeting each other with a kiss on the cheek or a hug. You make your lemonade with limes. Your mountains are really hills, and your hills are only mounds. Your rivers are the size of streams. You carry an umbrella for the sun instead of the rain, and when it rains, everyone takes shelter. No one goes out in the rain, so everything comes to a standstill until the rain stops.

"Your Cross Road is a T-junction, not two roads crossing. Every direction you give is 'just a piece up the road,' and when I ask how far a piece up the road is, the answer is always 'quarter mile.' And I would not exactly call Congo Bridge a bridge. It is just a culvert, a tubular concrete channel through which a little water trickles. But I must admit that it's a creepy place. The capital of the island is not Town; it is Saint Ann's Town.

"Some people seem to think that every word I say is a curse word. One of the church members told me that I should not say *lie*; I should say *untrue*. And how come no one is overweight? Does anyone here ever get fat? My mother believed that fat could have saved the world from sin—if Adam and Eve had filled up on the other fruits in the Garden of Eden, they might have been overweight, but they might not have eaten the forbidden fruit. And why—"

"Did you come looking for me because you like me?" I interrupted.

"Yes. I like you."

"Why do you like me?"

She thought for a while. "Because you recognized that I just needed peace and quiet. In addition, because you have a stillness that does not intrude on other people's space. You question, but you don't judge."

I did not respond. But I felt a tingling on the top of my head, and I permitted myself to enjoy it. It was at this point in time that in her presence I began to develop that same feeling I got when I was in church. She had not made me her disciple, so I decided to make her my mentor.

"I'm running away from a man," she said quietly—so quietly that I had to turn my head to hear her. My ear was close to her mouth.

"I met him in New York City a few days before I set sail. He offered to pay my fare on a ship sailing to the West Indies. He's married with three children. He is old enough to be my father, but he liked me and would do anything for me. I saw no harm in letting him pay my fare. It made him happy. I needed to leave the United States. My life was not going well. I needed a change of scenery. He's not a very attractive man. What he lacked in looks, he made up for in personality. He could make me laugh. In the daytime, he made me laugh. At night, he made me sad. At night, I made him cry. At late night, I could hear him scratching my cabin door and calling, calling my name. The loneliness in his voice moved me to tears several nights. 'I just need to talk,' he would say. 'I won't touch you.'"

Chapter 8

"Come, chile, put on yu church shoes. We ah go visit Ma'as Charlie."
It was Sunday afternoon.

"Yes, Nanna."

"Bring mi blue hat, an' tell yu maddah she mus' come too."

"Yes, Nanna."

"An' don't take yu notebook dis time. Leave it behin'."

"Yes, Nanna."

The sun had cooled somewhat by the time we set off down the road. We walked in single file on the shaded side of the street. Nanna led the way with her favorite lace handkerchief flapping in hand and the blue hat pinned firmly on her head. I walked behind my mother.

For a short time, the only sound to be heard was the gravel shifting lethargically beneath our feet until the majestic sound of the Jacobs's organ loomed, pumping a grand and mystical ambiance over all of Naggo Head; its notes separating and then closing, pitching, swelling, and attacking; its complaints ranging from gentle to strong and unencumbered, like a slow-moving haze tinged with tears. The Jacobs family lived on Porter's Mountain, and the mother, a poorly and weak woman who refused to tell anyone how she had mysteriously come to own an organ, played mostly on Sunday afternoons. There was a rumor that she played with dainty white gloves on her hands.

I dragged my feet with apprehension. I had a fear of Ma'as Charlie's house. I was a fearful child at fourteen, so fearful that Nanna said if I was not careful, I would soon be afraid of my own shadow.

Ma'as Charlie lived about a quarter mile below us, in the farthest house inside Calypso Gully, but by the time Nanna said how-de-do to everyone who was alerted by the shifting gravel beneath our feet and came out to see who it was, it had taken twice the length of time it should have. Nanna's walking down Naggo Road, aside from her trips to and from church, was a rare event and something her peers, the kindly neighbors—all busybodies and their uncles—wanted to behold.

It was the main road and the only constructed road—all others were earthen footpaths. Naggo Head Road started at the Cross Road and was a very slight, gradually rising gravel road mixed with river rocks that ended abruptly two and a half miles up. Because of the gravel, it was impossible for anyone to enter or leave Naggo Head in secret. Ma'as Charlie had never married, and he lived alone. Years before, he was set to marry a young lady from another village, but on the day of the wedding, he had not shown up at the church. He was nowhere to be found all day. He had eventually been found late that evening, wearing his khaki work clothes and water boots and hiding in his mother's chicken coop. Since then he had worked as a shoemaker at a small stall he had set up at Cross Road. His father, whom I never met, had passed away several years earlier, and it was rumored that a part of his father's nose had been eaten away by a disease due to his association with loose women in the Blue Bay seaside town.

The shifting stones on the road caused Miss Pem Pem on Cherry Hill to come out and peer down to see who the travelers were.

She chanted down to Nanna. "Goood afternoooon, Nanna. What a gloooriouuus sermon in church todaaay!"

"Ah, Pem Pem, it was heavenly!" Nanna called up to her. "T'ank the Lawd!"

The rolling slopes at that region of the island destined the majority of the houses along Naggo Head Road to be either on a hill or in a valley, except for Mill Yard. At the time I did not know how unique this was, and outdoor conversations between neighbors could range from delightful greetings and pleasantries yelled up or the occasional poisonous curses yelled down. We turned off Naggo Head Road onto the narrow foot-path of Calypso Gully, passing banana trees with huge bunches of green bananas hanging from them—a lush, green ginger field. The front veranda floors of the small, unpainted wooden houses were dyed deep red from the logwood tree bark and buffed to a high sheen. Colorful rag mats lined some of the top front steps. Several houses were surrounded by coconut trees that had had the bottom halves whitewashed, as were the stones that lined the flower beds. "Charliiiee!" Nanna sang about fifty yards away from the house. That was how it was done in Naggo Head; one never crept up on one's neighbors.

"Ma'as Charliiiee!" My mother echoed the song.

Pretty soon we were sitting in the house that I dreaded and smelling beeswax, glue, and leather. The house was built over a water well. It had no back door, only an entrance door, and the back end of the house was nearly jammed onto the side of a hill. Donkey-brown-colored curtains hanging in doorframes separated the front room from the back. A framed photograph of a young Edward VIII and George VI that hung slightly crooked on one wall and an embroidered religious panel on another wall reading "Rock of Ages Cleft for Me" were the only decorations.

Ma'as Charlie was a delicately thin, parched man of average height. Tiny lines meandered all over his skin, creating patterns rivaling a crocodile's. Two deep creases began at the corners of his nose and bracketed his mouth, around which a graying beard and mustache struggled. The arrangement of his facial features told of a not-so-long-gone average-looking young man.

He lifted a thin, loosely braided coconut-leaf mat from the floor and pulled up an earthenware jug attached to a twine from out of the well. He offered us freshly squeezed sugarcane juice in earthenware mugs. It was cool and delicious and lessened the rigidity of my spine. When Nanna mentioned the exceptional drink, Ma'as Charlie said it was the grated ginger and the fresh lime juice that he had added.

I was seen but not heard as we sat on small, hand-carved chairs in the front room around the deep, dark hole in the floor. Every once in a while, a gurgling sound could be heard coming from deep in the well.

Ma'as Charlie was very polite, and he spoke softly. His shoe-making business was doing well; soon he might have to look for an apprentice. But he had lumbago; so did his mother. He was thinking of moving back home to take care of her. Nanna spent the rest of the visiting time giving him natural remedies to help in providing quick relief from lumbago. She told him to crush cabbage leaves well, until they were very limp. Mix them in a container with a bit of warm milk, leaving to sit for ten minutes. Then place the leaves on the lower back, with a bandage to hold them in place. Leave on for about fifteen minutes. He could also fry garlic cloves in mustard oil, strain, and use the oil to massage the aching areas.

Chapter 9

It was Saturday evening, and the usual merriment and palavering at Cross Road was in full swing. The men sat around tables playing dominoes; children were running and playing hide-and-seek; mothers sat on small, low stools with babies held softly and safely in their laps. Shoes were optional, but greasing the hands and legs with homemade coconut oil was a must.

Miss Beck sat around her striped candy trays, stretching, pulling, and twisting the striped confection to make her peppermint candy. Young men and women tried to make their rare and perhaps their first bottled cola or ice cream cone last as long as possible. Younger ones drained the last drop of ice cream from dented tin mugs. Unruly boys ran around picking up discarded cigarette butts. The evening air was ripe with music from a four-piece calypso outfit, candy sellers calling out their wares, giggling teenagers, squealing kids, and men in khakis and water boots slapping dominoes on wooden tabletops.

In a field across from the clinic, a schoolboy's cricket match was in progress; the few onlookers whooped, and other boys climbed nearby trees for the thrill of a panoramic view. In the background was the faraway rumble of the Sweet River as it made its way over a small waterfall. The intermingling of splashes of colors with the sedated evening sunshine, the cool breeze from the river, and the waves of sound would undoubtedly shape a young person's imagination and remain in memory forever.

It had been three weeks since Nanna had last given me permission to join the Saturday evening gathering. I was with Comfort, my classmate from the neighboring village. We watched two girls from our church sing and dance to a forbidden worldly song. We were having such a good time that the time slipped by. I usually headed home before the last bus from Blue Bay arrived because Pootus usually got off that bus.

Pootus lived about a mile up into Naggo Head. She was a spinster, short and wiry in stature. She never attended church. She dressed only in men's clothes, hat, and shoes, smoked a pipe, and worked her produce field during the week. On Fridays she would go into Blue Bay to sell her produce and come back on Saturday evenings with a cow's head in a dishpan balanced, hands free, on her head. The cow's head would be left exposed, and its wide-open, staring eyes would drive blood-curdling fear into me.

That Saturday I did not even see her get off the bus until I felt someone brush my left arm. I looked around, and staring at me from the dishpan on top of her head were the cow's black eyeballs. The only thought that came to my mind was to get home to Nanna fast. I began to run up Naggo Head Road. Later, when I was asked why I hadn't stayed my ground and allowed Pootus to walk ahead and go home, my reply was that I did not know why.

Besides balancing her load on her head while traversing the rocky Naggo Head Road, Pootus possessed one other skill: she could do all that while walking at fire-rapid speed. I heard the gravel shifting, looked around, and saw that she was bearing down on me. I took a deep breath, gathered strength, and let out a howl. I was desperate; I panted, howled, and ran. Then, to my left, I glimpsed the pink house on Pill Hill and thought, Dove will save me.

With this thought in mind, I did something out of character, something that would have brought shame on Nanna. I pushed opened the pink-and-cream ironwork gate and raced uninvited onto a stranger's property. The hill was steep, and I completely disregarded the curving driveway and ran nonstop through the tired, half-dead flower garden without looking back at Pootus.

I raced through the huge columns and across the veranda. As I reached the front door, it opened abruptly. I fell into the doorway and into Dove's arms. The howling was like nothing she had ever heard before, and she had come out to investigate it.

After following my pointed finger and finding Pootus hesitating on the road with the cow's head and looking up at her, she ducked out of sight and joined me on the floor.

"Is de pickney ahright, ma'am?" Pootus called up toward the house from the road, and when she got no reply, she sucked her teeth and went on her way.

At fourteen, my idea of mansions came from storybooks. The house on Pill Hill did not quite have sweeping stairways, sky-high ceilings, marbled walls, or gold chandeliers and plates, but by

Naggo Head's standards and mine, it was a mansion. The exterior was painted pale pink, and the interior soft beige.

Dove tied the sash of the floral-painted silk robe she wore tightly around her, swept wide-open arms at the furniture and drapes with a white layer of dust, and said, "This is it. This is where I'm staying."

The entire floor, from kitchen to veranda, was shiny beige tiles that cooled the soles of my feet. The four bedrooms were decked out with four-poster beds over which hung delicate, web-like mosquito nets. Every room had several of what were once lush potted plants but were now dried twigs and large dead leaves. The kitchen had an empty icebox. The kitchen cupboards, too, were empty, but the bedroom closets were full of clothes.

She opened one of the bedroom closets, pulled out several frocks, and then removed a bedsheet that covered a full-length mirror. She held the frocks up to her body and twisted and turned in front of the mirror.

"Mrs. Rutherford was a flapper girl!" she declared.

"Flappah girl?" I asked.

"Yes. Young fabulous women in the 1920s. They wore short skirts, bobbed their hair, and danced day and night to jazz music. They were the most feared group of people in the 1920s."

I had never seen my body from head to toe before, and the vision in the mirror rendered me speechless. All the mirrors I had ever seen were just barely large enough for me to view my face. Now, rising from two large feet that were planted haphazardly on the floor, I saw two very long sticks that ended abruptly at the base of knobby knees. Above the pencil-like neck was a nose sprinkled with freckles, and below were small, narrow shoulders from which the shapeless, donkey-brown-colored dress with a sailor collar hung.

I became aware that Dove had stopped speaking and was staring at me, so I repeated the last coherent thought that I had. "Flappah girl?"

The gathers from the yoke seam above my chest hid my breasts as they were meant to do, so basically my chest looked flat. My lips hung loosely open between two chunky braids. I saw for the first time what Bulla saw when he looked at me.

"Mi going home now," I announced. The sun was setting fast, and twilight was falling. Dove waved as I ran down the hill.

"Come back again soon," she called. "We will model Mrs. Rutherford's flapper dresses next time."

"We will clean an' dus', too," I called back. I ran home to Nanna.

Chapter 10

"Remembah de new dress yu promise' me, Mama?" I asked two days later as she steered fabric through the sewing machine with her left hand and spun the handle of the wheel with her right.

She nodded. "Yu birt'day present."

I asked if I could have a green sleeveless dress with a belt at the waist and a wide, flared skirt. The last word left my lips, and the sewing machine wheel slowly came to a halt. My mother lifted her head and looked at me with narrowed eyes. Her face was set. She stared at me for a long time. I made a motion to shrink away, but before I could, her face softened suddenly. She lifted a hand and brushed her fingers very softly under my chin. I looked up, she smiled, and I knew then that she understood.

Oh joy! I felt then, for the first time in a long time, a warm, sweet affection coming from my mother. My mother had shown me again that she loved me!

We set about planning for this dress. First of all, since I was getting to be a young lady, I would go to Blue Bay that day by myself to choose the fabric, but I would have to ask Nanna's permission. Secondly, a sleeveless dress would not do. If I would like to wear this new dress to church, it would have to have short, puffy sleeves instead. I wanted Bulla to see me in this dress, so of course I agreed to puffed sleeves.

Nanna gave her permission. But don't buy green, she told me. We were already surrounded by a multitude of green trees, green grass, and green leaves, she said. Would you want to blend into the bushes? She told me to buy something soft and sweet like me—like the young lady I was to become. Buy a soft pink or pale yellow, she said. Perhaps something with small, dainty flowers.

Several neighbors had relayed to her my running and howling incident with Pootus's cow's head, and when I had gotten home that night, she had comforted me in the sweetest way she knew how: she had dribbled a spoonful of honey into a bowl-shaped water cracker and placed it tenderly in my hand. And it was truly comfort food. Biting noisily into the pale, crispy cracker without letting the golden honey drip and then pausing the deafening munching only to lick sticky fingers clean would have been more than enough to take one's mind off any misery. Then as I took the last bite, Nanna had begun humming. It was her usual soft and gentle lullaby, interrupted only by the usual whir of my mother's sewing machine in the back room.

The thought of the new dress was so exciting that I forgot to be apprehensive of travelling to Blue Bay alone for the first time.

"Go up to Sistah Lady an' see if she want anyt'ing down Blue Bay," Nanna called after me as I left Mill Yard.

Sister Lady was sitting on her front steps sunning herself, her skirt hiked up to her thighs and tucked between there.

The thatched-roof house had belonged to her long-gone mother. A large wooden mortar and pestle sat outside her zinc kitchen, and she was lazily sifting through a wash pan of dried cocoa beans. I knew then that later that evening my mother and I would help her beat those seeds into greasy cocoa balls while she sat and chatted with Nanna. She wanted nothing in Blue Bay.

I traveled over the rocky road out to Cross Road as though I had wings. Nanna had tied my transport fare money in one end of her handkerchief and the money for the fabric at another end. She had told me to hold on tight to the handkerchief since I didn't have a bosom to put it in. My notebook and pencil were in Nanna's straw basket, and her umbrella was gripped securely in one fist. I glanced up at the house on Pill Hill as I passed; that was all I did, just glanced. My head was full of what I would see the next time I looked in that full-length mirror.

Ma'as Charlie was also waiting on the transport at Cross Road. He told me to tell Nanna that his mother was very ill and he was going home to spend a few days taking care of her.

"Yes, sah, Ma'as Charlie," I promised him.

I did everything right. I took the Mayflower transport, paid the correct fare, sat in the same seat in which my mother liked to sit, and enjoyed the scenery we passed: women chatting and washing clothes under the yellow sun in the Sweet River, with their skirt hems looped between their legs and tucked in their waistbands to keep them out of the water; men in sleeveless undershirts, water boots, and straw hats chopping sugarcane with gleaming machetes, the sweat glistening on their muscled arms as they hurled the sugar cane in piles; the wide, squat, whitewashed gates that led to the sugar factory, its chimney swirling smoke far in the distance; women with a gentle rhythmical swing in their hips gliding gracefully, carrying gourds of drinking water on their heads without spilling a drop.

The farther one moved south of Naggo Head, the better-dressed individuals one saw, along with more public transportation, more private vehicles, streetlights, bigger shops, and a bigger marketplace with the one and only stop signal. One also saw fewer men dressed in water boots riding on donkeys and carrying machetes to do their cultivating; one saw fewer women balancing baskets of produce or with water jugs resting on rolled-up and coiled pieces of fabric on top of their heads.

I got off at the correct stop and crossed the street safely to the haberdashery store on the other side. I lingered at the entrance of the store, where each item was displayed strategically in the wide doors to lure me inside. The two-burner snow-white kerosene-oil stove gleamed at me, and I could have sworn that the ceramic on top of the tin goblet and washbasin set, embellished with purple and white flowers, winked. The pink comb-and-brush doll dresser set was no longer displayed there, and I imagined a lucky little girl brushing her doll's hair. Farther inside the shop, a fan whirled and cooled the air. Customers stood patiently in a queue.

I stood still and stared at the rows and rows of fabric bolts on top of the counter. Take your time, I told myself. And then I saw it. A bolt of pale-pink color sprinkled with very tiny and very pale yellow flowers.

"Good day, mister. Please sell me three yards of that one," I said to the storekeeper, pointing to the bolt of fabric in the pile at the left end of the counter, and pleased that from my many talks with Dove, I was now remembering to pronounce my *th* and *er.*

"Ah! The dusty rose," he said. "Good choice."

While untying the money from Nanna's handkerchief, I remembered that my mother always asked questions before she purchased anything, so in my best English-speaking voice, I asked the storekeeper, "Mister, the one shilling and sixpence marked on the cardboard, is it for one yard or for the whole thing?"

"One and six per yard," he replied.

"T'ank you, sir," I replied, happy I'd managed the *ir* in *sir* and disappointed that I had skipped the *th* in *thank*.

I walked out of the store with a brown paper package tied with twine under one arm. I walked out with my head in the clouds and bumped headlong into a mass of white shirt and beige pants. Inside these clothes was a man with two patches of sweat at his armpits. Underneath the Panama hat was a bearded face that I had seen several weeks earlier.

I apologized and picked my package up from the sidewalk where it had fallen. One hairy arm that protruded from the rolled-up shirt-sleeves dug into his shirt pocket. The black-and-white photograph he pushed toward me was of a young girl. She had shoulder-length, light-colored hair. Her eyes were sad, and I knew immediately that had the photograph been in color, the eyes would have been gray. The girl in the photograph was Dove.

He spoke, and his accent was thick and strange; the words sounded jumbled in his throat before they got to his lips. I had heard it once before.

"Girl," he began, and even though I could not understand the rest of what he said, I knew he was asking if I recognized the person in the photograph.

I could not look up at his face because I knew I was about to commit a sin. I was about to break one of the Ten Commandments. I focused my eyes on the hand that held the picture instead. It was large and soft, and I could see tiny beads of sweat on the pink skin under the straight black hairs.

"No, sir," I replied, certain that I was immediately heading straight for hell in a handbasket.

He wiped his face with a large handkerchief and walked on.

The sun was at its hottest exactly at noon on our island. The temperature could climb so high at this time that if one sat in the shade and stared continuously out into the sun, one would see the sunrays shimmering in the distance.

Any self-respecting islander knew to avoid hard physical labor around this time. It was at this time of day that everyone and everything seemed to move in slow motion. Farmers and sugarcane cutters, who had already been working since 7:00 a.m., would put down their machetes and hoes, sit under shaded, broad-leafed trees, and eat lunch from their thermoses and drink rainwater from canteens. Women washing clothes in the river would spread their soapy whites on river boulders or on top of bushes on the riverbanks to catch the heat from the blazing sun, which would boil and whiten them.

It was at this time of day when one's cotton dress or shirt would cling to one's perspiring body as if it were a man dying of thirst and sucking on a dewdrop. It was at such a time of day that Bro' Man had seen my mother hanging out the wash on the clothesline and told Nanna that her daughter could be in an Archibald Motley painting. That night, by lamplight, I wrote in my notebook, "Bro' Man told mama that she could be in an Archie Ballmutly painting. Who is he? One day I will know who he is." Years later I would find that the women in Archibald Motley's paintings had round and shapely arms and legs, round and shapely bosoms, and round and protruding backsides.

It was at such a time of day, about six weeks earlier, that a tourist had made his way to the grocery shop in Naggo Head.

Bro' Man had just settled himself on his favorite stool, wearing his crisply ironed khaki clothes. The shopkeeper had been attending to a customer. Out of sight and in the shade of the breadfruit tree's lazy branches, with one's eyes closed, one would have heard the shopkeeper's metal scoop slicing through the brown rice in the jute sack and the grains falling onto the brown wrapping paper in the scale. One would have heard even the rustling of the paper being folded over the rice in a neat rectangular bundle. I doubt that the sound of the cleaver slamming into the cutting board as it chopped through the tail of the stiff, dry salted codfish could ever be duplicated.

I had not attended school that day due to a toothache and was sitting outside under the breadfruit tree at the side of the shop with my pencil and notebook in hand. For several years, I had been quietly listening to Bro' Man's conversations and jotting down his interesting declarations and theories.

The tourist had greeted everyone quite cordially. His name was Helmut Wagner. He had spoken his first and last names with a long pause between them, as if he were unsure of his name or taking time to part it carefully down the middle. I had not understood most of what he had said, but I had gotten the gist from the responses from those in the shop.

He had been doing a lot of walking because the driver of the private car he had hired had not shown up. He was a private investigator, and he had wanted to know if anyone had seen the girl in the photograph he had shown them. She was wanted for larceny from a charity organization. When they had said no, he had ordered a cold bottle of cola. Mistress Ferguson had popped the bottle cap, and I had heard him sucking thirstily on the mouth of the bottle. Mistress Ferguson had noticed the boil on his neck and had advised him to pick a leaf from the Scotch bonnet pepper tree, heat it slowly over a low flame, and apply it to the boil. She had told him to change the leaf three times during the day to draw blood to the affected area. This would bring the boil to a head in a day, and the pus would drain.

"Poppycock!" Bro' Man had protested. "Piffle! Pepper leaf nothing. What you need, my trusted tourist, is to learn how to love the sunlight. One should never be afraid of it. The sun can improve your health. It increases your vitality and your mindfulness. Plant your feet firmly in the earth. Look the sun dead in the eye, and inhale deeply. Draw the sun's yellow energy into your eyes, throat, and lungs, into your heart, into your gut. Hold it in for as long as you can to let it soak into the vital organs. Then…exhale the impurities."

The tourist had thanked everyone and headed down the road toward Cross Road. The gravel had shifted sluggishly under his heavy feet.

"*Schönen tag*," Bro' Man had called to him, and had explained to his companions that the foreign language was German and that the phrase meant "have a good day."

"Never trust a man under thirty with a beard," Bro' Man had declared as soon as the tourist was out of earshot. "Getting up every day and pulling a razor across one's throat first thing in the morning gives a man character! Notice how his index finger was bent when he pointed it at the picture? A man who cannot straighten the joints of his finger when he points is a troubled man. Pointing should be a minor rebellion. A dominant gesture. A rebel yell. There is no half and half—you either point or you don't point."

Someone in the group had said that it was impolite to point, so perhaps he had been trying to be polite when he bent the finger. Another customer had stated that he had been pointing at a photograph of a person, not at a human, so politeness should be discounted.

"A man should always point with a fixed finger," Bro' Man had replied. "A soldier goes into battle with his gun erect and ready; he does not go into battle with his gun at half-mast or with his gun wagging. Who wags fingers?"

"Woman!" the group of men had replied in unison.

"Who get fingers wagged at them?" Bro' Man had asked.

"Pickney!" the group had replied again in unison.

The tourist's visit had provided Bro' Man and his cronies conversation for several days.

⋏

The trip back home from Blue Bay with my fabric, Nanna's straw basket, and umbrella was barely memorable. I got off the bus at Cross Road. Breathlessly, and without invitation, I knocked on the door of the house on Pill Hill, but no one answered. I wrote a note on a page from my notebook and pushed it under the front door.

When I arrived home, Nanna was in her rocking chair reading the latest newspaper. She had a visitor. It was Sister Lady. I greeted her correctly, as Nanna had taught me, and her eyes followed me as I made my way along the veranda to the back of the house. When I was out of sight, she turned her attention back to Nanna.

"Go on, Nanna," she ordered. "You stap where de man from Germany wit' de moustache, write to de president *h*of *H*america an' sey '*h*apply de pruning knife.'"

For the rest of the day, I waited on the riverbank for Dove. But when twilight fell and she had not come, I went home to Nanna.

CHAPTER 11

The next day, my mother and I designed and sewed my new dress. Every cell in my body stood at attention during this experience. And when I thought that it could not get any better, every cell began to pulse—a slow pulse that vibrated softly and consistently until my face burned hot and my mouth watered. Several times my mother touched my face with cool, feather-like fingers.

First she drew the style on paper with pencil. Then she took my body measurements while I wrote them in her notebook: "Chest: thirty-three inches. Waist: eighteen inches. Hip: thirty-three inches."

I watched as she cut the dress pattern from old newspapers and then lay the pieces of paper on the fabric and cut around them.

For two days, I knotted threads at the end of seams, I put on Nanna's thimble and made tiny, neat hand stitches at the hem and sleeves, and I sewed on buttons. By the time Nanna said prayers at bedtime that second night, the dress was ironed and hanging on a homemade hanger of dried twig and twine in my room.

I had just put out the flame of the oil lamp and settled into bed when I heard the scratching outside my window. It was Dove.

I put my finger to my lips and climbed out through the window. The stillness in the air surprised me. Not a leaf stirred on the trees. The moon was low and full, and its light shone silvery blue on her face.

She was dressed in full black, with her hair pulled back in a ponytail. When she spoke, there was an urgency in her voice.

She told me that she had gotten my note, and she thanked me. She did not say where she had been for two days. And when she said that she had walked all the way from Pill Hill along the riverbank, I gasped. The gasp seemed to frighten her. Her eyes grew round and large.

She explained that she had walked along the riverbank from Pill Hill and spent the entire day on the riverbank several yards down from Nanna's house. She had fallen asleep, and when she woke up, it was dark, and she did not know how to get back home without everyone on Naggo Head Road seeing or hearing her. She asked me to spend the night with her on Pill Hill. She needed company. It took me only a second to consider this. I crept back through the window, wrote a note to Nanna, and then added "and Mama." I changed into my day clothes and grabbed a kerosene-bottle torch and matches. I was about to take my new dress but decided that whenever that dress walked out of that house, I was going to be in it. It would not be carried out folded and crushed.

I showed Dove a much less treacherous route along the riverbank to Pill Hill. It was the route where we had crossed the river over to the other side in a shallow area, and sometimes we walked through neighbors' backyards. Mostly we walked in silence, except for my wincing because of the sometimes-rock-strewn path. I had forgotten my shoes.

The house on Pill Hill was in darkness. She lit the petrol lamps. First, she had to lower the lamp from the ceiling with its rope pulley, and then she pumped a metal piston situated on the side of the lamp into the reservoir, and the euphoric aroma of what I thought was petrol drifted over me. She lit the huge wick under the glass chimney, and the house glowed in the most spectacular lamplight I had ever seen.

Dove glanced at the huge smile on my face. "I heard the Rutherfords describe how they lit this lamp many times," she explained.

She showed me how the indoor toilet worked: pull the chain attached to the iron water tank high up in the ceiling with the word *Niagara* embossed on it. Dove laughed and said that I did not have to be frightened by the noise the water made as it rushed madly down from the tank into the toilet and swirled down the hole.

"I have something for you," she told me, leading me by the hand to the master bedroom.

"It's time you start wearing one of these," she said, pushing a garment that she had removed from a bureau drawer in my hand. It was a brassiere. It was of a pale-blush silk fabric, with gossamer lace insets and tiny golden hooks. Noticing that I did not know how to put it on and did not want to remove my clothes in front of her, she demonstrated how to put it on over her dress.

I removed my dress in the bathroom, slipped the delicate bra straps onto my shoulders, and fastened the hooks in the back, and instantly the soft fabric completely and absolutely wrapped itself around my breasts. It cupped them like two silky hands. It caressed my nipples. I bent forward to reach for my dress to pull it back on, and the sensation of my torso muscles straining ever so slightly against this silken harness that now gripped my breasts and brushed my nipples was new and electrifying, and for the first time I became aware of another part of my anatomy stirring other than my lower lip separating from my upper lip.

It was while we were modeling Mrs. Rutherford's clothes in front of the full-length mirror that Dove slowly peeled the red hair from her head and laid it on the bed as though she were handling precious treasure.

"I wear a wig," she said in a low, hesitant voice.

"I already know dat," I said.

"Really?" she asked, spinning to face me, her eyes wide. "How did you know?"

Her face seemed smaller and paler with the lighter-color hair pulled back and piled high on her head.

"The German showed me yu picture in Blue Bay," I replied.

At the mention of the German, she sank to the edge of the bed and sat with her hands in her lap, the back of one palm resting in the other palm. She ended the modeling. She wrapped and secured a tightly knotted scarf around her head, threw a sheet over the mirror, and led the way out of the bedroom and through the back door. We sat in the moonlit backyard on the grass and chatted. We lay on our stomachs and chatted. We lay on our backs. We sat back to back. I did not ask her about the man who hunted her. She did not offer food or drink as was the neighborly custom in Naggo Head. Nanna would have been shocked at this.

Instead, she showed me how to tell which men had cabbage by the way they dressed, walked, and talked.

"You know the kind of men I mean?" she asked.

I shook my head.

"The butter-and-egg men, the yum-yum type," she explained.

She explained the difference between men who dressed to the left of their trouser fly and those who dressed to the right. She showed me how the girls on Fifth Avenue in New York City dressed and walked as opposed to the girls on Double Fifth.

"Double Fifth is Tenth Avenue," she explained.

She showed me how to dance the Lindy Hop. Her mother had taught her. But after her mother had an attack that had left her unconscious on the floor, she had not danced anymore. After she came back from the hospital, she had not done much of anything anymore.

Dove chatted throughout the entire night. The longer she spoke, the coarser her language became, and the stranger her accent sounded.

We fell asleep in the backyard. When I woke up the next morning, I shook Dove awake. Before I left, I asked her what was to happen next.

"I don't know," she replied, her scarf-wrapped head bowed low into her chest.

I ran all the way home, wearing Mrs. Rutherford's flapper frock and the brassiere. After the rough terrain along the riverbank, my feet cherished the fresh caress of dew that was still on the soft, carpet-like grass in Mill Yard. I slipped through the window just as Nanna finished singing the spiritual melody and called through the thin walls, "Let us pray."

"Let us pray," I replied loud enough for her to hear.

CHAPTER 12

I slept most of that day, so much so that Nanna kept waking me to ask if I was feeling unwell. In Naggo Head, one slept during the daytime only if one was ill. There was halfhearted talk of an approaching hurricane, but no one truly believed it. It was too early in the season. The whipping of the clothes drying on the clothesline could only be due to an unusually strong sea breeze.

It was only when the chirping, the calls, and the flapping of wings from the birds whirling about in the skies got louder and faster that the threat of a storm became worrisome. Then, toward the late afternoon, sudden high winds whipped the branches in the trees and the sugarcane stalks. The skies grew ominously darker, causing everyone to scurry around moving their cows, pigs, and goats closer to their homes and to higher ground. They carried and stored buckets of water from the river or from wells. Fish and meat that had been hung to dry over the fireplace in the kitchens were taken inside the houses.

At Mill Yard we gathered the delicate produce; peas, eggplants, and tomatoes were picked from their vines. We collected eggs from the chicken and battened the coops with the restless chickens inside.

Later that night, after Nanna prayed for the safety of everyone in Naggo Head, the entire island, and the whole world, I climbed out my bedroom window with a bottle torch and a box of matches. The yard was barely lit by the faint moonlight. I ran the mile along the riverbank to Pill Hill. The house was in darkness and was scarcely visible from the riverbank. The winds had gotten louder. I shouted and banged on the back door.

The door opened, and someone grabbed the wrist of my hand that held the torch, pulled me inside, and pushed the door shut without saying a word. The face that looked back at me through the torchlight was Dove's. Her head was wrapped with the scarf. She put a finger to her lips, took the torch from my hand, and pushed the lit wick into a dried-up potted plant; we were plunged into blackness.

"The German came here today," she whispered, locking the door. "He may come back tonight."

"Dey say hurricane coming!" I whispered back.

"Do you have matches to relight the torch later?" she asked. I nodded.

"Good. We will wait here."

"But de hurricane coming!" I cried.

"Will you shut up about the hurricane!" she hissed.

And so, shrouded in darkness and disbelief, I sat on the kitchen floor beside her and waited. How could a German be more dangerous than a hurricane? Could a German in a strange land with a boil on his neck and with an inability to point with a fixed finger overturn houses? Could he uproot trees, blow the roofs off houses, and cause the Sweet River to rise and overflow its banks? Could he push the wind so that it went howling and wailing through the keyholes and cracks in the sideboards?

I truly cannot remember how long we waited before we heard the back doorknob slowly turn; it could have been fifteen minutes, or it could have been fifty minutes. The doorknob jammed, and then we heard faint footsteps moving along the left side of the house going toward the front. The thrashing of the leaves on the trees had gotten louder by then.

Then, almost simultaneously, I heard running footsteps and the splintering of wood as the back door burst open upon the night. For a mere second, the dim moonlight silhouetted the German in the doorway before he tripped headlong into us.

Dove screamed. I may have screamed, but it could have been the kitchen table that I ran into scraping the tiled floor as it fell over. In fact, I am sure now that I screamed. We ran toward the front of the house and through the door, forgetting the torch. I still had the box of matches gripped in my fist. We ran down the hill and headed up Naggo Head Road. My foremost thought was to run home to Nanna.

"Nanna," I said to Dove; my panting made it sound like "Nan."

She struggled over the gravel on the road. Her breathing was erratic. I had no problem running on the gravel, so I took her hand in mine. I knew the German was close behind us because I could hear the gravel shifting under his feet. Then it occurred to me that if we could hear him, he could hear us. We had to get off the graveled road.

We turned the bend at Calypso Gully, and Dove stumbled over her feet. She fell facedown into the gravel, and one of her shoes went flying in the darkness.

"My shoe!" she cried, looking up at me. "I can't...run... without my shoe. I can't..." I bent to pick her up and saw two long streaks of tears glistening on her stained and dusty cheeks. I dragged her to her feet as the urgent shifting of the gravel drew closer to us.

"Let's go to Ma'as Charlie," I said. Without letting go of her hand, I dashed onto the footpath into Calypso Gully. The wind whipped the bushes, the ginger plants, and the coconut trees around us as our footsteps fell soundlessly on the soft earth and grass, alerting none of the neighbors sheltered safely inside their homes. Much later on, when Nanna asked me why I had not stopped at the first house and called for help, I told her I did not know. But I did know why. Naggo Head citizens could handle hurricanes but nothing more; anything worse than a hurricane they were not prepared to handle, and this man chasing us did strike me as worse.

I did not look back for the German, nor did I hear his footsteps. We were just a few yards from Ma'as Charlie's house when I felt the first raindrop. It was large and cool and fell with such an unbelievable force that it stung my shoulder. It was a relief when I saw that the house was in darkness. The hurricane-like rain and wind began just as I slammed the front door shut and fixed the wooden latch on the inside.

I lit one of the matches. The dim light from its small flame fell on Dove as she lay panting on the floor near the doorway, gripping her only remaining shoe. The scarf had fallen off, and her blond hair that perhaps was piled at the top of her head was now hanging in straggly bits about her face. She saw me staring and raised one hand up to her head.

"My scarf!" she gasped.

I put a finger to my lips and motioned for her to follow me. The match flame went out. I lit another match, lifted the braided-coconut-leaf cover from the mouth of the well, and motioned for her to look down the hole. She did. The well gurgled, and the sound echoed eerily in the strange house, pounded outside by whipping winds and pelting rain. She fell away from the well and back onto the floor with her eyes big and round.

"What's that down there?" she gasped. "Is that a stream down there?"

"A water hole," I said.

"A water hole?" she asked, creeping back over to the hole again to look down. "You mean a well?"

I nodded, putting the cover back in place.

"But why?" she whispered. "Why did he build his house over a well?"

I shrugged my shoulders. She saw that it was a careless shrug, and she fell silent.

We sat in darkness and in silence after that, our backs resting against the wall and our feet toward the well. Our vision became accustomed to the room, and due to the slivers of light that came through the numerous chinks and open spaces between the planks along its sides, we no longer needed the matches.

Dove's breathing changed suddenly; she had fallen asleep. I sat there in that darkened room near a hole in the floor and concluded that fear was not permanent. The hole in Ma'as Charlie's floor, the hole that had been my second-biggest fear, was all it was, just a hole in the floor. Fear made the hole bigger than it was. Was it possible that few situations and things deserved the fear we have of them?

I began typing on the phantom typewriter:

Even though I walk through the valley of the shadow of death, I will fear no evil, for you are with me; your rod and your staff, they comfort me. (Psalm 23:4)

For I am the Lord, your God, who takes hold of your right hand and says to you, Do not fear; I will help you. (Isaiah 41:13)

Moses answered the people, "Do not be afraid. Stand firm and you will see the deliverance the Lord will bring you today. The Egyptians you see today you will never see again." (Exodus 14:13).

I have learned over the years that when one's mind is made up, it diminishes fear—determination diminishes fear. Now I know I must not fear. Fear is the mind killer. Fear is the assassin that brings quick and total destruction. I have decided I will face my fear. I will permit it to pass over me and through me. And when it has gone past me, I will turn the inner eye to see its path. Where the fear had been, there will be nothing. Only I will remain.

I became aware of a new presence in the room when I glimpsed what I thought was a bat's wing floating silently downward until its dark velvety tip brushed my arm, which rested on the floor. I mechanically reached out to touch it and felt the hard knot of Dove's head scarf beneath my fingers. And that was when I saw the hulking shadow moving toward Dove.

At that instant the gusting wind blew the door open with such a force that it sent the braided-coconut-leaf lid smashing into the nearby wall. Dove sat up with a start, but before she could spring to her feet, the German grabbed her and pressed her down into the floor.

The moonlight and the flashes of lightning that came through the opened door revealed the German leaning with his entire weight on Dove's body and her legs flayed beneath him as he tried to put handcuffs on her wrists. Then, without warning and with astounding strength, Dove flipped her body over and on top of him. She had the upper hand but only for a short time, because the German threw a solid fist into the side of her face, sending her reeling. The house shuddered, followed by the shrill tearing of fabric and the splintering of wood as she flew backward into the table and the wall.

I was not prepared for the wild fight that followed. And as I could see from the shock on the German's face, neither was he.

The volleying of the gusting winds that rattled the tin roof, and the pounding rain of the hurricane, were no match for the rumble inside Ma'as Charlie's house that night.

The German threw two hard-driving punches. Each blow staggered Dove, but she remained on her feet and returned each one, though with less force. Then she began moving quicker and avoiding his punches, which put her nearer to the hole in the floor.

She sidestepped a punch, and he grabbed a hold of her dress instead. He ripped off the little bolero and one of the shoulder straps of Mrs. Rutherford's flapper dress, exposing the upper half of Dove's body. The German hesitated. He stared at her breast, and Dove, like a ball of fury, hurled herself on him, grabbed his right arm and twisted it around his back, and wrapped one bare arm around his neck from behind and dragged him struggling down to the floor. The muscles in her arms bulged as she locked both around his neck. Her lips were pulled back, baring her teeth, and the veins in her neck looked as though they were about to pop. Two veins pulsed in her sweat-drenched and bloody forehead as she tightened her grip around his neck. She jerked his neck backward in her death grip twice, and each time she jerked it, she let out a guttural, beast-like growl.

When the German's eyes began to bulge, and his tongue protruded big and dark through his lips, the thought did register in my mind that I should stop her, but I could not move. A sudden sense of my uselessness washed over me as I sat and watched in silence. It was only after his body jerked one last time and then was still that she loosened her grip and rolled away from the lifeless form on the floor.

Then there was silence inside the house—dead silence. And it was only with this stillness that I became aware that for a few minutes there were two separate waves of sounds around me that had converged into one—the hurricane outside and the fight inside—and now that one was silenced, hearing only one was even more frightening than the two. The silenced one was lying dead with his face down on the floor.

"You killed him!" I cried.

"I know," she replied, panting and clutching the ripped dress around her body.

"Oh Lord! What we gwine do now?" I wailed.

At my question, Dove sprang into action again. She rolled him over, took his wallet and passport from his pockets, removed the money and identification from the wallet, and put them in her bra. She took the shoes off his feet, dragged the body over to the hole in the floor, and without hesitation or consideration, she pitched it unceremoniously headfirst down the well. The thuds and thumps of the body hitting the rocks on the sides and then splashing into the water were the most horrible and unforgettable sounds I have ever heard. I screamed. I screamed until Dove's bloody and swollen palm connected roughly with my mouth and stopped all sounds from leaving my lips. The screams piled up in my throat with the now-rising bile, and I emptied the contents of my stomach fast and furiously onto Ma'as Charlie's floor.

The shoes were about three sizes too large, but she laced them onto her feet. She threw the wallet down the well.

"What we gwine do now?" I asked again, and my voice echoed in my ears as if it came from deep in the well. It sounded weak and faraway.

She pried her head scarf, which I still clutched, from my fist and tied it around her head. Then she fastened the broken shoulder straps of her dress around her neck. She reached her hand toward me. I did not take her hand. Instead, I shifted my body and settled it more steadfastly on the floor. She extended the hand farther out to me, this time more aggressively. But I could not take her hand. I could not hold the hand that had just strangled a man to death and thrown him down a well; the hand that was blood drenched and now looked muscular and powerful and dangerous.

Without uttering a word, she grabbed my hand firmly and dragged me off the floor and through the door. We stepped out into the raging hurricane and ran all the way home to Nanna, struggling against the rain, the uprooted bushes, the broken tree limbs, and the loose stones that washed downward on the sloping road. The storm was just beginning.

Chapter 13

All of the next day and into the night, the storm raged, and when Nanna pushed her bedroom windows open after morning devotion on the second morning, she looked at the speck of sun peeping from behind the gray clouds, at the uprooted plants, the broken branches hanging from the trees, and the fruits scattered on the grounds, and she inhaled deeply, exhaled, and repeated the opening lines of her morning prayer: "Thank you, Lord, for the blessings you have bestowed on our lives. Thank you for granting us access to the place of your peace."

There was a certain force that a hurricane always left hanging over the island after it passed through. It was a fusion of limpness, grayness, and the awful silence of defeat. Any sense of victory or triumph would come later for me, but for Nanna, her feelings of gratitude and blessings were always instant.

She and my mother had been in the sitting room long after their bedtimes, with the oil lamps lit, when Dove and I had run up the steps and across the veranda two nights earlier. The wind and rain had blown severely through the front door as they pulled us inside. Anxiousness had lined the grooves that were already on Nanna's face, making them deeper.

The head scarf, the skimpy strap dress, and the men's shoes, illuminated by the pale lamplight, made it difficult for them to recognize Dove at first. Even I had difficulty recognizing her. The lamplight cast eerie shadows on her bruised face and busted lips. Her skin, darkened by the harsh island sunshine, was stretched tautly over the exposed muscles in her neck, arms, and shoulders, emphasizing them. The two extended veins were still visible on her forehead.

"Dove is afraid to stay alone on Pill Hill in de hurricane, Nanna" was the only explanation I offered. They understood immediately and jumped around, getting her towels and dry bedclothes. Dove was put in my room, and I shared my mother's bed. I fell quickly into an exhausted asleep and slept soundly.

The next morning Nanna's voice was not strong enough to carry over the howling wind and the beating of the rain on the tin roof, so she kept devotion later than usual, and instead of being in our separate rooms, we gathered in her bedroom. Dove watched in amazement as we sang and prayed, and she did her best to sing and pray along.

I ate very little of the ackee, salted fish, green bananas, and herbal tea that my mother had braved the storm to cook in the detached kitchen. One's visitors always deserved the best of everything, storm or no storm. Dove's appetite was not affected by the events of the night before. She left Nanna and my mother nonplussed when she liked her coffee with "sugar, no moo juice."

She ate and asked for a second serving. Nanna was pleased.

After breakfast, with the hard-pouring rain, the only place to go was in the sitting room, where we had two choices of activity: either sit and look at one another or read a book by lamplight. My mother chose reading her Bible; Nanna, Dove, and I chose sitting and looking.

Then Dove got to her feet and began strolling around the room, picking up objects, putting them down, complimenting and commenting on them; Nanna kept explaining and telling little stories about each piece.

Papa Doc had hand made all the furniture from the blue mahoe tree. The sturdy chairs, tables, beds, and cabinets were all hand turned, with delicate curves and embellishments. Later on, I discovered that the chairs were made in the Windsor style. Instead of paintings, cushions, or pillows, there were embroidered white linen doilies and crocheted runners. Of all the windows, only the two in the great room off the veranda were glass; the others were wooden double half doors that we pushed out to open and pulled in to close. None had curtains or needed curtains. The overhead hand-hewn beams and visible nailheads provided one with a sense of everlasting safety and shelter. Among the luxuries were a hand-propelled sewing machine and a writing table, three blue-and-white china pieces, and a blue glass oil lamp.

The floorboards were irregular in width but smooth and were stained to a deep wine red with logwood tree dye and buffed to a high sheen. Keeping one's floor this red and at this high of a luster was a source of pride in Naggo Head. All the doors had large, weathered outside hinges, with beautifully carved wooden latches that turned to open and close from a single nail in the middle—there was no need for lock and keys.

Again I noticed Dove's sun-kissed skin. How dark her complexion had become! Nanna noticed it too and mentioned it, and

Dove playfully picked up a piece of brown wrapping paper and held it to her tanned face.

"I am as brown as this paper," she joked.

Nanna and my mother threw their heads back and laughed heartily, but Nanna noticed that I had not laughed and suggested that we all make rag mats to pass the time and to keep away boredom. But I did not want to make rag mats; I wanted Dove to talk to me. I wanted her to notice that I was still wearing the bra she had given me. I wanted to know about the secret she was hiding, the secret that had caused her to strangle a man to death—a man who had been about seventy pounds heavier and about six inches taller than she was.

But Nanna and my mother were already running around gathering scissors, large pieces of burlap, and scraps of brightly colored fabric. We cut the scraps in one-half-inch-wide strips, interwove them into the burlap, and tied them individually, leaving two-inch-long ends that formed a soft, plush surface. We spent most of the day making these mats until my mother left to cook dinner.

That was when Nanna pulled up her chair and sat facing us. "Cherrimina, Dove," she began, "you have somet'ing to tell me?" Her face was inscrutable.

Dove went stock-still for a few seconds, and then her body began to vibrate. I felt a heat rising up off her body. Just at that moment, my mother hollered from the kitchen. It was barely audible above the beating rain. Nanna wrapped her shawl around her shoulders and went to the back veranda to see what my mother wanted.

I looked at Dove; she did not look at me. She hung her head instead. I stretched my hand toward her, touched her wrist, and said something that I had heard Bro' Man say a thousand times, one of his phrases that I had written in my notebook: "Tell her de trut', de whole trut', an' not'ing but de trut'."

Nanna came back in the room and took her seat.

Dove took a deep breath.

"I killed a man," she began.

Nanna looked at me, looked at Dove, and then looked back at me. Her eyes were wide, and her lips moved but produced no sound. I nodded.

"I strangled a man to death last night in Ma'as Charlie's house and threw his body down the well," Dove said in a cracked voice.

She continued. She had been born and raised in New York City, on Tenth Avenue, between Thirty-Ninth and Thirty-Eighth Streets. Her mother had been very young and could not take care of her properly, so both of them had drifted from home to home until she was seventeen. Then one day men in uniforms had come and taken her mother away. The night before the men had come, her mother had seemed terribly disoriented. She had alternated between weeping and cursing.

"Then she pulled me tightly to her bosom and told me that she wished I was never born. And that she loved me."

The pause here was so long that I thought Dove had fallen asleep, but she continued.

She had found work in a speakeasy on Fifty-Fourth Street as a cigarette girl. The Icepick, it had been called. She had hated the place at first. Everyone had called her a "glass of milk" because she was so young. Then Jimmy, a tall job from Chicago, had started coming in. He had been plenty rugged, with gorgeous blue peepers. He had just gotten out of the pen on good conduct and wanted a fresh start in the Apple. He did not drink booze and always ordered a dog soup.

"Can you believe a guy like that drinking only water?" she asked.

I shook my head.

He had had eyes only for Dove, but a canary at the club had started blowing her wig over him. She had been a real crumb who had thought of herself as a vamp. She had bubs, but Dove had the stems. Furthermore, Dove had heard rumors that she was on the gong.

"Gong?" Nanna asked. I had decided to stop interrupting her story with questions, but I, too, had been lost on that one.

"Opium pipe. Drugs. I heard also that she was a lunger. Tuberculosis. I deliberately helped to spread that one."

At least once a night when she would walk by Jimmy, he would look at her legs and say, "Nice stems, Milk!" She and Jimmy had just been bumping gums, but the wheat with the bad gams from Idaho had gotten it wrong and started making trouble. She had begun reporting lies about Dove to the authorities. She had reported that Dove was a quiff, but Dove had yelled back that it was a lie and that she had never slept with anyone, much less for money. She had also told the authorities that Dove was retarded, a third-generation imbecile, and should not be allowed to bring another retarded kid into this world.

Looking back now, I can almost tell her story word for word, having heard it numerous times over the first twenty-two-year period of our lives together. She told it when she was happy, when she was sad, when she drank too much wine, or when she was angry, but only when we were alone, and never once did she cry over her past life. But she did have one regret: she regretted that she could only tell her story to me because no one else would believe it.

And so, while the storm raged outside, we snipped strips of fabric and made rag mats, and Dove told her story.

"It was immediately after the wheat had told everyone that I had been involved with men of color that I had begun noticing a lanky gumshoe hanging around the building in which I lived and around the speakeasy. Six weeks later, on my way to work one Friday evening, a vehicle with a covered-wagon-like back area pulled up alongside me, and two ugly pills jumped out, pushed me inside, and drove off. That was the last time I was to see my neighborhood.

"They drove me across town and then over a bridge. I knew it was a bridge by the different sound the tires made. It was about nine o'clock that night when they stopped the motorcar and hustled me into a brick building. The room they pushed me into was dark. After my eyes adjusted to the dark, I saw six hospital beds and five girls, one girl to a bed. The room was cold. On the sixth bed was a night dress. I put it on and put my coat back on over it. None of the girls spoke to me or to one another. The last sound I heard before I fell asleep was one of the girls sobbing.

"When I woke up the next morning, I was alone in the room. Three of the mattresses on the other five beds had been rolled up. The walls were clean, though a drab gray, and the bare windows were dirty only on the outside. My purse, shoes, and clothes were gone and had been replaced by fuzzy bed slippers. I tried the door, and it was locked on the outside.

"Breakfast was on a tray near my bed. I ate the eggs and toast but left the half of grapefruit untouched. I washed that down with the glass of milk.

"About ten o'clock later that morning, a female aide with extremely thick glasses ushered me to a bathroom, where I was made to take a shower and given a plain shift to wear. The aide took away my underwear and did not replace it. Any attempts on my part to speak or to communicate were squashed or ignored.

"So, wearing only a shift and the fuzzy bed slippers, I was escorted by a younger woman in a white overcoat to the back of a room on the second floor. Men in suits and women with bad stems in white flat-heeled shoes and stockings, doctors with stethoscopes around their necks, and nurses in white uniforms were assembled in this room that looked like a gymnasium. A banner with the lettering 'Race Betterment Seminar' ran across the platform where a projector had been set up. Films were shown of feebleminded, drooling, and crippled children; drunken men staggering on the street; and homeless men and women with bundles, talking to themselves. They showed images of round heads and labeled them low intelligence, and they showed images of heads shaped like a ball that had been stepped on and labeled them high intelligence. A Caucasian woman holding the hand of a mixed-race child was described as one who did not have the 'normal aversion of white women to colored men.'

"Speakers with titles such as attorney, scientist, doctor, geneticist, and historian, from groups such as the American Breeders Society, quoted lines from laws and acts with titles such as the Model Sterilization Act and were applauded long and heartily.

"They used terms such as *eugenics, race degeneration, race suicide, Anglo-Saxon heritage, paupers, illiterates, criminals, sterilization,* and *racial hygiene. Dregs of society* was a popular phrase. Large maps and charts were displayed of normal and degenerate lines of pedigreed and defective families.

"At the end, the audience was able to ask questions. Irate, loud men stood up and asked questions about castration, hazardous medication, horror, misery, and engineering humans like agricultural templates—like cattle.

"Then one audience member stood up and asked if anyone had thought of what would become of society in the not-so-near future when all humans were perfect. When all those with the imperfect genes had been eliminated, he continued, and society was eugenically sound, and the gene pool had become limited, wouldn't the result be somewhat like inbreeding? And with inbreeding, wouldn't that result in mutation and diseases?

"'We all agree that mutation does not create new genes,' the man had said, stepping into the aisle and raising his voice; 'it only exposes the already existing ones. Supposing those exposed genes prove to be even more defective than these existing today. What do we do then?'

"It was at this point that a man in a white lab coat saw me in the audience and rebuked the young attendant for having me in the wrong place. I was rushed out of there and into a small office in the basement, in which I was locked.

"There was a hard, leather-covered table equipped with leather straps and metal stirrups. The wait was fairly short. The key turned in the door, and a man entered. I recognized him as one of the speakers from earlier in the seminar.

"He was very professional—not friendly but not threatening either. I decided then that he deserved to be called *sir*. He asked me questions and wrote nonstop in a book. He asked my name, date of birth, and address.

"'Where is your mother?'

"'I don't know, sir.'

"'When was the last time you saw her?'

"'Almost four years ago. Men in white uniforms took her away.'

"'And your father?'

"'I have never seen him.'

"'So you have been on your own since you were almost seventeen?'

"'Yes, sir.'"

"'What do you do for money? Do you work?'

"'Yes. I am a hatcheck girl in a speakeasy.'

"The questions then became more personal and about my mother's illness, until at last he opened the door, and the same young attendant wheeled in a cart on which were laid out all kinds of shiny metal tools. The man stepped out, and the attendant told me to climb up on the hard leather table. I climbed up with my back to the attendant and sat on my haunches with my legs folded beneath me. The attended laughed out loud and told me to turn around, remove my slippers, lie on my back, and put my legs up in the shiny stirrups.

"I had just put my feet in the stirrups when I remembered that I was not wearing my underwear, but the attendant threw a white sheet over my torso and legs, and I felt more at ease. Then a doctor with a stethoscope around his neck came in and without a word took a seat on a small stool in front of the stirrups and directed a bright lamp under the sheet.

"Surprised at his bizarre behavior, I struggled to sit up, but before I could remove my feet from the stirrups, the doctor gasped. After the gasp, he stood still and silent for several seconds. He stood so still that that the young attendant walked from her side of the table to look under the sheet. She, too, gasped. The doctor motioned to her, and she bolted out the door.

"Too frightened to move, I lay still until the attendant rushed back in with three other doctors and a nurse. They, too, stared under the sheet. It was then that I began to struggle to get off the table. It was just as I removed the sheet from my legs and began screaming that I felt the prick in my buttocks and looked up to see the nurse with a needle.

"The next thing I knew was waking up in the back of a vehicle, strapped to a metal table. My mouth was dry, and I was hungry. Two male attendants flipping through magazines glanced at me. Their faces were kind. One of them lifted my head, and I sipped cool water from a cup he put to my lips. Then the vehicle turned into a property full of whitewashed buildings with rows and rows of barred windows, with the sign 'Virginia Colony for the Epileptic and Feeblemindedness' above its entrance. It was late afternoon.

"Four times in the next three days, I was subjected to examinations in several offices on tables with stirrups, attended by men and women in lab coats and carrying stethoscopes. They wrote in notebooks. Photographs were taken of me spread-eagled on the tables. Other times I was mercifully rendered unconscious for these examinations. I was questioned and prodded, yet no one told me why they were so interested in me.

"In the meantime, I was housed alone in a room with a single bed and a table with chipped paint. I ate my meals in the cafeteria with almost sixty others. I was given plain, nondescript clothes and shoes; some fit better than others. My movements were restricted, but only slightly. I was allowed freedom within the compound, but the entrance was out of bounds, even though it was not heavily guarded.

"I made friends with an older woman named Maria White. I learned that Maria was a mother to a little girl who was mentally challenged and who lived on the compound but was housed in a separate building. The doctors had sterilized Maria about three months earlier, so she could not have any more children. They had taken her to a room with shiny metal instruments, and when she had woken up later, she had had stitches on her stomach.

"She had been allowed out daily to go to the maid job she had at a rich woman's house.

"Maria loved to talk, and I let her talk. She told me which bus she caught and where to get to the neighborhood where she worked as a maid. She knew other maids and also other wealthy folks who were looking for maids to do their cleaning. She also told me about advertisements for maids in the newspaper. There were even live-in maid jobs. 'You will need references,' Maria told me. Rich folks always wanted references. She showed me a written reference that she had lost and had had to have replaced by the matron, only to find it a few days later. She even told me how easy it was to get to the train station.

"Two days later I was summoned to one of the doctor's offices. He told me that after all the examinations, it was determined that they might not have to proceed with the sterilization surgery they had planned. However, they had discovered complications that needed further studying. This was why they would have to transfer me the next day to a more specialized hospital in Maryland for further study and tests.

"He showed me images of male and female external genital organs that were placed on one wall. Then he put photographs of my genitalia beside them. I had seen the difference before he explained it.

"I didn't know I was different!" Dove then declared to Nanna. She was near tears. "I had never seen mine or any other."

"That same night I escaped. The plan had been simple: steal money from Maria; write a fake reference; don several items of her clothes for warmth, just in case the weather turned chilly and to avoid carrying a bundle of clothes; wait until dark and climb the fence at the rear of the building; walk the almost one mile out to the street; hop on the streetcar to the train station, where I would stay all night; buy a wig and a newspaper; and look for live-in maid jobs.

"I got the first job for which I interviewed. Mrs. Rutherford was a small, frail woman with two little girls, and I knew instantly that she would not bother to check the names on the reference letter that I had forged. Her kindness was obvious from that first day, and so was her need for a friend. The doctor had told her that she needed more sunshine to get better, but Mr. Rutherford had had some bad luck recently, and they could not afford to go back to the West Indies, where they had lived for five years while Mr. Rutherford supervised a sugar factory on an island. They had moved back to the United States when Mrs. Rutherford was expecting her first child, and everyone had told her that the best place for prenatal care and to raise children was the United States. They had planned on going back to the pink house on Pill Hill for vacations.

"At nights, they told me stories about their time spent on the island, about the house, the villagers, and their culture. They had good memories of their time spent on the island. For five weeks, I cooked, washed, cleaned, and cared for the two little girls. Mrs. Rutherford was kind enough to overlook my shortcomings in some areas of the work, but I learned fast.

"Then one day I was sent to shop for vegetables at the community farmer's market and bumped into Maria. She was with a well-dressed woman. I was shocked that Maria recognized me straightaway, even with the short auburn wig I wore. Maria could not talk very long, not with her superior waiting and watching, but she shared with me that it was rumored that a private detective had been assigned to find me and take me back to the compound. She told me that some of the doctors and nurses considered my dimwitted escape a blight and a disgrace on the Virginia Colony for the Epileptic and Feeblemindedness and on them personally, and the only redemption they could accept was to find me and bring me back as soon as possible, dead or alive. Maria told me that it was said that the detective they hired was one of the best. He could find anyone and anything.

"I went home and told Mrs. Rutherford a story that I needed a few days to visit my sister in Hackensack, New Jersey. I said she was down on her luck and was now ill and needed my support financially and physically. I left with the five weeks' wages and some secondhand clothes that Mrs. Rutherford had been generous enough to donate, and I rode the next train to New York City.

"It was cold, rainy, and gray when I arrived in New York City. I immediately felt at home and purchased a soft pretzel and a hot dog with mustard and sauerkraut. But I knew that I could not stay in New York, so I purchased a ticket on the next ship leaving for the West Indies. I booked a room in a motel and spent the next two days walking the streets of my old neighborhoods and enjoying my favorite haunts: the skyscrapers, the Brooklyn Bridge, South Ferry, bums sitting on benches at Battery Park, tenement stoops near the East River, fire escapes, stores on Broome Street, store windows in Chinatown, Italian bakeshops below Canal Street, peanut sellers' pushcarts, produce trucks lined up end to end at Washington Market, delivery trucks' traffic jams on Thirty-Seventh Street, the various languages of immigrants yelling warnings as they pushed carts with hanging clothes around the garment center, clotheslines crisscrossing in the skyline of six-story backyards, the bright glow of the signs of Times Square movie houses, barber shops, and lunchrooms. I don't know how they tracked me to the island. Perhaps Maria told them something. Maria loves to talk."

Dove finished her story, and all three of us sat in silence. I had forgotten about the storm raging over the island. Then Nanna spoke.

"What did de doctor say was different wit' you?"

"He said I have...atypical genitalia."

"What is dat? I don't know what dat is," Nanna replied, shaking her head from side to side.

Dove made several attempts to explain and then gave up and did something quite unexpected and shocking. She reached under her dress, pulled her underwear down, stood up from the chair to face Nanna, and stepped out of the underwear. Then she lifted one foot and set it down on top of her chair seat, and she lifted the front of her dress. Nanna sat stock-still at first, and then she slowly reached out and pulled the oil lamp from the center of the table toward the edge closest to her and stared for what seemed like an eternity.

I waited for Nanna to speak, and when she didn't, I moved toward her chair, prepared to see what she was seeing from her angle because I could not see anything from my angle. Before I could take the second step, Nanna put out her hand palm outward and stopped me in my track.

"Stay, chile!" she ordered.

I shrank back into myself at the uncommon authoritarian quality in her voice. She noticed and took that time to say something endearing.

"An' button you lip, sugar plum," she added as Dove quickly put her clothes back on.

I sat in my chair and banged out the word on the phantom typewriter: a-t-y-p-i-c-a-l g-e-n-i-t-a-l-i-a. I typed it again, this time in uppercase letters.

Just then my mother entered the room with a gust of wind and rain and a steaming pot of gungo-pea soup.

Chapter 14

By nightfall the storm had lost its frenzy. By the next morning, Nanna's daily devotion had gone back to normal, and we worshipped in our separate bedrooms. After singing a chorus, she began with a quote from the book of Numbers, chapter thirty-five, verse thirty: "Whoso killeth any person, the murderer shall be put to death by the mouth of witnesses: but one witness shall not testify against any person to cause him to die."

And she ended it with Proverbs chapter seventeen, verse nine: "Whoever covers an offense seeks love, but he who repeats a matter separates close friends."

After our final "amen," I heard Dove start to applaud, then stop suddenly.

The storm had also ended, and one by one the neighbors emerged from their doorways to compare damages. The Sweet River had overflowed its banks in several places but stayed within its usual course; it had changed its course during the 1912 storm. Coconuts and branches dotted the ground, six goats were killed by uprooted trees, and two houses were destroyed; one house had its entire roof blown off, and Ma'as Charlie's was completely demolished—a tree on the hill at the back of the house had uprooted and fallen on top of it. We were told that it had been flattened to ground level.

We at Mill Yard were lucky. Besides fruits blown from their branches and littering the ground, only the citrus tree that Papa Doc had grafted was destroyed. He had cut a piece out of the trunk of a lime tree and inserted it into a gash he had cut in an orange tree trunk and tied it in place with twine. The tree did eventually bear fruit, but the roughly dimpled peel was an ugly mustard color, and the inside was a washed-out maroon. Also, it had very little juice and an unpleasant taste—somewhere between the tartness of the lime and the sweetness of the orange with a dash of soil. One of its branches had caught the clothesline and broken it.

But life quickly came back to Naggo Head. The roosters began crowing. The birds came back from wherever it was that they went during a hurricane and were flying from branch to branch, shaking the leaves, chirping, and singing. Small wild creatures scurried and romped under the bushes and shrubberies. My mother opened the coop to free the chickens, and they strutted and hopped around, clucking, scratching the ground, preening, and pecking.

It was just after breakfast that we heard masculine voices calling Nanna from the entrance of Mill Yard. They were two police constables in full uniform attire sitting astride beautifully groomed horses. By this time the sun was no longer peeking out from behind the clouds; it was radiant and daring in the sky, and they shaded their eyes with their hands. Two policemen in full official uniform sitting on large horses at the end of one's property can be intimidating if you witnessed a murder the night before.

Nanna had told Dove to stay indoors and out of sight after morning prayers, and at the sight of the constables, she hustled Dove to the back of the house. She used a small crowbar to pry out two wide planks of the flooring near the back steps to reveal a closed-off space about four feet high and about six feet long, and she told Dove to get in. I had had no idea that this private hidey-hole existed.

"It's damp," Dove whispered, and Nanna assured her that it would not be long and she would be safe there.

I pushed Dove's clothes, her wig, and the German's shoes in the space with her. My mother set about sweeping the floor with the broom.

Nanna greeted the constables.

"Good mahning, Constable Mannings. Good mahning, Constable Burton."

She invited the men onto the veranda; she offered coffee or tea, which they refused.

They put questions to us about a missing German tourist who had been seen searching for a young woman around the Blue Bay area and in Naggo Head. I listened and typed on my phantom typewriter.

They said that they had information that the young woman was a friend of Nanna's granddaughter, as she had been seen at the house on Pill Hill, and the young tourist had been seen visiting Mill Yard. The German had last been seen getting out of a car at Cross Road and making his way to the house on Pill Hill.

They had paid a visit to the house, but it was empty. The hurricane must have hit it hard, because the front and back doors were thrown open, allowing the wind and rain inside, and it had overturned and broken the furniture.

Nanna said yes, the young lady had visited Mill Yard, but that had been about three weeks before. She was known to like lying on the banks of the Sweet River—perhaps she had fallen into it. Had they searched the river? No, they had not searched the river, but a single woman's shoe had been found just a piece down Naggo Head Road from Mill Yard, and someone had said it looked like the shoe the young lady had been wearing a couple of days earlier. It was not a type of shoe that anyone in Naggo Head would have worn, and it was similar to other shoes found in the closet on Pill Hill. Also, they had found a wet German newspaper that seemed to have been dropped on the floor of the house at Pill Hill. They knew the newspaper did not belong to anyone in the house because it had directions to the house scribbled with pen in the margin of the front page.

Nanna asked them if they would like to come inside and search her house. They turned her down but wanted to confirm with all three of us one last time that we had never seen the shoe before. We shook our heads in unison. After they had mounted their horses and left, Nanna went to her favorite chair to read her Bible, and my mother went to take Dove out of hiding. I had been raised to obey every rule of the Ten Commandments, but of late it was getting harder and harder to do so. It used to be so easy. I intended to find a place to kneel and ask God to forgive me for lying about the shoe, but first I had to take Nanna's urgent message to Barabbas—a message that was for his ears only. A coconut telegram, Bro' Man named it. She wanted Barabbas to come see her quietly and as quickly as possible.

Barabbas was busy helping his Naggo Head neighbors restore their runaway animals, their broken fences, and their water-logged properties and told me to ask Nanna if she could please allow him to come around dinnertime. I ran all the way back to Nanna with his message. She said it was acceptable. I ran back to Barabbas with this reply and then ran back home. Nanna told me to go back to Barabbas and help the neighbors. I was happy to be neighborly because I was still not sure what to say to Dove. I was still not truly comfortable around her. And I was sure she would be happy for a little time to be with her thoughts. It was a small and close space in Nanna's house.

By late afternoon the sun had dried out the water-soaked soil, and by dinnertime, when Barabbas walked through the Mill Yard entrance, the smell of wet wood and leaves and mud and clay had almost vanished. Barabbas gifted Nanna with a bunch of fresh jelly coconuts he had salvaged.

Because we still had a visitor, we ate inside the house instead of in the detached kitchen. Barabbas was a little uncomfortable with eating inside the house and even more so with doing it in front of a foreigner. He once told me that eating inside the middle of a house was like a rat eating inside its hole.

As soon as Nanna began explaining why she had summoned him, his nervousness went with the wind, and something else took its place.

Nanna had a plan. She told it to us but mostly to Barabbas as he carefully loaded enough food on his fork for an extended chewing.

The nice lady foreigner, Dove, needed to get off the island and get home to America without anyone except us seeing or knowing anything about it. Nanna had already checked the newspaper for the arrival and departure schedule of the ships, and there was a ship leaving Blue Bay for Cuba in two days. If Barabbas could get someone to purchase a ticket in Dove's name, she could board the ship safely and set sail home worry free.

Barabbas chewed his food in silence, his eyes shifting back and forth between the four of us women sitting and staring at him.

Then I became convinced that if he did not speak soon, we would all be hypnotized into a trance by the sound of tongue licking against food, teeth, and gums and the hammering of jawbone. At last, I heard the opening and closing of the esophageal sphincter as he swallowed. Then he spoke.

"Sonny Bwoy cum back frahm dung ah Blue Beya todeh an seh de wharf swahming wid de police dem. Dey looking fah a missing touris'. Ei noh safe dung deh."

Seeing the puzzled look on Dove's face, Nanna nodded to me, and instinctively I knew the nod meant that I should translate this for Dove.

"Sonny Boy came back from down Blue Bay today and said dat police is searching all over de wharf looking for a missing tourist," I said. "It is not safe dere."

Nanna continued. If Barabbas could not find anyone to purchase the ticket, perhaps he knew someone who could ferry her to Quail Isle, where she could wait in hiding for the ship, and when it made its stop, she could secretly climb aboard and stow away on it. Everyone knew that all the ships leaving the island for

America usually made a stop at Quail Isle, which was just about two miles off the coast of Cuba.

Barabbas's gaze narrowed. It narrowed in such a sinister way that I became aware of this one troubling fact: Barabbas might no longer be a thief, but he still thought like a thief. He was suspicious and distrustful. Still, he remained silent.

Nanna continued. Everyone knew that Barabbas had had his problems, she said, but that he had put his troubled past behind him and was now one of the most helpful, kindest, and most respected people in Naggo Head. Everyone came to him because they know that he was dependable, and that proved that he was not a "boogooyagga boy."

Barabbas sat as if he were waiting for more, as if he knew with all certainty that there was something missing. We all waited. He was no longer chewing because the food on his plate was gone.

Then Dove's voice penetrated the dense silence that was barely contained by the four walls.

"Last night I killed a man," she said. "He tried to kill me first. It was either his life or mine. I have committed an unforgivable sin, and I will spend the rest of my life begging the Lord for forgiveness. Now I must get back home, or they will hang me here."

Barabbas perked up. He sat erect in his chair, his eyes big and his mouth opened wide.

"Lawd ah massi!" he finally exclaimed.

"Lord have mercy!" I translated, proud to be contributing to the conversation between adults.

"Wha'?" he exclaimed again.

"What?" I translated.

Then finally Barabbas's face rested and fell into a soft, gentle place.

"Doah cry, pretty lady, ma'am," he begged. "Doah worry— mi wi help yu get back to Mericah safe an' soun'."

"Don't cry, pretty lady," I interpreted. "Don't worry—I will help you get back safe and sound to 'Merica."

"Dankey seh dis worl' noh level. Hill an' gully yahso; hill an' gully over dehso," my mother declared.

"A donkey says dis world is not level. Hill and gully over here; hill and gully over there. This world is full of ups and downs," I translated for Dove.

With that said, Barabbas took charge—a charge that was dictatorial in its credentials and epic in its proportion. Foremost, he bragged that after he'd seen the pirate movie in the movie house in Blue Bay three years ago, he had spent time planning this same adventure. He had perfected how to escape the island by boat to America without being seen or caught. He laid out this plan to us, and in this production he was the writer, director, and star.

First, Dove would have to dress like a man. She should cut her hair short. Neither he nor any other man in Naggo Head had the proper clothes for her to wear, so he would steal clothes, a hat, and shoes from Pootus. Dove should rub a little earth over her face and hands to darken her skin a little. He had seen that in a movie at the movie house in Blue Bay.

I translated all of that to Dove, who listened with a constant stream of emotions fluttering about her mouth and the corners of her nose.

"I already have a pair of man's shoes," Dove informed Barabbas.

Next, he would take a trip to Blue Bay seaside later that night to see a half-Chinese fisherman named Squid. Squid earned extra money by sailing to Cuba several times a week at nights to pick up and deliver suspicious-looking cargo for a businessman in Blue Bay. Barabbas had accompanied him on several of these trips. Squid would take them to Cuba in his boat, but he would ask for money. The connecting man in Cuba and the one on the freighter would need to be paid too. Did the pretty lady have money? Good. He would find out the total cost and let her know.

They could not take public transportation to Blue Bay, nor could they trust anyone to give them a motorcar ride, so they would go by his bicycle. Could Dove ride a bicycle? Good. Four miles was a very long way for one person to tow another on a bicycle. It would have been better if they had two bicycles, but since there was only his, they would take turns pedaling if necessary. Furthermore, if they used two, how would he get the second one back to Naggo Head? Dove would meet him at Cross Road around eight o'clock the next evening. It was a good little ride, and that should put them in Blue Bay in time for Squid's trip.

Nanna should prepare food for Dove: hard-boiled eggs, drinking water (preferably rainwater or coconut water), a few fresh fruits (but mostly dried fruits and nuts), corn pone, smoked fish, crackers, cheese, and bread. The voyage from Cuba to New York might take five to six days, and since the boat was mainly a freighter, she would be traveling among the cargo, and she would be responsible for her own meals.

"I have someone's passport and identification papers that I could use." This from Dove did not even cause a pause in Barabbas's pitch.

Do not put the food in a straw basket or straw bag, Barabbas warned—she would look like a lost tourist and would attract too much attention. Nanna should tie the food in the warmest and darkest-color bedsheet she had, as Dove would need something to cover her body or to rest her head on at nights. Did anyone know how to tie a cross-body bag? No? Fold the sheet in half, tie the food in the middle of the sheet, and then tie the sheet across the body like a sling for a broken arm. He had seen that in a movie at the movie house in Blue Bay.

The nearer she got to New York, the colder it would be, so she should dress in all the clothes to keep warm. He had seen that in another movie at the movie house. Also, the smaller and lighter the bundle she was carrying, the less suspicious and curious people would be. Oh yes, she should not wear any perfume. She must remember that she was a man now and should smell of musky sweat. Every now and then she should curse, spit, grunt, and scratch.

"Alphanso…" Nanna's attempt to interrupt was disregarded, and he continued.

Dove should keep in mind that she would be in the bottom of a freighter in the middle of the ocean, surrounded by huge containers filled with possibly dangerous cargo worth millions of dollars, so it was possible that she would be tossed about by turbulence and get seasick. Cargo ships didn't have stabilizers, so they rocked more than passenger ships. Nanna should pack ginger or peppermint candy to help with the seasickness. Some people were lucky to have the rocking put them to sleep; he hoped she would be one of the lucky ones. Also, cargo ships had been known to get hijacked by pirates, but this rarely happened nowadays.

After she got to New York, she would be on her own. Did the lady know her way around that city? Good. He would see us all later that night when he brought Pootus's clothes.

He started to walk away as if he considered the discussion closed.

"Alphanso!" Nanna cried, putting a shaky hand out toward him. Barabbas turned to face us.

"T'ank yu for yu help," Nanna said. "Dis is a very great plan. Yu t'ink of everyt'ing. But dis fine plan, it is for a man. A woman can't do all dat."

"Wan fingah cyaah kill louse," my mother interjected.

"One finger alone cannot kill lice," I translated.

"I have someone's identification papers that I could use." This was again from Dove.

Barabbas's stiff back and tight mouth highlighted his tyrannical stance. His gaze flashed around the room. I knew he saw Dove's limpness and Nanna's shakiness. My mother's stillness would be hard to read. I swallowed the bile that was then rising in my throat.

"Yu right, Nanna, ma'am," he admitted, and relaxed his stance. "It is a tough plan. But don't worry, mi can fix it. Noah mug no bruk; noah cahfee no dash weh."

Nanna nodded and whispered thanks.

"De mug is not broken; derefore, the coffee is not spilled. Do not make a mountain out of a molehill," I translated.

Barabbas said he would make changes to the voyage part of the plan, but in the meantime, we should carry on with the food preparations. Then Nanna excused herself from the room, motioning that she would be back shortly. When she came back, she was carrying Papa Doc's pocket watch. She set its time to her clock on the shelf, and then she gave it to Barabbas.

"To keep time wit' de ship dem," she told him. He opened and closed the flap several times as he grinned from ear to ear. He thanked Nanna profusely.

"Good evening, Nanna, ma'am. Good evening, Mary Mary. Good evening, pretty lady. Ta-ta, Cherrimina."

We sat in silence and listened to the sound of his rapid footsteps kicking and pushing the loose stones, sending them scattering, and then stomping and grinding them into the ground as he walked, whistling a jolly tune up Naggo Head Road.

When we could no longer hear him, Nanna and my mother talked about him. They knew that he would keep his word. After all, he had kept his word when he promised that he would no longer steal from his neighbors or stir up any more trouble in this peaceful place that kind and gentle folks called their home. When Uncle Cobey had accidentally cut his toe off with his field fork while working his field over at Matilda Walk, even though he was wearing water boots, wasn't Barabbas the one who had pushed him in a wheelbarrow under the hot sun all the way to the clinic at Cross Road? Remember how scrawny and underfed he had been at sixteen when the Fergusons brought him home wearing pitchy-patchy pants? Yes, he had truly grown into a kind-hearted man. They knew that it was because of his brashness and tyrannical attitude, even though he had kept his shenanigans with Squid hidden over the years, and that Dove would be transported safely on her voyage from Blue Bay to America.

Nanna set to cleaning the oil lamps' glass chimneys, and my mother went to clean up the kitchen. I was exhausted from all that translating from patois to proper English and wanted to just sit, but Dove wanted some fresh air, so we sneaked out to the back side of the kitchen, where we knew we would be safe from inquisitive eyes.

Chapter 15

Behind the kitchen I was surprised to see that the pile of stones that I had heaped there a few weeks earlier were still there and had not been washed away by the hurricane. They were a type known to display a soft white gleam when in the dark. I told Dove how we could use the stones to create a moonshine baby. The water-soaked soil was dry by then, so she lay on her back on the ground with her arms outstretched to the sides, and I arranged her skirt wide around her extended legs and then began placing the stones in single file along the outline of her body.

As I worked at arranging the stones, we connected and talked as we had that night on Pill Hill. The bond between us that I thought had been broken had only been stretched to its limit. She seemed much like her old self again; she was gentle and kind.

"What do you want to be when you are grown up, Mina?" she asked me, sighing.

"I want to write stories," I replied, "but that's not a real job. So I should be a postmistress." I had been told many times, and was now convinced, that postmistress, teacher, and nurse were real jobs. After all, I didn't know of, or had never seen, a banker, a singer, a dentist, or a lawyer.

"I wanted to be cabaret singer," she said, sighing. "There were times when I would have this scene playing continuously for days in my head: I'm standing on a dark stage leaning against a white piano; the house is packed with a beautiful, classy crowd ordering champagne. They've come from all over to see me. From Paris, London, the Netherlands. At the entrance is a full-size picture of me. The marquee in lights reads, 'Miss Dove Diamond.' Me, Dove Diamond, the star and toast of New York City!

"Bored bachelors in tuxedos and with manicured nails line the bar at the back, exhaling clouds of smoke as they wait for the show to begin. I am wearing just a touch of my favorite perfume, Soir de Paris—'evening in Paris.'

"I am draped in a sleeveless, curve-hugging, steel-blue, floor-length gown. It is weighted down with eight hundred beads from top to bottom. The neckline is high in front and plunges low to the waist in the back. I am wearing long black gloves that go way above my elbows. On my feet are dyed-to-match steel-blue shoes made in France, with Spanish-type high heels and silver buckles. My hair is pulled back to a low, sleek chignon. Diamond earrings are glistening at my ears.

"Then the drum rolls, but I won't have an entrance. The emcee announces me from backstage. Suddenly, a baby spotlight is turned on and hits the stage. It searches the stage as if intoxicated or disoriented. Then it collides with the piano—all that is to create anticipation and suspense, you see. The room grows hushed; the clinking of glasses and chatter stop. You can hear a pin drop.

"I lift a glove-swathed hand from the piano and bring it slowly into the spotlight. Between my fingers I am holding a long, long cigarette holder, with smoke curling up from the cigarette at the end of it. The spotlight brightens and engulfs me. I put the other hand low on my thigh, the piano player hits the first note, and I begin to sing. Oh, how I sing! The lyrics are hauntingly beautiful. The tune is at first full of love, then of angst, then alarm, then love again. By the last note, the piano player is weeping, and the mesmerized audience erupts into cheering and applauding—'Encore! Encore!' are their cries. I step forward, and I am flooded with spotlights. I blow kisses, I smile, I wave, and then I give a small bow to the left, lowering my head about twenty degrees, and a faint trail of my perfume wafts into my already-amplified senses. I turn and bow to the piano player. Then I take one step backward and make a very deep bow to the center. And the curtain drops."

At the end of it, I wanted to cry. Mostly because she spoke of another place, another life, one that was foreign to me and to which one day she must return. She did not talk about the island, about us, nor about the event that had taken place at Ma'as Charlie's house. I wanted her to tell me about the secret that Nanna knew, but she didn't.

With the stones now completely arranged around her, Dove got up to see the result.

"I love it. What a great idea! But she looks sad," she remarked. "She looks like an orphan. Can we do anything to make her look a little happier?"

I suggested we use smaller stones to make a ribbon for her hair or make two braids hanging to her shoulders.

"How about a crown?" she asked. I added a crown, and she was happy with her moonshine baby.

🙵

Just before devotion that night, Nanna suggested we go swimming in Mullet Hole early the next morning. This was something she had loved to do after a hurricane since she was a child. It was always a treat to go swimming with Nanna. Her regular swimming sprees were early Sunday mornings, before church, but whenever Sweet River overflowed its banks, like it had during the hurricane a few days earlier, Mullet Hole, an area of the river just above Nanna's house, would be deeper and wider and was just perfect for a before-dawn adventurous swim.

After devotion that night, when all of Naggo Head was asleep, when I lay in bed listening to the creaking walls and floors, the crickets, croaking frogs, and hooting owls, Barabbas tapped on my mother's window and dropped off a bundle of Pootus's clothes. He told us to tell Nanna that he was still working on changing the plan, but the date and time still remained as planned. We did not hear him come, nor did we hear him go.

It was a few minutes to five o'clock when Nanna woke us up to go swimming the next morning. We did not own swimsuits since that particular item of clothing was frowned upon even by the nonchurchgoers, so we donned full underslips. The moon was low and splashed a cool, silvery-blue light over all, even the shadows, and we did not need torches or lanterns. We trudged the almost hundred yards or so up toward the riverhead through the profusion of undergrowth and the tall, damp weeds, crushing snails and succulent plants underfoot and sending small bush creatures scurrying. Excited as Dove was, she was on unfamiliar terrain, so she had a little difficulty keeping up with us.

Mullet Hole was deep and shaded, with huge overhanging trees blocking out some of the moonlight, but I liked it because it had several perfectly placed overhanging rocks to allow pleasurable and satisfying diving from different heights and then was shallow and wide to allow swimming in circles.

Dove had publicized the fact that she could not swim very well, but it turned out that she could not swim at all. So, while my mother and I dove in Mullet Hole, Nanna took Dove to the shallower water and taught her to swim. Nanna had been an excellent swimmer in her younger days and for the most part still was. In a short time, Dove was swimming and wanted to attempt the diving, but Nanna advised us against it. Our squeals and laughter seemed to echo and easily pierced the shadows and the water as stilettos would sand but were kept in place by the surrounding trees.

We arrived back home after our swim, and Dove set to unpacking the bundle of Pootus's clothes. The pants and shirt-sleeves were a bit short, and the waists were too big, but my mother got out her sewing machine and made the necessary adjustments. The hat was a good fit, but Dove did not like the style. She said it made her look like an escapee from a chain gang. The shoes were too small, so she put them aside and took out the German's shoes.

Nanna and my mother went about the kitchen preparing the foods suggested by Barabbas for the trip later that evening.

They roasted yams and corns, removed the husks from dried nuts, chopped the top off Barabbas's fresh jelly coconut, and poured the pure water into a bottle. They seasoned dried shrimps and boiled eggs, and they baked pones and filled a calabash with rain water. The kitchen was roasting hot, and smoke billowed from the one window.

Indoors, Dove borrowed my mother's scissors, stood in front of the tiny mirror, and tentatively began to cut her hair. She dropped clumps of hair on the floor, and I picked them up. The long, flaxen hair was soft to the touch, and the silky ends curled around my fingers.

"I would like you to keep that to remember me, Mina," she said when she noticed that I had tied them in one bunch with sewing thread.

"I will always remember you, Dove. Forever," I said timidly, lowering my head.

"They say that forever always falls on a Saturday, Mina," she replied, turning to look at me.

"Really?" I asked.

She put out a hand and gently touched my bottom lip with one finger, raising it up to its rightful place.

She sat on the edge of the bed, smiled kindly at me, and took both my hands in hers. "You are a beautiful and kind girl, Mina," she told me. "And don't let anyone tell you otherwise. Please don't judge me too harshly for not talking to you about all that happened to me here on this island. There is so much going on in my head, so much I have to sort out, that I am having a hard time keeping track of who I really am. I am not sure who I am anymore, so I can't talk about me. I can't tell you how I knew to fight the German like I did or from where the physical strength came. Do you understand, Mina? I suppose one day all these loose bits and pieces of me will fall into place and make me whole again. One day, Mina, when you are older, you will come into your own person too; you will have your own style, and everybody better watch out. You will be a force to be reckoned with."

⟂

With all the preparation and all the chatter, and even with the cutting of Dove's hair, the feeling of loss and change did not really hit home until I saw her dressed in Pootus's masculine clothes. She had just rubbed the soil all over her body, hands, and face, and I had stepped outside to get more soil. When I returned, she was completely dressed and was bent over tying the shoes' laces. She straightened up, and I could not believe what I saw. It was a new Dove; it was an almost terrifying Dove.

Nanna announced that my mother should accompany Dove to Cross Road instead of me, and since Dove was in disguise, they could walk on Naggo Road instead of along the treacherous banks of the Sweet River. I protested, and she went on to explain that the people of Naggo Head were more familiar with my mother walking down the road with a friend. I always walked alone, and it would just raise their suspicions if suddenly I were to be walking with someone.

In the last few minutes before it was time to leave, Nanna and my mother gave Dove some last-minute advice. Nanna reminded her to say a prayer morning and night and ask the Lord for guidance and enduring strength for the trip. She also suggested that she tie the money in a handkerchief and then tie the handkerchief to the shoulder strap of her brassiere, but Dove told her that she was not wearing a brassiere. My mother suggested to her that if she should have difficulty understanding Barabbas's speech, she should ask him to write it or spell it; she could even ask him to draw it or act it out.

"I'll write to you, Mina," she said to me. "And perhaps one day you can visit me in New York. I am hoping that when we see one another again, my life will be better, more respectable. What do you say? Will you promise to write to me?"

The impulse to fling myself at her neck rose up in me, but instead I lowered my head in what I thought was a nod and scraped my feet on the floor. My heart felt as if it were about to burst with sadness, and this rendered me speechless. But I managed to raise my gaze again, and in doing so, I noticed that the portions of her ears not completely covered with the soil were beet red.

Nanna had followed Barabbas's instructions closely, and just before the sun sank golden, blood red, and purple into the sea, Dove said her goodbyes, and her last words to us were, "Here goes. Up or down; make or break."

She headed down Naggo Head Road with my mother. The food tied in a sheet and slung across her body was heavier than any of us had anticipated. The cap visor was pulled low down into her face, even though it was past twilight and facial features could not be easily recognized. Her oversize shoes bumped awkwardly against the stones as she walked hesitantly beside my mother. She looked smaller than I had come to believe she was.

Chapter 16

We waited for three whole days without seeing or hearing from Barabbas. Nanna prayed constantly and consistently for them, both in her morning and evening devotions. The Fergusons asked every customer if they had heard anything of his whereabouts. No one had. It was as if Barabbas had vanished from the face of the earth.

When my mother came back from Cross Road the night she had taken Dove to meet Barabbas, all she had had to tell us was that Barabbas, wearing the watch, had been there waiting for them. He had taken one look at the bag across Dove's body and said it was too heavy; he would have to remove some of the food when they got to a more remote area on the way to Blue Bay. Then Dove had sat sideways on the bicycle's back saddle, and Barabbas had pedaled off.

That night I went to my bedroom to sleep for the first time in three nights, and there was a brassiere tucked under the pillow—a white, silky brassiere. It was not mine, so it had to be Dove's. I smelled it, and to my shock it had a scent. All along I had thought that there was no trace of a scent on her person, not even an underarm perspiration smell from the steaming island sun. But there was one—an almost bland one but still a distinct one. It took her absence for my senses to recognize that, like all members of the human race, she did have a presence marked by a byproduct of the metabolic process of microorganisms.

I put the bra on and slept in it that night. The next morning I placed the clump of hair and the red wig in a tin pan and hid it in the cubbyhole under the back steps.

So it was with great joy when late evening on the third day, a rumor flashed around Naggo Head that Barabbas was back home after the fishing boat on which he had gone to do some work had been taken by pirates at sea and held captive for two days. And it was with greater joy that we welcomed him when he walked into Mill Yard that Saturday morning, just in time for breakfast. The wide grin on his face foretold that he had good news for us.

"G' mahning, Nanna, ma'am," he said. "G' mahning, Mary Mary. G' mahning, Cherrimina."

"To Gawd be de glory!" Nanna replied, raising a hand and her eyes toward heaven.

I waited impatiently as he took his first couple of sips of steaming hot coffee and his first bite of callaloo and boiled green bananas; the callaloo had been cooked in coconut milk and seasoned with Scotch bonnet pepper, garlic, scallion, and thyme and melted in the mouth.

"Nanna, ma'am, i' went like dis," he began, taking a deep breath. And this time he was the director, writer, star, and stuntman. It took him three mornings of breakfasts to tell the complete story. It was epic and dramatic.

The ride to Blue Bay had not gone as planned. Having to tow the pretty lady alone on the bicycle for four miles would have been fine, but towing her and the ton of food had been almost impossible. The going was slow for two miles, making him run behind time. Since he didn't have the heart to throw away good food, he held on to the back end of a Farmall tractor transporting sugarcane, allowing it to pull him slowly along. But the pretty lady became afraid, saying that the load of sugarcane could break loose, fall out of the carriage, and impale them both to death.

When they reached Blue Bay, he took her load from her and carried it. They made their way down to the seaside, where he hid his bicycle under the mangroves, and waited at the prearranged place on the beach and watched the sun as it died on the horizon. One of Squid's men, Osbel, rowed a canoe out to them and took them to the boat. The Caribbean Sea was still choppy from the hurricane, and the canoe tipped and dipped dangerously.

They set foot on the boat, and immediately Squid asked for payment; he had had to prepay Heddou, his connection in Cuba. The pretty lady settled that money matter with Squid and also the exchange of the US dollar to the Cuban currency, to purchase the ticket without attracting unwanted attention.

Then they set off toward Cuba. The "Paris of the Caribbean," Squid called it. There was a thick fog off the coast of Cuba. They waited for an hour and a half out at sea, just off the coast of Havana, with the lights on the boat off, watching the glow from the city, but Heddou never appeared. To make matters worse, the fog had begun to lift, and stars had begun to appear in the sky. An airplane passed overhead.

Squid cursed the absent Heddou. He stomped the deck with his bare feet, and since he disliked wearing shoes, his toes were fat and round, like baby wild yams, and spread wide since they rarely felt the constraints and discipline of shoes. He swore he would find Heddou and extract the money out of him with a table fork. His language was foul, and Barabbas, forgetting for a few minutes that the pretty lady was now posing as a man, whispered to Squid to take it easy with the foul language. Luckily, Squid's head on his thick, short neck was too full of violent thoughts and furious curses to pick up that Barabbas had made a blunder, and instead he cursed louder and stomped harder with his squat bowlegs.

Exhausted and limp from the cursing, he rested for a while. Then he sprang into action and moved the boat closer to land, toward the west of the island. However, that area of the coastline, he told them, was considered perilous and was always deserted because it was also a cleaning station for stingrays; they would gather there in multitudes to have the blue wrasses and Spanish hogfish eat parasites and mucus from their bodies. At nights the stingrays slowly grazed over the sandy ocean floor, so if Barabbas were to stay afloat and off the ocean floor and swim quietly and slowly, they should be safe. When they reached shallow water, to wade ashore, they should shuffle their feet through the sand, and the stingrays would simply swim out of the way. He told them to be mindful of the undercurrent because it was strong and would carry them eastward. Squid would be making his next trip to Cuba in two nights and would stop back at this same spot to pick up Barabbas.

"Here, take dis flashlight," Squid had said.

He told Barabbas that on the second night from that night, at this same time, Barabbas should flash the light twice, and Squid would send a canoe out to get him. Also, there would be a man named Sanchez who worked at the pier. He didn't speak much English, but Barabbas should contact him if possible and ask him to tell Jey Jey to tell Squid one word: *yes*. The *yes* would mean that Barabbas was ready and waiting at the place and time as planned. He told Barabbas not to worry about recognizing Sanchez, because he had a wooden leg; the missing leg was perhaps still in a shark's belly somewhere in the Caribbean Sea.

They swam the quarter mile to the shore without any incidents. At first the pretty lady had struggled; she had been scared to death but had never once said she couldn't do it, and very soon she was keeping up with him. They got dressed, and Barabbas used a branch from a young tree to obliterate their footprints in the sand, while Dove rubbed soil over her body. Already he could smell the island air; the vegetation, the spices, the seabirds, and the insects were abundant. Smelling new places was something he was good at doing.

They walked the near mile to the empty warehouse, sticking always to under the mangroves, and climbed through one of the rear windows away from the road. Barabbas was thankful that he had remembered to put the pocket watch in the tarp. They ate and then lay down to sleep, and over the rats and insects scurrying about them, they heard the waves pounding and spraying the coastline relentlessly.

The next morning at first light, before Dove woke up, Barabbas took some money and went out to look around the harbor, dodging behind buildings and trucks, while keeping track of the time with his pocket watch. He walked for miles along the harbor but kept off the main coastal paths.

He stood and watched the hustle and bustle of ships: ocean liners, barges, tugboats, pleasure boats, and freighters unloading, embarking, and disembarking; cargoes of cane sugar bags being hoisted and swung high on pallets; men in overalls sipping steaming hot coffee, and liquids being poured into cups; engines running and horns honking at the truck depot; men in hard hats with folders and rolled-up plans under their arms.

Just up the road, he passed a newspaper stand and saw a picture of the German on the front page—the same picture as the one in the newspaper and posters on our island. He stole a paper and rushed back to tell Dove that she couldn't use the German's identification because the authorities had been alerted to his being missing. He told the pretty lady not to worry about a thing.

They ate sitting on the floor of the dark, dusty warehouse. Then he left once again to scout the area, taking more money with him. By then the streets were alive with Cubans and tourists. He walked the thoroughfares to familiarize himself with the neighborhoods. Street hawkers yelled their merchandise, and fishmongers shouted in the market square. Blue parrot fish was popular, but they called it another name. The Caribbean waters provided rich reefs that had become excellent feeding and breeding grounds. Housewives were shuttling prams and bags of groceries carefully between motorcars, under the guttural roars of buses, delivery vans, and lorries delivering gas, surrounded by the smell of hot tarmac and diesel. Cab drivers were shouting to each other. There were beautiful curvy women with shiny black hair. Wolf whistles. The smell of the ocean air mingled with the syrupy smell of confectionery and fresh bread baking. Nothing beat the smell of fresh-baked bread.

He had searched for and quickly located Sanchez but had not spoken to him; he had just wanted to be sure he knew where to reach him. "I, Barabbas, surely have a God-given gift for finding places and people," he boasted.

He had walked down narrow streets with narrow sidewalks sloshing over with throngs of people walking and talking their language—wide streets with rows and rows of large, glossy motorcars; tram cars; pushcart vendors; a guava jelly factory; cigar factories; military men; beautiful and fine-looking women; tall sculptures with men on horseback at the top; tall, tall buildings with people looking down from high balconies; men and women dancing to sweet, sweet music. The music! Ah, the music! Cubans could dance! The rumba was what they called the dance. Women lifted up their wide frilly skirts and stomped their feet, and their male partners in ruffled shirts swirled and twirled to the music, which had gotten inside his head and which he could still hear.

Most of the business places opened out onto the streets. Crowds of tourists were sitting on high stools drinking long, cool drinks at bars that spilled out onto the sidewalks. The beauty parlors opened onto the street, and he watched women sitting in rows getting their fingernails painted blood red. A true fact! Blood red! Grocery shops with shelves piled high with canned goods were right there within reach of the sidewalks.

He wandered toward the beach and found Heddou. He was sure that Heddou would not remember him; it had been over a year ago that they had met for a few minutes on Squid's boat on one of his deliveries. He remembered Heddou only because he spoke English very well and would tell everyone he met that he had been born in America. He was a good-looking, well-dressed young man with tendencies toward being a gigolo, so Barabbas was sure he would find him on the beach.

He was hot, and the turquoise Caribbean waters looked inviting. The smell of meat cooking over hot charcoals was rampant on the beach, and he bought a sandwich made of sliced roast pork, thinly sliced ham, cheese, salted cucumbers they called dill pickles, and yellow mustard pressed between two slices of Cuban bread. He washed that down with a bottle of pop. He sat on a bench in the shade and ate and burped.

He trailed Heddou for the rest of the morning, waiting outside hotels and cabanas. What he wanted from Heddou was not with him in the streets; it was at his home. To Barabbas's delight, around midday, he trailed Heddou to his first-floor side-street apartment. So, while Heddou and others living on that street were taking an afternoon nap with the windows and doors opened, lying facedown as if dead, Barabbas crept in and stole Heddou's passport from a chest of drawers.

There was money in the drawer, but he did not touch it, leaving it so that Squid could take it from him with a fork. Then he stopped at a clothing store on one of the back streets and spent the money sparingly, purchasing a secondhand suitcase, brand-new men's clothes, and a hat and shoes for Dove and for himself. They would need to fit into the Cubans' and the tourists' seemingly rich lifestyles.

He went back to the warehouse, showed Dove the passport, and helped her pack the few personal items she would need. Dove pointed at the picture and with her eyes wide and round asked him who Heddou Famosa was. He told her not to worry; the sun had darkened her skin so much that she could easily pass for a man.

But she insisted on finding out who Heddou Famosa was. Squid had talked a lot about him, and Barrabas told her as they packed.

"Heddou is a lover bwoy, not a prison house criminal," he began.

He then took her to the public bathhouse he had seen on one of the back streets, and they emerged fresh and clean in the more fashionable getup.

They then took a cab down to the pier, and she purchased a passage on the next ship departing Havana that evening for Florida. They chose Florida because it would be the shortest trip; the shorter the trip, the sooner she could stop the masquerading. From Florida she would ride the trains to New York.

They still had a little time before the ship sailed, so the pretty lady wanted to take a walk in the cool evening breeze with all the other rich, beautiful people promenading along a beautiful paved walkway with lush green trees and grass.

As they strolled together like two gentleman friends, she talked about her homeland: the New York City skyline, a building called the Empire State and another called Woolworth, Times Square, the Stork Club, a hall named Radio City Music Hall, a statue called Liberty, the Yankee Stadium, a famous university, a big museum of art, a Holland Tunnel that ran under a river, Wall Street, and a big, beautiful park named Central.

Then it was time to board the ship to Florida. The pretty young lady hugged him and thanked him, and he had to remind her not to cry.

⋏

Later that night he had gone back to the empty warehouse, eaten, and slept all the next day until it had been time for him to meet

Squid at the coastline. He had disposed of all evidence of their stay in the abandoned warehouse. At the exact time arranged, he had flashed the light twice, Squid had flashed his light once, and Barabbas had entered the waters of the Caribbean Sea, erasing his footprints in the sand with a tree branch, and then swum out to the boat, his clothes and his watch tied in the tarp and strapped to his back, just like in the movie he had seen at the movie house in Blue Bay.

After Barabbas left that morning, Nanna and my mother talked about him. They wondered about his account of certain parts of the trip. Heddou's money, had he left it untouched? And after he and the pretty lady had had to swim a quarter of a mile at night against the current in stingray-infested water and then walk a mile under mangroves, had Barabbas really left Heddou lying there sweetly sleeping in his bed and resting up for another bout of lovemaking on the beach for money? They could see him not taking the money, but they weren't sure that he had left Heddou untouched. They said that he was a better thief than he was a liar but that he was an honorable thief. That night in devotion, Nanna asked God to forgive her for distrusting Barabbas.

A few days later, Barabbas made the newspaper for the second time. The headline for the small article read "Man Kidnapped by Pirates?"

Chapter 17

In just a matter of days, the summer holidays were over, and the new school term had begun. This was to be my last year in school. I went back to school wearing a brassiere. Besides Mable, a big-boned, big-bosomed, big-bottomed girl, I was the only other girl in my class wearing a bra, and with this came status and a reputation, especially when I said I had two of them; Mable from the Stable had one. You would think that unbuttoning my blouse during recess and showing my bra to small groups of girls would soon become old and tiring, but instead it went to my head.

By the end of the year, two facts about me were paramount in my mind. First, the attention and limelight that I had once shied away from, I now enjoyed immensely. I could understand the reason for this attention; it was only the everyday, common-place attention I did not understand. And second, I had become possessed with a potent need to take a look at my private parts, to get to know that part of my anatomy that was never seen by anyone, not even by me. The idea was to view it and then compare to another's in order to confirm my authenticity, to ensure that I had all the right parts and that they were in their right places and that it would never be necessary for doctors to perform tests on me or take pictures, put them up on a wall, and stare at them.

I searched the school library and the public library in Blue Bay for biology books that might contain photographs and drawings, but all I found were images of the internal reproductive organs. With the failure of each leg of this stealthy pursuit, my curiosity—and fear of being born with a physical gaffe—grew stronger and more terrifying. I wondered if other girls had this problem. Then I realized that other girls' changing diapers on their younger sisters would have satisfied their curiosity, if any. But I had no baby sisters and couldn't seem to find the right words to discuss this topic with my peers. Or could it be that they just didn't care about the private parts of their anatomy? Perhaps they had no idea what misfortunes awaited them if they had happened to be born with a strange or different physique. Yes, Bro' Man had been right all along—ignorance surely was bliss. I racked my brain day and night, and a couple of mornings Nanna told me that she had heard me tossing in my sleep during the night. She wondered if I was getting ill.

Then I hit upon the idea to use Nanna's mirror. If I waited until Nanna and my mother were out of the house, probably while they were in the kitchen cooking dinner, I could finalize one leg of my mission. The opportunity came, and I carefully took the mirror from the bureau in Nanna's room and placed it on the floor. But the lighting was not right and provided very little visibility. Lighting a lamp and placing it strategically on the floor was still not enough, so I lit a second one.

No, do not blush, I thought. Blushing is a visible sign of man's basic fight-or-flight posture when in survival mode. Choose fight, for God's sake!

Then I squatted and gazed at the revelation in the mirror on the floor. It took quite some time to absorb all the details, but after I did, I came to a conclusion, a rapid and irreversible conclusion. The image in the mirror was ugly. And for the first time, I sympathized with Sister Lady—with her being in a position to have to look at that image more than once. Once was all I needed.

Looking back later on in life, I can say now that the whole process could be compared to producing a film—lighting, manipulating, focusing, and directing. The only thing wanting was a score. And if I had been asked to suggest a musical instrument for the score, it would not have been the suave, breathy violin, nor the weighted majestic notes of the organ, nor the sorrowful retreats of the bagpipes. It would have been African drums— the furious, feverish jungle beats warning of danger, calling for war—mysterious, shadowy, and imperious, yet alluring even to the drummer herself. And learning to drum was easy, I found.

The first part of this mission was completed, but I still needed to take that image in the mirror and conduct a comparison test for normalcy.

⁂

All this time the moonshine baby behind our kitchen had remained intact except for the crown. The small stones we had used for the crown had disappeared. Perhaps wind, rain, or small bush animals scurrying over it were responsible for this.

It was the summer holidays again, and as children do, those of Naggo Head loved playing in old ruins and any place that they were told not to play because it was dangerous. And it was one of those kids who found a shiny silver treasure in the ruins of Ma'as Charlie's house. I heard about the discovery of this treasure, and with a fair idea of what it was, I went to investigate it one morning among a group as they played ring games in the front yard of houses near Mill Yard.

And as I suspected, it was the pair of handcuffs that the German had had that night in Ma'as Charlie's house. I bought it from the little boy for threepence. I stood for a while and watched them play, their laughter and singing ringing out free and clear as they played a traditional children's ring game of the West Indies, "Brown Girl in the Ring":

There's a brown girl in the ring
Tra la la la
There's a brown girl in the ring
Tra la la la
There's a brown girl in the ring
Tra la la la
For she likes sugar
And I like plum

Then you skip across the ocean
Tra la la la . . .
Then you show me your motion
Tra la la la . . .
Then you show me your partner
Tra la la la . . .

The group of kids held hands and formed a ring, and then one child went into the middle of the ring and started walking around as the group sang. When the players sang "Then you skip across the ocean," the child inside the ring skipped around the ring. At "Show me your motion," the child in the center did his or her favorite dance. When they sang "Show me your partner," he or she picked a friend to join him or her in the circle. At the end of the song, the first child in the ring stepped out and rejoined the circle, while the second child walked around the ring, and the song began again.

Away from the group, Portia stood alone. She was never chosen to play along in any of the games on account that she could not go barefoot, and her thin, narrow shoulders would shake as she coughed after she ran or jumped. At the other side of the yard, Bunchie also stood at the fringe. After he had been caught interfering with himself behind the star apple tree, it was widely believed that his next unnatural act might be with an animal. For a while, Naggo Head residents were watching out for their dogs, goats, hogs, and even their chickens.

The kids asked me to join them, and I did. I skipped and danced and laughed as I had never done before. I watched the older children play another ring game called "Manuel Road":

Go dung a Manuel Road, gal an' bwoy,
Fe go bruk rock stone, gal an' bwoy.
Go dung a Manuel Road, gal an' bwoy,
Fe go bruk rock stone, gal an' bwoy.
Bruk dem one by one, gal an' bwoy,
Bruk dem two by two, gal an' bwoy,

Finga mash, no cry, gal an' bwoy,
Memba a play we a play, gal an' bwoy

They formed a ring on the ground by kneeling, each player having a rock before him or her. They began singing, and each child took the rock before him and passed it to the person closest to the right to a set rhythm. The game continued until that unfortunate someone got his or her finger smashed, or the one who lost rhythm and got more than one stone piled before him or her was dismissed, until one only person was left, and this would be the winner.

Partway through the game, a fight broke out. Patsy had done the unforgivable and swung the hem of her frock over Tan Tan's head while he was crouched over in the game. She should have wrapped her frock hem close to her body when she walked by him. Everybody knew that a girl's frock tail passing over a boy's head would stunt his growth. He would not grow even a fraction of an inch farther.

I walked away. I had begun feeling that I was too old for ring games. The kids playing were between six and twelve years old, just getting interested in hidden treasures, still playing among ruins, and perhaps still wetting their beds. Later in the afternoon, they might chase one another down to the banks of Sweet River, strip themselves down to bare skin, and jump in to splash, laugh, and scream. Then that evening, perhaps, they would sneak into their neighbors' fields and climb their fruit trees to plunder and pick sugar plums, mangoes, and guavas, and then settle in their secret meeting place to split the booty. Then tomorrow the boys might play marbles, while the girls might hand sew clothes for their dolly babies.

I did not belong with such a group anymore, and yet I could not say to which group I belonged or where I belonged. Nanna wanted to teach me to crochet and embroider, and I did try, but I did not belong in that group either. I was somewhere in between these two groups, and it was a lonely place.

I walked home listening to them sing and laugh. I stored the handcuffs in the tin can I had hidden in the cubbyhole under the back steps. I found myself envying the kids' carefree existence. It was only a year earlier that I had lived such an idyllic lifestyle, but the times they were a-changing on the British West Indian islands.

CHAPTER 18

For months, there had been discussions of labor conflicts and discontent among the farmers and farm workers. A huge number of the agricultural workers owned or leased their small plots of lands and also worked full time on larger farms or sugar estates.

The chief grounds for this discontent were overall dissatisfaction with working conditions, low wages, underemployment, and the arrogant and prejudiced attitudes of the colonial overseers and employers toward the islanders in their employment. Lack of adequate representation and structure for resolving industrial disputes also played a large part in these conflicts. Another factor was the world economic crisis, which had started in the United States and by the early 1930s was having a residual effect internationally.

It was Sunday afternoon, and Bro' Man and Miss Priyanka made one of their visits to Nanna. Bro' Man strolled into Mill Yard with a silk ascot knotted at his throat and flourishing his walking stick. Chest out, toes pointed out, he escorted Miss Priyanka up the steps like a gentleman should. She brought an egg custard cooked in an earthenware pot.

Nanna and my mother entertained our guests, and I was seen but not heard as I sat mesmerized by Miss Priyanka's beauty. Her jet-black hair was pulled back in a single thick braid that swung below her waist. The bangles she wore at her wrists tinkled delicately as she expertly handled the bright-yellow, traditionally embroidered, and braid-trimmed outfit she wore. I would learn much later that it was called a sari.

As usual, the reading of the newspaper and discussion of current affairs began, from which I came to understand that in December 1937, workers on a sugar estate at the eastern end of the island had refused to start harvesting the sugarcane crop at the pay rates offered. What began as a simple go-slow had eventually led to an outright riotous strike. Police had been rushed to the area, and over sixty of the strikers had been arrested over a period of three days. Several had been tried before the resident magistrate, and the three ringleaders had been sentenced to one month's imprisonment with hard labor.

A small farmer who had returned from Cuba had formed an organization called the Poor Man's Improvement and Land Settlement Association, which had a membership of nearly eight hundred. This organization had published a letter in the newspaper addressed to the governor.

Nanna read the article. "'We are the sons of slaves who have been paying rent to the landlords for fully many decades; we want better wages, we have been exploited for years, and we are looking to you to help us. We want a minimum wage law. We want freedom in this the hundredth year of our emancipation. We are still economic slaves, burdened in paying rent to landlords who are sucking out our vitalities.'"

A crusade to refuse to pay rent to landlords had begun to spread, and in some areas people had captured estate lands.

A widely held belief that Queen Victoria had promised that one hundred years after their emancipation, the slaves who had gotten nothing at the time of the abolition of slavery would inherit the land had been revived and powered this crusade. Tenants and others who had seized lands erected fences around them. Some had offered to pay taxes on the captured lands.

The British government had sent the West Indian Royal Commission to inquire into the rates of wages and working conditions of the laborers in the British West Indies.

Then an increasing number of workers had begun converging at the western end of the island, not far from Blue Bay, attracted by the possibility of employment by the construction of a new sugar factory, and thus the unrest was brought closer home to Naggo Head.

After they had exhausted political topics, Nanna and Miss Priyanka discussed herbal remedies. Nanna told her about the book Barabbas had given her, and she offered to lend it to Miss Priyanka anytime she wanted to borrow it.

Sister Lady stopped by Nanna's for the usual weekly reading of the newspaper and discussion of current affairs one afternoon. She had taken to talking with Nanna in codes or whispers when I was in her sight or within earshot.

"Nanna," she would begin, "did you hear about hmpf, tiick, hmpf, tiick tiick?"

"But dat's not the whole story," Nanna would reply.

"Yes, Bertie wife say, 'Hmpf, tiick, hmpf, tiick tiick.'"

That particular Sunday evening, I put the dusty pink dress on but was so busy trying a new way of wearing my hair that I had seen in a magazine in the library that I was not ready when our visitor arrived. I could hear their conversation through the plank walls.

Nanna read several articles published in the daily newspaper that she had in a pile at her feet.

An article on May 2 said, "One thousand laborers, a large proportion of them engaged in the construction of a giant central sugar factory estate...went on strike Friday..."

On May 3, another article in the newspaper reported,

> The old factory on the estate, which up to Friday had been grinding canes, is entirely in the hands of the strikers... I hear rifle firing, followed by shrieks and cries...I can see men on the ground. Some are motionless, others are staggering to and fro or crawling away on their hands and knees. The strike has culminated in stark tragedy. A few minutes later I hear that three are dead, eleven wounded, and that the police are making many arrests.

The wounded might have been more numerous than reported, as it was understood by all that anyone who sought medical treatment would be identifying himself as a participant and inviting arrest.

Next, the governor ordered the arrest of a popular and daring rebel who had been leading public protest meetings and writing letters to British Members of Parliament disclosing the troubling economic conditions on the island.

This arrest caused a rush of further strikes and disturbances. A week later, the government granted him bail after realizing that the only way to ease the situation was to release this leader. But by that time, it was too late; the soul of revolt had spread throughout the island, and strikes and demonstrations were occurring in every parish.

British troops were stationed on our island to supplement the police, and they were called into action. Despite this, the strikes and demonstrations continued. Workers were killed and injured, and many arrests took place.

An announcement came in early June that a royal commission would be arriving shortly to investigate conditions. Later that same month, the acting governor announced that two loans would be raised to finance land settlements and other infrastructural developments.

I went to ask Nanna if she had seen my hair ribbons, and as I turned the corner of the veranda, there was Sister Lady sitting alone looking at the newspaper, which she kept rotating, and cocking her head to get the right end of the paper up. Nanna had gone to fetch some refreshments.

"Good evening, Sistah Lady," I greeted her, pleased that someone would finally get the chance to see me in my new dress but hoping that I was not exhibiting the eternally sinful "vanity" that I was constantly being warned about.

"Evening, chile," she replied, folding the newspaper and placing it on Nanna's chair.

"'Ow *h*is school, Cherriminah?" she asked.

"School fine, Sistah Lady, ma'am," I whispered.

She looked me up and down. I smiled in a manner that I hoped was friendly. After all, I had recently come to understand through a reflection in a mirror that she had a good reason for her meanness, for her spitefulness.

"Yu granny mek yu wear yu hair open now?"

"No, Sistah Lady, ma'am. Just looking for ribbons to make pigtail."

"You maddah mek dat dress, gal?"

"Yes, ma'am. I help her make it."

She had a sudden attack of spasmic rage and then gripped her walking stick and sat quietly with her head cocked to one side as if listening to her heartbeat.

"Dat *h*is *h*a dress fi *h*a 'arlat," she said at last.

I stood looking at her, not understanding what she meant. I racked my brain. Arlat? Arlat? Sister Lady would eat the consonant *h* that began her words and add *h* on the words that began a vowel, so could it be h-a-r-l-a-t? What was a harlat? Was there such a word?

I banged the letters on the phantom typewriter and still did not understand.

"'Harlat,' Sistah Lady, ma'am?"

She cut her eye in that gesture of contempt of turning one's face away abruptly while closing one's eyes.

"What is a 'harlat,' Sister Lady, ma'am?"

She picked up a handheld fan from her lap and began mixing the airflow near her face furiously.

"I agree wit' dat warmongah in Germany. We mus' 'break de body, break de spirit, break de 'eart,'" she said, picking up all her pent-up hostility and setting it loose in my direction.

Then, at my left elbow, I heard the sudden tinkling of drinking glasses. Nanna was carrying a wooden tray with glasses full of frothy fruit punch. She was shaking. Her chest heaved. Her face was pinched and furrowed.

"What yu call har?" she asked Sister Lady.

Sister Lady jerked her head around and looked up at Nanna and then sat paralyzed like a snake on a hot rock below eye level for what seemed like an eternity. Her lips moved but made no sound, so she stomped her foot, and the words came pouring out.

"Mi no know wha' de chile been telling yu, Nanna!" she rattled off.

"She tell me not'ing, Matty! Cock mout' kill cock!"

The exchange that took place between the two respected citizens of Naggo Head, if it could be called an exchange since Nanna did most of the taking, was unforgettable.

First of all, I learned that Sister Lady's government name was Mathilda—Matty for short. Nanna took hold of my hand and dragged me front and center of the two, pointed at my dress, and told Matty to look at the neckline, look at the childish puff sleeves, look at the length of the skirt, and tell her which harlot she knew who would wear a dress like that. She took a bundle of my hair in her hand and asked Matty what she wanted the child to do with her hair—should she chop it off to please you, Matty? God made her hair like this; why should she hide it?

She told Matty that she was evil wrapped in skin and that Matty had bullied everyone up and down Naggo Head Road ever since as a young woman she had beaten Pearl when she had rivaled her over a beau. And Matty had known the truth that the beau had chosen Pearl over her because Matty was innocent of reading, writing, and arithmetic.

Nanna told her that she had suspected for some time now that she had been verbally abusive to her only grandchild but had no proof, so she had kept quiet and had given her the benefit of the doubt. And she was wrong to have kept quiet. Because of what she heard coming out of Matty's mouth that day, she had to take sides. Neutrality helps the oppressor, never the victim. Silence encourages the tormentor, never the tormented, she told Sister Lady.

"You want to break de body, break de spirit, break de heart, eh?"

Sister Lady wiped the corners of her mouth with a thumb and forefinger and opened it to speak, but Nanna beat her to it.

"Shut dat mean, nasty mout', Matty!"

Matty hung her head.

"Now, buzz off!" were Nanna's final and most shocking words.

Matty took her walking stick and carefully walked down the steps and bent over from the waist as if suddenly gravity and her heavy bosom were working against her. I felt pity for her and hoped that she would get to the bottom step without falling. She dropped the fan, and I ran down the steps, picked it up, and handed it to her, and I doubted if she even knew that her fan had fallen. Nanna watched her go, and there were tears in her eyes. I placed my arms around her shoulders, and her entire body was trembling—and I understood then that the part of her that it took to say those words to Sister Lady, that same part had broken her heart because she had emptied it, and now there was nothing left in its place. Her prayers to the Lord asking for forgiveness and tolerance at worship that night were heart-wrenching.

The next day my mother was preparing clothes for ironing. I helped her, scooping up handfuls of water from a small basin, sprinkling the water over the garment to lightly dampen it, and then rolling the garment into a ball and tucking it into a covered zinc pan. We chatted. I asked her the meaning of *harlot*, and she said a harlot is like a low-hanging fruit in the flesh trade. She said harlots devote themselves to making many men happy instead of one man miserable. I asked her if she knew the story about Sister Lady, a.k.a. Matty, and Pearl, and she told me the story.

The story was that Sister Lady had been about eighteen years old when she had fallen in love for the first time. His name had been Sparrow, and he had been from same place there in Naggo Head. Pearl had been from Little London, two villages over, and had met Sparrow at a dance. Sparrow had fallen in love with Pearl and written her a love letter. Matty had heard about this and gone to Little London to confront Pearl. Matty had been completely unprepared for Pearl's aggressiveness because Pearl had been tiny and lightweight and Matty had been a heavyweight. Pearl had sprung into quick action and won the first round when she had told Matty that Sparrow had never written her a love letter because Matty could not read. Matty had taken the second round when she had told Pearl that her hair was so short that in school she had an ounce of hair and a pound of hair ribbon. Pearl had quickly doled out another zinger and told Matty that her breasts were so large that the sun rose over one and set over the other. A scuffle had begun and ended quickly. There had been no biting, no eye gouging, and no hair pulling, and the story would have died there if Matty had not slapped Pearl in the face, or if she had used her hand. Instead, Matty had pushed out her bosom, jumped up in the air, and slapped Pearl's face with her breasts. In that era, young, unmarried females had not been expected to wear brassieres, and Matty's large breasts had been hanging, swinging, and lethal under her loose-fitting frock.

At the end of the story, my mother said Sister Lady was going to hell with kerosene-oil drawers on.

Soon Nanna began objecting to my wearing the dusty-rose dress, saying that lately it seemed as if I was thinking too much about my body, the brassieres, and that dusty-rose dress. And that my mother's behavior had had such tendencies just before she had gotten in a predicament with me on the way. She lectured me on the sins of the flesh. Her prayers at devotions seemed filled with asking God to give me direction and guidance. But every once in a while, I would put the cursed dress on and wear it around the house just for a few minutes.

Halfway through the second school term, we heard from Dove. Nanna received a mysterious letter from a Mr. Justin Johnson in the United States of America. She read it aloud before devotion that same night. It was from Dove, thanking Nanna and family for sending the wonderful food and gifts with his friends for him. The US dollars were a token of his appreciation. A named portion was to go to the friend of the family who had helped her out on the boat trip. The letter writer advised her not to write to the address, as he would be moving soon. She should say hello and thanks to everyone. It was signed Justine Dove Johnson. I was never mentioned by name.

My mother tried to persuade Nanna to spend some of the money on a store-bought mattress or an oil-burning stove, but Nanna refused. She did not trust store-bought mattresses and oil stoves. "Can one roast a breadfruit on an oil stove?" she had asked.

The next day Nanna put on her blue hat and made one of her rare trips to Blue Bay, where she exchanged the currency at the bank. After returning home, she summoned Barabbas and gave him his portion of the money. Two days later Barabbas came to Mill Yard wearing a brand-new pair of shoes and a hat that he wore cocked jauntily to one side. He had spent some of his money on a book about herbs and plants used in medicine, cosmetics, and cooking and presented it to Nanna wrapped in brown paper and tied with fresh green creepers he had picked in the back woods. And Nanna wept.

CHAPTER 19

Girls, keep away from boys, the educators ruled. Boys are the carnal enemy, the sob sisters wrote.

The groom-to-be would take no interest in the wedding because he would only be thinking about the intimacy he would get on the wedding night, the adventurous schoolgirls whispered as they clustered in the school yard.

Boys are only after one thing, the virgins would write on pieces of paper they passed around. Men are the enemy, and sexuality is a woman's only weapon against them, the revolutionaries would prophesy.

"Romans eight, seven to eight: 'Because the carnal mind is enmity against God: for it is not subject to the law of God, neither indeed can be. So then they that are in the flesh cannot please God,'" they would expound from the pulpit.

"Romans eight thirteen: 'For if ye live after the flesh, ye shall die: but if ye through the Spirit do mortify the deeds of the body, ye shall live,'" they would recite in their morning devotions.

"Galatians five nineteen: 'Now the works of the flesh are evident: sexual immorality, impurity, sensuality,'" they would preach.

They would say all these things. You as a fifteen-year-old girl in Naggo Head in the 1930s would have heard all these things that they said.

The concerned folks warned, they preached, they expounded, they worried, and they fretted. They did all these things. All these things they did, but no one told you what to do when you obeyed the rules and stayed away from boys, but the boys kept coming after you and would keep coming. No one told you what to do when they caught up with you, when they touched you—when they touched you, and you liked it. When you wanted more of their touches. When their touches lit your insides on fire. And when the fire raged for days after.

Don't be the girl they experiment on, your mind would try to say to you, but you wouldn't listen. You are five feet from that group of boys over there; it's time to preen, to parade, to giggle, to wiggle, your cresting brainwaves would keep repeating. Sexuality is power, your walk would say. The attention is an important part, your glances would tell them. Your lips would pucker. Please watch me, the new pout in your bosom and the new cinch in your waist would plead. Let them look but *never* touch, your body would yell every other day; on other days it would just burn hot and tremble.

No one ever told you that you should not like boys. No one told you that boys would keep coming after you even though you were staying away from them. They did not say, "Do not like boys." They did not say, "Do not like a boy's touch." They never said, "No matter how tender a boy's touch is, and no matter how warm it makes you feel, don't ever like it." And would they have believed you if you had said that your thoughts never once went past the stirring physicality of touching? That you harbored no interest beyond a laying on of a hand on the body? "Was once lost always lost really true of chastity?" one author asked.

Chastity. Chaste.

There is that unnatural word again. Can anything or anyone remain chaste in life?

Where does it come from, this violent change, this newness in a fifteen-year-old's body, a fifteen-year-old's mind? That terrible imbalance of body, mind, and age? Why? How? Was this change a brilliant blooming of a thing to replace a dank, decaying one? Or was it the dank, decaying one replacing the thing that had been blooming brilliantly for the first fourteen years? Was this change meant to fall faintly, fall happily from the sky in drops of yellows and ecru, like the rain shower does while the sun is still shining brightly, but instead it sat multiplying in a dark corner for years, waiting for the right time to pounce heavy and hard?

Why must things change? Why does life change? Why does one's body change? What was a fifteen-year-old girl to do when the crayfish hiding under the river rock no longer interested her? When the legend of the fairy flower no longer frightened her? What was she to do after she was finished with what could be the final level of schooling? What was she to do when everyone seemed to be watching her and waiting?

What a fifteen-year-old girl could do was put on her brassiere and her dusty-pink dress with the belted waist, fix her hair, and find excuses to ride the motorcar transport into Blue Bay.

"Let me go buy the sewing needles for you in Blue Bay, Mama, an' you can stay home an' rest," she would plead. And her mother would look at her strangely, as if she knew her true thoughts.

"The blue thread is almos' finish', Mama. Let me go to Blue Bay to buy some for you."

Then her mother would relent and give her the money.

"Don't go to de Syrian store," her mother would warn her. "Go to de Indian store. An' don't stay too long. Come back soon before Nanna start asking for yu."

"Yes, Mama," she would promise.

But she would go to the Syrian's. And the Syrian would say she was a pretty girl. Then another time he would offer to take her body measurements to see how closely she measured to the mannequin he kept in the back of the store, behind the burnt-umber-colored drapes hanging in the doorway. By this time she knew what time of the day his store would have few or no customers.

Then one day he would pull the neck of her dress away from her chest, peer down the dress, and say, "Let me see what you have in your house." And he would put his hand down the neck of her dress and fondle her breasts. Then he would give her transport fare to come back to Blue Bay another day. She would ride the motorcar transport back home, still feeling the rough fingers on her chest. Yes, she took delight in his fingers defying the high neckline of her dress and ravaging her body.

She would be so entrenched in her erotic thoughts that the once-adored scenery on the way up from Blue Bay was unseen by her; she would not see the women chatting and washing clothes under the yellow sun in the Sweet River, with their skirt hems looped between their legs and tucked in their waistbands to keep them out of the water; nor the men in undershirts, water boots, and straw hats chopping sugarcane with gleaming machetes, the sweat glistening on their muscled arms as they hurled the sugarcane in piles; nor the wide, squat, whitewashed gates that led to the sugar factory, its chimney swirling smoke far in the distance; nor the women with a gentle rhythmical swing in their hips, gliding gracefully, carrying gourds of drinking water on their heads without spilling a drop.

What was a fifteen-year-old girl to do when bored?

She could go to church on Sundays and sit in the line of vision of a certain preacher's son. She would see the surprised look on his face the first time that he saw her in her dusty-pink dress with the belted waist, and he would follow her when during the sermon she went out to get a drink of water from the rainwater bucket.

He would smile at her as she drank, and he would say, "Gawd didn' know when to stap when he make yu," and laugh quietly, showing strong, white teeth under his young mustache. Then, as she walked past him, he would move to get his drink of the water from the wooden water bucket, and he would brush his body forcefully all along her lower back and on one arm. Her body would shudder, and she would become unsure if she were slipping or walking. He would smile at her over his shoulders. And as she sat in church for the rest of the sermon, her lower back and arm would throb and ache as she relived all the nuances of his stroke. At the end of each episode, her mind would race to start over again.

The throbbing and aching would eventually spread to her entire body, and it would glow as close to cherub pink as possible, and when the minister would announce the next song after a spirited sermon, "Hymn numbah one hundred an' t'irty one," she would grip the pew in front of her and rise with the rest of the congregation. And when the voices of the choir soared in song, she would be afraid to open her lips lest a feral moan should escape from them. And when she could trust herself enough to open her mouth, it was with the name of the preacher's son on her lips and his face in her eyes.

Later that night, in her room after devotion, she would stay on her knees and silently beg the Lord for forgiveness, for guidance, and for humility—and for those who cared and worried and fretted to understand that her craving never once went past the stirring physicality of touching, beyond the laying on of a hand, with its ambiances of temperature, pressure, and vibrations on the largest organ of the human body. She knew that there was something that came after the throbbing and aching, but it was out there somewhere far and away, not of her present realm.

This fifteen-year-old girl on her knees would reason with God to the best of her ability, asking him why love, romance, or marriage did not interest her as they did her peers. She would beg to understand where this sudden and awful sense of superiority to the citizens of Naggo Head had come from, because she had begun feeling as if she could take Naggo Head apart and put it back together again. Because there was a time when she had felt like she was the one who would tie the lace on the shoe of the person who would take that giant step for mankind, but now she felt that she was that person wearing the shoe to take that giant step, and the person tying the lace had no thumbs. She was royalty who gave to the peasants with one hand while the other hand was straightening her tiara.

Then she would rise from her knees and lie on her bed in the dark thinking that perhaps she needed to find another mentor, but then her body would begin to throb to the rhythm of her heartbeat. And she would lie there in bed, in the darkness, in limbo, knowing that there was a crack somewhere inside her, somewhere in her body, but unable to tell if there were a leaking out or a seeping in. Strange how the whole body quivers around one point. But by now she had gotten over the shame of it, and all that remained was the guilt.

She would learn how to keep her secret thoughts and behavior hidden. No one in Naggo Head should know her goings and comings or who she really was. She would learn how to walk on Naggo Head's gravelly road without making a sound, like a thief in the night. Over to the left side of the road, at Miss Zeppa's house, were the embedded, quiet river rocks; she would stay on those for thirty footsteps, shift to the middle of the road for ten steps, and so on. By this time, she would be eyeing all men. Rich man. Poor man. Beggar man. Thief.

"You should give dat dusty-pink dress a res'," her Nanna would say to her one day. "You wear it so often, dey gwine take yu picture in it. Wear yu blue dress nex' time."

Then one day she would go to the Syrian's store, and he would take her picture in the dusty-pink belted dress. First he would show her photographs of partially clothed girls from the neck down, their faces missing, and take her picture partially clothed. Then he would show her photographs of girls with their legs spread, and he would take hers with her legs spread. Then he would show her close-ups and graphically frank photographs of the part of the anatomy that she had seen in the mirror that day.

And that was how she would come to confirm that anatomically she was normal. True, none of them was identical to what she had seen in the mirror that day, but neither were they identical to one other. She would be so pleased that she would break out in a big, wide smile. The Syrian would then tell her she had a lovely smile. Lovely toes. Lovely feet. Lovely legs. Lovely thighs.

It was then that she would see a familiar pair of shoes in one of the photographs. A chill would go up her spine, and she would sit up, the smile vanishing from her face. She had seen those same shoes hidden under her mother's bed. And if the photograph had been in in color, the shoes would have been black and tan. There was a tiny scar or a birthmark on the girl's leg, just above her left knee at the inner area.

Her blood would run cold, and the chill along her spine would get colder by the second, and she would adjust her clothes and leave the store abruptly. She would ride home on the motor-car transport thinking about the shoes under her mother's bed. And about that time her mother figured out that she had bought the tape measure from the Syrian's store, even though she had told her that she had bought it from the Chinese's. The manner in which she would rant and rave about it would be unusual because she was usually of a quiet, reasonably pleasant personality.

That fifteen-year-old girl would go home and, for the first time, question her mother about her father. Who was he? Where was he from? Where did she meet him? What did he look like? Did she have any photographs of him? Was he tall or short? Fat or slim? And when she did not get any satisfactory reply, she would vow she would search her mother's room the first chance she got. And she would sit close to her mother during breakfast and dinner and would bend down often to pick up spilled pins and buttons near her feet under the chair on which her mother sat sewing.

Then, at the next early Sunday morning family swim in the Sweet River before church, she would swim closely behind her mother, and she would climb out of the river closely behind her mother, and she would see a tiny birthmark on her mother's leg, just above the inner area of her left knee.

With that sighting her mother would fall to the bottom of the fifteen-year-old's mind. And each time that her mother would try to get back up to her rightful place, she would stumble over a dead log. And she would keep falling.

Then this fifteen-year-old would meet a trio of youngsters visiting Blue Bay from Town with access to money, transportation, and a home on a private beach. They, too, would seem to have been watching her and waiting. Ninety false smiles between the trio, sixty acts of deception, and fifteen false promises in two weeks; then one false smile from the fifteen-year-old and then a second and then another.

Her saver would be the guilt that she still felt, but she didn't know it then.

CHAPTER 20

By then Naggo Head had a new and regular visitor. Bulla had begun taking almost daily trips up into Naggo Head and specifically to the grocery shop. The grocery shop was in spitting distance from Mill Yard, so I was made aware of all his visits. He would gallop into Naggo Head on his father's horse like a dark knight.

It seemed that he had taken a shine to me, and several times I had quietly made my way to my favorite listening spot on the breadfruit tree root at the side of the grocery shop and eavesdropped on their conversations. But some things are not said; some things are just heard. I knew why he was visiting Naggo Head, he knew that I knew, and the group of men in the grocery shop suspected that he was a serpent slithering into the Garden of Eden.

Then one day he quietly came around the corner of the shop where I sat listening. He grabbed me roughly by the hair at the top of my head, tilted my head back, and without saying a word, he buried his mouth deep into mine. He finally extricated his hand and his mouth and went back to the front of the shop, leaving me unable to breathe and dizzy because my heart had rushed up into my throat and lodged there. Then slowly and sweetly, it fell back into place, leaving me wanting it to rush up again.

Despite the group of men warning him about "no monkey business wit' Naggo Head gals," he came back again shortly, but this time when I heard his horse coming up Naggo Head Road, I ran away before he could get a hold of me. I ran home to Nanna.

The regular group in the grocery shop soon concluded that Bulla was cocky and was a troublemaker. He would address them as "old man" or "gramps" instead of by their names. He would strut around the shop picking up objects and manhandling them. Once he had picked up Bro' Man's walking stick and fiddled with it, which had led Bro' Man to lecture him about walking sticks.

"The prehistoric man struggled to walk upright on a walking stick," he could be heard telling a group of men in the grocery shop. "Since then man has hunted his food with a stick; it is with a stick that he has defended his life and his freedom. He has pursued recreation with a stick.

"It's a proven fact that the walking stick has its origins in tropical countries. There is good evidence dating back almost four thousand years to the Egyptians, the Romans, the Ethiopians, and the Aztecs to prove that games were played with a stick and ball. How many games can you name that have a stick as their mainspring for scoring points?"

By the time Bulla had left the shop, the walking stick had had a nick in its decorated head, and the last three statements had provided Bro' Man and his friends with debate topics for several weeks.

I survived for weeks on that one kiss. It was my first kiss and was more than I had read it would be, and along with that realization came fear of its intensity, of Bulla's concentrated passion. And when he realized that I would slip away from my listening post whenever I suspected he was making his way back there, he began visiting Naggo Head with a creased forehead and leaving grinding his teeth. He became meaner at each visit, and one day as it was setting up for rain, and the group of men disassembled and scrambled home, the opportunity opened, and he rushed around to the side of the grocery shop, grabbed my arm, and pulled me to my feet. It was as though he were held together with loose, wobbly stitches and were now bursting at the seams.

"Dere is a fire burning inside mi," he whispered in my ear through gritted teeth. "Mi hungry an' can't eat; mi tired an' can't sleep."

The sudden burst of beaded sweat on his upper lip, the gritted teeth, the wild eyes, and the searing pain in my arm drilled massive fear in me, so much fear that I fought harder than ever to break free out of his grip.

"'And I find more bitter than death the woman whose heart is snares and nets, and her hands as bands'...Ecclesiastes seven, verse..." he recited from the Bible. It was then that I decided to sink my teeth into his knuckles. My teeth hit bone, and I tasted his salty blood on my tongue.

"Mi naw come back to Naggo Head," he called after me as I sprinted through the trees and fallen leaves toward home and Nanna.

But he did come back. The horse galloped faster and louder coming and going. His language grew fouler, his views sleazier and more shocking, his voice louder and more passionate, and it excited me. I wallowed in it. Behind Bro' Man's back, he told the group in the shop that Bro' Man and his wife had neither chick nor child because his wife was far too dignified to be ridden. And that having her as a wife must be as unrewarding as the bottom half of a mermaid. And when one of the men warned him to be more respectful to Bro' Man—he was the richest man in Naggo Head—Bulla sucked his teeth and said, "Bedclothes have no pockets."

He laughed at the farmers' calloused hands, holding up his to show soft, clean palms. He did not know what Seabiscuit was. He thought that Seabiscuit was a biscuit baked out at sea on a ship, and the group of men roared with laughter at this. Then Bro' Man told him that he fiddled with everything he could get his hands on because he was not up to speed with current affairs and so could not take part in a conversation between grown men.

Mr. Ferguson advised him to stop his tomfoolery and begin reading the newspaper, and Bulla retaliated by nicknaming him "Piggy Chops," due to the shape of his mouth, and pointed out that when Mr. Ferguson spoke, his tongue and lips flapped like four-string drawers drying on a clothesline on a windy day. This caused Mr. Ferguson to start tucking in his lips; he gave it up after two days because there was just too much lip.

And the day that Bulla took his shirt off to show the group his well-built muscles and young, tight skin, one member of the group ordered him to put his shirt back on, and Bulla told him that he couldn't take his shirt off because he looked like the type who would have toes on his back. And when Day Ghost laughed hard at this and was unfortunate enough to end in a fit of coughing, Bulla pointed a finger at him and told him that he was a one-man leper colony. He told the group of men that the only thing he had in common with them was spittle.

He even made fun of Pootus. Ever since she had found that several pieces of her scanty wardrobe were missing, Pootus had become obsessed with thieves, and when she told a story to the men about a burglary in Blue Bay, Bulla told her that she didn't have to worry about burglars because her face looked like an attack dog. Barabbas was the only one to whom he showed any respect and restraint.

Several late nights I lay in bed and listened to the clip-clopping of a horse's hooves slowly kicking up and turning over the stones up and down Naggo Head Road, and my heart raced to the rhythm.

Then he turned up one day with his young, sparse mustache trimmed in the manner of Adolf Hitler. The shocked men asked him why that style, and he said he had seen the photograph in the newspaper and wondered how he would look with it. They asked him if he had read the story under the photograph, and he said he had not. They told him to read the story—only then he would understand why he should shave it off—but he raised his voice and told them that no old man was going to tell him what to do. He told Old Man Egypt that he had only two or three haircuts left before he kicked the bucket.

They told him that if he was not careful, he could become a laughingstock of the entire western end of the island, and that even people from Pidgin Cove, whom everyone else laughed at, would laugh at him.

"Careful, Bulla. Yu on yu way to becoming de village idiot."

Bulla sucked his teeth and stormed off home. They agreed among themselves that Bulla was a boogooyagga boy and that the devil had breathed on him.

For a whole week, Bulla did not come up in to Naggo Head, and when he finally galloped up to the grocery shop and dismounted from the horse, he was still wearing the mustache, and the men were prepared for him. Four men roped him to a chair in the grocery shop. The Fergusons had warned them not to do it in their shop but had changed their minds. The men told Bulla to keep still or he might not only lose the hair on his lip, but he might also lose his nose and a lip or even his tallywag, and they shaved his mustache clean. He vowed that if the men ever laid a hand on him again, they would have to be picked up off the ground with a sieve.

Then suddenly I lost all interest in Bulla. Just like that and *poof*, my interest was gone. We had never held a conversation and had had only three physical contacts—once at the church water bucket and twice at my listening post. In mature reflections on those days, I have told myself sometimes in moments of pathos that it died a natural death, a natural crib death; other times, I have believed that this short-lived, red-hot flame had consumed itself, which was better and safer than continuing to burn only to explode months or even years later and claim innocent casualities. Then at other times, in moments of grand attempts and immense efforts in God-level thinking, I have told myself that it died because of Bulla's cerebral malaise.

Chapter 21

What happened next was not my mother's fault, even though the whole of Naggo Head blamed her. I learned then that it was easier to blame the dead, and blame was the most popular and easiest way of coping when people were confronted with trouble or misfortune.

We all had the sense that trouble was coming to Naggo Head, because Mother Woman had made another one of her middle-of-the-night trips about a week earlier. She had been in rare form that night; she had delivered her prophesies in a call-and-response manner, except she had been both the caller and the responder. Her baritone voice had carved out the night air, punching it, crumpling it.

I had listened along with everyone else and placed little importance to her words until she had compared someone or something in Naggo Head to the "flesh pot of Egypt."

There had been that word again—*flesh*! That flesh-colored word. That word that caused gooseflesh. Such an ugly word. That word with a gladiatorial attitude, a large mouth, and a volcanic appetite for sanity. That vulgar word propelled by pious egos to attack the daring and the alive and so driving shame and guilt into the conscience again and again, rendering it shaky and toothless. Against this one must fight, I had believed then. How was I to have known that to maintain our human kindness, we needed a little of both shame and guilt?

Nanna had time and again warned anyone she saw with a lit oil lamp about the dangers of running with a lit lamp or torch. I can still hear the fear-tinged reflection in her voice. Perhaps she had foreseen this mishap?

It was Saturday evening. I had climbed through my bedroom window around eight o'clock and was stretched out exhausted on my bed in the dark. I had removed my shoes earlier, and they were still clenched in my fists. I was still fully clothed in my dusty-rose dress with the tiny yellow flowers. The walk up from Cross Road had drained the last bit of energy that I had had left in me after the crowded and frenzied dance in Blue Bay. That was the fourth consecutive Saturday afternoon beach party that I had attended in four weeks.

I closed my eyes and was savoring the memory of the last month and must have fallen asleep. The next thing I knew, I felt a warmth near my face. I opened my eyes to see my mother bending over me. In her left hand was her blue oil lamp, the one with the words "Home Sweet Home" etched on the glass chimney. In her right hand was Papa Doc's two-inch-wide leather belt, which I had not seen since he had passed away; the end with the buckle was wrapped around her knuckles. Her mouth was tight and twisted off-center of her face.

Without a word she lifted the belt swiftly, but before she could bring it down I instinctively rolled away to my right. The belt struck the bed and sounded like an ax splitting through wood. I bounced off the bed and stood in shock with my head reeling, unable to comprehend the situation fully. Her face, in its violent intent, was like that of a stranger. Still without a word, she lunged at me and hurled the belt the way a reptile aims its tongue. The belt caught my left shoulder and coiled itself around my neck. I sprinted out the door and toward Nanna's bedroom. She followed me; the sound of our bare feet forcefully striking the wooden floor and rattling the loose planks was like the rolling of thunder. The house shook on its foundation.

"Nanna!" I wailed.

And so, in the dead of the night, Nanna was awoken by the stampede of a mother and daughter, a daughter and granddaughter, locked in a wordless battle. I had just barely leaped into Nanna's bed when my mother stomped into the room. The lamp illuminated her face and cast a giant shadow on the wall nearest to her. I crouched on the bed on all fours, now expecting my mother to call off the attack, but the light and that giant, looming shadow kept coming toward the bed, toward me, with incredible speed and rage. The look of astonishment on Nanna's face and the sight of her sitting up in bed with her hand over her heart was to be the last vision that I would have of her. In desperation, I sprang from the bed and leaped out the opened window. I hit the hard ground and lay stunned for a moment. Then I heard screams. The first two were long and in unison...and then another scream and then another and another and then no more.

The fire spread quickly. The red flames rose high, licking the leaves on the nearby mango tree; the smoke was thick. By the time the first neighbor arrived, Nanna and my mother were no longer living. I remember someone grabbing me by the back of my dress on the veranda and pulling me all the way across the yard and out to the side of the road. I remember being aware of an absolute lack in logical progression about the entire scene that night: it seemed to me that sections of the house were crumpling to ash before it even caught fire. Even though the fire was raging red and hot and spitting embers in the sky, turning solid structures to ashes, and people were running and obviously screaming, there was no sound, just a certain dumbness. It was as if someone had reached out and turned the audio button to off.

The water carried from nearby wells and from the Sweet River was too little and too late. There was nothing more anyone could do except stand and watch the shimmering embers helplessly. The nearest fire station was seven miles away, and this was the first house fire ever in Naggo Head's history.

And when the sun rose pink and golden the next morning, I was still wandering dirty and ragged in my dusty-pink belted dress around the burned crust of Mill Yard, wandering among the ashes, among the broken pieces of blue-and-white china dishes, the husk of the sewing machine, and the smell of over-cooked human flesh. The six broad, solid stone-slab steps led up to nowhere. I picked up the charred pieces of mahogany chairs, the broken pieces of blue vases and oil lamps. I picked them up and dropped them, feeling as though the heart beating in my chest were as dark and broken as they were because I had caused this ruination.

It was because of me that Nanna was no longer with us. She was supposed to have passed away naturally and peacefully in her bed, in her sleep. Wasn't that how grandmothers were supposed to pass on? I had truly loved her and had made plans to take care of her, just as she had taken care of me.

Many days I had lain on the banks of the Sweet River in the splendor of innocence and planned. I was going to be successful and buy a new house equipped with electricity for Nanna. Everything would be contained in this beautiful house, surrounded with a lush, rich lawn, flowers, and vegetable gardens. The bedrooms would still be in close proximity to each other so we could hear her voice clearly during devotions. She would no longer have to chop wood or cook over a smoky fireside or have to bend over a washtub full of dirty clothes under the blazing sun. All she would have to do was go to church and conduct morning and night devotions in the lovely house that I had bought for her.

But while I was making my plans, another with a pruning knife was also putting his plans into action. This was my punishment. Wasn't I the one who had caused the best person I had ever known to commit sin after sin by bringing a killer into her home and causing her to lie to the authorities to cover up a murder? Before I brought Dove home to Mill Yard, wasn't Nanna pure and sinless? It was because of me that she had had to be unkind to Sister Lady. And hadn't I brought vanity, lust, and fleshly thoughts under her roof, causing her to worry and fret? But why punish Nanna to punish me? And wasn't my mother punished too? Didn't this mean then that everyone who had ever died was someone's punishment?

Then I heard Bro' Man's and Barabbas's voices. It took a while for me to realize that they were speaking to me.

"You should get some rest now, child."

"No punish yuself, Cherrimina."

"Bro' Man sey mi ft carry yu up to Cocoa Walk."

"You are staying at my house, child. Come."

"Get up off de groun' Cherrimina."

"Miss Priyanka is getting the bed ready for you, child."

"Come on, gal pickney!"

"Pick her up, Barabbas!"

Then I felt the sensation of flying through the air and landing limply head down over something alive and solid, then a whirling dizziness as my disorientated internal compass spun to navigate to the set direction. I heard the shifting of the gravel under footsteps and felt the dream-inducing bobbing motion of a long, strong stride.

Nanna's relatives who lived several villages over in Little London came to take charge of the funeral arrangements. I had seen several of my cousins and aunts before when they had come to visit Nanna. They could not afford to take me home with them, and Bro' Man and Miss Priyanka suggested I stay with them in Cocoa Walk, in familiar surroundings, at least until after the funeral.

The elders of Naggo Head held a meeting and discussed my situation. Bro' Man had a spare room, they told me, and I would make good company for Miss Priyanka because she had always liked me.

Mill Yard was now a dead yard.

Neighbors, relatives, and church members set up tables and chairs nightly in what was left of Mill Yard, but since no one now lived there, and since it was near the grocery shop, the gathering spilled over to the shop. I attended the nine-night ceremony.

The nine-night was the ninth night of the dead, counting from the first night after the person died to the ninth night. It was an extended wake that lasted for nine days, with roots thrown all the way back to the African tradition. It was believed by some that the dead needed to rest for at least nine days and nights and prepare for their spirits to pass over into the afterlife, so we did not bury the dead until the spirit rose on the third day, grieved for itself, and gathered all its possessions that it wished to take with it. The ninth night was the most sacred of all the nights, since the deceased was usually buried the day after.

On the ninth night, Nanna's relatives and friends set up tables with food and beverages in the dead yard. They prepared fried fish and bread, very hot and very strong coffee, and cocoa tea sweetened with coconut milk and sugar and spiced with nutmeg or cinnamon sticks. Visitors, supporters, friends, and church members sang hymns and choruses. There were stories, condolences to the grieving family members, and fond memories about Nanna. Prayers were offered up to heaven.

Usually the bed and mattress of the deceased were turned up against the wall to encourage the spirit to leave the house and enter the grave, but since there was no bed, someone took the only piece of a corner post left standing and leaned it against the tree at the front of Mill Yard. Then an older relative steeped in the nine-night tradition used a piece of white chalk to draw a cross over the exit that the spirit should use to leave, never to return. It was believed that the spirit of the deceased passed through the celebration, gathering food and saying goodbye before continuing on to its resting place.

No alcohol was served out of respect for Nanna, who was religious, but the men slamming dominoes, the grave diggers, and such poured liquids from bottles and flasks into their mugs of coffee.

Exactly at midnight the mento band stationed on the front steps began to play and drowned out the chatter. The hands beating the drums flew over the stretched skin, and the beats exploded loudly and quickly; the flurries of the banjo soared into the night; the gourds, the tambourines, and rumba box kept time; the man scraping table forks on tin graters boogied.

I had read somewhere that the drumbeat could be healing, that the drumbeat was the same as our heartbeat, that they had the same pulse—that it was a supernatural force that entered into our bodies and nibbled at our souls and roused our spirits so that we responded immediately to therapeutic suggestions.

For the healing process to commence, we lay our bodies down on the earth, relaxed all our muscles, closed our eyes, and let our bodies surrender to the rhythm, allowing the drum spirit to control our spirits.

I knew with every fiber in my being that I needed healing, but healing from what, I was not sure. I stretched my body out on the cool, dark earth in Mill Yard, on top of the green that was above the brown, closed my eyes, and relaxed my muscles and let the spirit of the drumbeat take control and heal my spirit. I heard later that my behavior was odd.

It was sometime during the nine-night, while relatives, church members, former teachers, and neighbors voiced sympathy for the loss of my grandmother and my mother, that I realized that I had never been able to separate my feelings for Nanna from those for my mother. Nanna had always been synonymous with love; my mother, comfort and security. Nanna loved me;

therefore, my mother loved me. Nanna provided comfort and security; therefore, my mother, too, provided all those. Had I disrespected and denigrated my mother all these years by lumping her with Nanna? I had so many things for which I had to ask God's forgiveness. Or should I be cursing God instead?

Everyone I saw I wondered why he or she was alive while Nanna was dead. Why should anyone be alive while Nanna was dead?

It was with all these questions, stinging guilt, and punishing blame and these rigorous traditional proceedings that I attended the memorial service. It was a Saturday. I had seen many beautiful days on our island, but I truly could not remember seeing one more picturesque. A light breeze stirred the balmy air, and the sun shone brightly through cumulus clouds hanging low, fluffy, and white in the sky. But soon my eyes began to hurt.

I wore one of Miss Priyanka's black frocks and hat, stood in front of the congregation at the pulpit, remembered to call Nanna by her rightful name, Cordelia, instead of Nanna, and read John 14:1–3: "Let not your heart be troubled: ye believe in God, believe also in me. In my father's house are many mansions; if it were not so, I would have told you. I go to prepare a place for you. And if I go and prepare a place for you, I will come again, and receive you unto myself, that where I am, there ye may be also."

I was doing great until the beginning of the last verse. It was at that point that my throat became dry, began to tighten, and then closed up painfully around the words. My heart shook in an effort to push the words out, and my sense of balance became warped, and I tottered on the edge of the platform, on the edge of myself, on the edge of tears. Then I felt hands around my shoulders. They were steady and peaceful and kind hands, just like Nanna's used to be. Miss Priyanka and a senior church member had foreseen my predicament and had come to lend a helping hand.

I mourned Nanna the only way I knew how. At the interment I carried a large handkerchief on my shoulder, with which I wiped the tears as they rolled down my face. This was the manner in which Nanna had mourned my grandfather at his funeral. It was the only example of grieving at a funeral that I had seen. It felt right, and there was no one there to tell me what was right and wrong. My beloved Nanna was not there to give me guidance. I would hear later that my behavior was odd.

The fire had given me a new song to sing. On a wash day, who would look at the clouds and know when they were set to rain and that we should take the clothes from the clothesline before they got wet? Who would know when I needed purging? Who would sit on the veranda and hold smart conversation with visitors? Whom would I visit? Who would tell me if the amount of salt in the spoon was too much to put in the pumpkin soup? Who would commence worshipping prayers at bedtime and at dawn? And when I got sick, who would know which herbal tea I needed? Whom would I love? Who would love me? What would I do? Where would I go?

Chapter 22

The morning after the funeral, I woke up with a headache, a headache so intense that I could not leave my bed. Miss Priyanka made a tea of boiled turmeric and milk, but still I ached. My skin began to ache with fever. And when the chills began, Bro' Man arranged for a motorcar to pick us up and drive us to the clinic at Cross Road. The doctor looked at me over his glasses and prescribed a liquid medicine in a bottle, but after the third day without any improvement, Miss Priyanka, troubled by my condition, studied the book on herbalism that Nanna had lent her and, with Bro' Man's machete in hand, went into the forest among the lungs of the earth in search of a Jamaican logwood tree. No one in Naggo Head went to the doctor for a headache or fever; instead, people took a trip to the woods to find medicinal herbs.

A tea or tincture made from the bruised or dry bark from this tree was used as traditional remedy for treating neuralgia, migraine, insomnia, anxiety, fear, and nervous tension. As early as 1844, Western scientists discovered that the Jamaican dogwood tree had pain-relieving and sweat-promoting properties, Miss Priyanka had read.

Later that night, at bedtime, she brought the cup of steam-ing hot tea to my room. I was too weak to hold the cup, and she held it for me. It was too bitter and too hot. She took it away and added more honey to sweeten, but it was still bitter. She fed me in silence, and I drank in silence, and my eyes watched her face in silence. Her kind face was drawn, and her gentle hands shook slightly, and I hoped she was not regretting taking me in. We still had a distance to go between us, being that it had been only two weeks since I had begun living with her, and I vowed at that moment to do my best to show my gratitude and not to displease her. I smiled at her uncertainly; she smiled back hesitantly and lifted a hand and cupped my hot cheek.

After what seemed like an eternity, I finished the tea. I apolo-gized to her for causing so much trouble. She brushed my apolo-gies aside and wrapped me in the bedsheets to sweat.

Then I fell into a troubled sleep—or what might be more correctly called a trance—that lasted for three whole days. For three days she fed me a cup of the hot, bitter tea at bedtime. And for three days, my flesh ached, and my scalp burned.

I remember being unable to open my eyes because the sunlight had laid giant fingers on my eyelids, putting pressure on them so that they stayed close. I could hear voices, and even though I could not hear what was being said, I would try to type the words on the phantom typewriter but kept mak-ing mistakes, and I would stop and start over again. I never typed a complete word; I just kept starting over and over again statically.

At other times I felt a sensation of moving through the air above everything else and a whirling dizziness as if the earth's center of gravity had gotten off track and was spinning desperately in every direction to regain focus and center.

On the third morning, I was still shaky, but I was able to get out of bed, take a bath, and eat breakfast. Bro' Man was overjoyed to see me up and about. Miss Priyanka told me that I had kept screaming about falling whenever she and Bro' Man had had to move me in order to change the soaking-wet bedsheets and when they had tried to feed me soup or tea, and that I had constantly spoken in my sleep.

She combed my hair and put me to sit in a chair under shade of a coconut tree. The sunlight still hurt my eyes, and she made an eye mask to cover my eyes.

This was the routine for a little over a week. I grew stronger steadily, except for around six o'clock every evening, when a strange weakness would overtake my body, and I would take to bed. Miss Priyanka, too, noticed this and told me what she had read about this in the herbalism book: our bodies have a twenty-four-hour temperature rhythm, and the highest temperature of each day occurs around six o'clock in the evening.

Then I began getting visitors. The word must have gotten out that I was no longer at death's door and could have visitors. The first to visit was Bulla. He gave a sigh of relief at the news that Bro' Man was not at home. We sat on the veranda, and even though we had never had the chance to have a long conversation before, it was not uncomfortable, because Miss Priyanka sat with us, and he spent the whole time charming her.

He seemed a much more mature person now and was truly happy to see that I was feeling better. He was considering moving out of his father's home to look for a job, or perhaps even go back to school to learn a trade.

Three of the young kids in the neighborhood came to visit. They sat in a row in the chairs that Miss Priyanka had provided and looked at me as if they were in a classroom and I was the teacher. They ate the raisin cakes, drank the lemonade, and did not say a word to me or Miss Priyanka throughout the entire visit, but I felt grateful that they had even had the thought and made the effort to visit. But that was how it was in Naggo Head—children were seen but not heard. Precocity had no place or name in our culture; it was good behavior, proper behavior, that moved a child to the top of the favorite list, not cleverness or brightness.

Barabbas visited also. He was very happy to see that I was comfortable in my new home. He missed Nanna because he had truly loved her, but I could see that he was trying not to dwell on the subject. Bro' Man was at home, and they had a drink of alcoholic beverage together, and then Barabbas did what he knew best: he entertained us with the latest story. This time it was a story about Squid the boatman.

Everybody had known that Squid had not liked wearing shoes, and whenever he had worn shoes, they had been sandals, so his toes had been used to being spread out free and wild all day long. So no one had known what had possessed him to purchase a pair of leather cowboy boots. They had had heels that were one and a half inches high and long, pointy toes. He had put the boots on that particular morning and gone about his business as usual. By midafternoon his toes had been swollen so badly in the shoes, under the hot sun, that he could no longer walk—nor could he remove the boots. He had been in so much pain that he literally could not put his feet on the ground. He had said he felt like his toes were caught in a giant rat trap. Barabbas had arrived on the scene just in time to suggest they use some of the old fishing nets Squid had in his backyard to make a stretcher and carry him to a nearby butcher shop. The butcher had used his meat cleaver to cut the boots off his feet and set his bloated toes free again.

Barabbas demonstrated how Squid had wobbled on his bowlegs in the high-heeled cowboy-boots-turned-rattrap.

Bro' Man's house was the only house in Cocoa Walk. From the outside the appearance was just like the other houses in Naggo Head—unpainted, weathered sideboards—but that was where it ended. The furniture, though not excessive in quantity, was tasteful, highly polished, and nicely arranged. And there was a well-stocked library. The water supply was from a well.

Behind the house was a large cocoa tree plantation; the acres of frightfully shadowy land with closely spaced cocoa trees was a low-maintenance business. The cocoa pods were picked when ripe and split open, and the seeds were removed and sun-dried and then sold to chocolate and cocoa powder manufacturers.

Bro' Man would wake up early every day and take a walk among the cocoa trees. We would have breakfast, and then Bro' Man might leave the house midmorning and return late afternoon for a late lunch or early supper, which he devoured with a freshly picked Scotch bonnet pepper right from the stem without shedding a tear.

Miss Priyanka would cook; she would embroider; she would read, meditate, take walks, and go for swims in the Sweet River. I would cook, I would embroider, and I would read, meditate, take walks, and go for swims in the Sweet River. Our existence was quiet, peaceful, and comfortable. Bro' Man said it was a lifestyle of simple living and high thinking. The key to this, he told us, was never thinking of the small things as silly.

Bro' Man and Miss Priyanka had met on a ship sailing from London to the West Indies. She had been on her way to visit relatives in Trinidad, and he had been coming back to his island home for the first time after years of world traveling. He had been born on the north coast of the island, to a sailor father and an islander mother who had died in childbirth. Raised by his grandfather and large for his age, he had left the island at fifteen when he got a job on a banana boat. There was a framed photograph of him on his bureau dresser in which he was sitting at a table with his legs crossed at the knees, dressed in high-buttoned boots and dinner suit, the pants sharply creased, his hair parted down the middle and brushed flat toward his ears, and his mustache big and curling up at the sides like the handlebars of a bicycle.

"That was taken a long, long time ago," he told me. "It was a time when modesty was a woman's greatest virtue. A few years after this picture was taken, a woman's greatest virtue altered, and I stopped reading fiction." This was the closest Bro' Man had ever come to advice or encouragement about behavior in womanhood. The other time was when he had been teaching me to ride his bicycle. After seeing my frustration at being unable to stay in the seat and keep the handlebars steady, he had slapped me on the back and said, "Aww! Buck up! Buck uuuuppp!""

Miss Priyanka said she had never seen anyone so confident, gallant, and persistent as he was. He entered rooms leaning forward, she said. And halfway between London and Trinidad, he had worn down the wall that she had put up against his dogged chasing of her, and she had followed him to our island. She had never returned to India since.

Never having lived in a house with a male before, I was taken by surprise the first time I saw Bro' Man with shaving-soap foam all over his face and throat and at the way he sharpened a razor before he pulled it across his throat. Another amazing thing was seeing the way they fawned over each other. Bro' Man's fawning would begin at dinnertime and Miss Priyanka's at breakfast. At dinnertime, Bro' Man was the earth and Miss Priyanka the sun, and somewhere overnight they switched, and at breakfast Miss Priyanka became the earth and Bro' Man the sun.

I became fascinated with the surprise gifts, the delightful, light-headed giggles through half-open doors, baritones in muffled moans, quick kisses, and long hugs. Watching their faces and peeking around corners became a past time. That was so until Miss Priyanka sat me down and explained why I should allow them privacy. Their love seemed to be just like I had read in fairy tales—the part about living happily ever after.

I asked Miss Priyanka what was it that made her decide to marry Bro' Man, and she said it had been when he had whispered in her ear that she wouldn't have to love him back, she wouldn't have to do a drop of work, she wouldn't even have to bear children if she didn't want to—all she had to do was marry him and wake up in the mornings. She said that for a few seconds after saying this, Bro' Man had looked stunned and even cross-eyed because prior to his proposal, he had believed that marriage was prison for men and slavery for women.

It was on a beautiful Monday morning that I told Miss Priyanka and Bro' Man that I was walking down to Mill Yard. This would be my first time setting foot out of Cocoa Walk since the day I had been taken to the clinic—four months since the funeral.

Naggo Head Road was quiet with the children already in school. Papa John rocked sleepily on his mule and cart on his way down to his fields. Clotheslines were gaily decorated with flapping, laundered kids' clothes and men's khakis by industrious mothers; each house veranda's floors shone dark red with logwood dye and hot wax. Bundles of cut sugarcane stalks were piled at the entrance of Calypso Walk and were waiting to be collected by the sugar estate. Sister Lady sat on a bench in her backyard husking corn. I waved to her, and she pretended not to see me, so I told myself that her eyesight was getting poor.

Ma'as Zachy was taking one of his rare outings. He had lived in England for years and one day had just quietly returned home unannounced, touched in the head and with only the clothes he wore on his back. It was widely rumored that he had stood too long and often under the chiming Big Ben clock in London and that it had affected his head. Some believed that he had hated the cold, gray English weather so much that he had had no emotion left for anyone or anything else. Every once in a while, he would quietly show up at the hospital in Blue Bay, and they would put him in a straitjacket for a few days and then send him home.

But Naggo Head Road was broken now. The familiar route of slopes, gullies, greeneries, and houses, then hills, valleys, greeneries, rock walls, and houses again, was now broken at Mill Yard. It stood like a dark gap in a pearl necklace or a missing key in a clavier. Mill Yard was like an old gray ghost.

The front step slabs that were once bright white were filthy and overgrown with clumps of dense green moss. And instead of six steps, there were now five, the top one having crumbled away. The few corner posts and windows that had been barely standing were now lying on the ground in splinters, and I surmised that Mill Yard had become the neighborhood kids' newest playground.

The footpath that led down to the Sweet River and the surrounding land was now a forest. Through that bushy footpath, under the shade of the poinciana tree, their feet pointing toward the calabash tree, under the brown beneath the green, Nanna and my mother rested.

I pushed through the vegetation toward the two small mounds that were now covered with small greeneries. I bent to begin pulling away the weeds and creepers but decided against it. The green over the brown soil was more soothing, more peaceful. They were safe from the world. From their resting place, they could hear the gentle running of the river.

The bumblebees were humming. The fairy flowers next to the fever grass and the sawgrass would soon bloom in the fields at the north of their heads. In a couple of months, the blossoms of the stately blue mahoe trees would change from bright yellow to orange-red and finally to crimson. The poinciana tree would sprinkle the mounds with its colorful blossoms. It would be beautiful.

Yes, they were safe from the world—safe from me.

I picked up ten dried jumbie seeds from where they had fallen under the tree and put them in my pocket and walked back up the footpath toward the burned-out house.

Without any fuss a stray nanny goat and a few hens wandered the yard with me. Under a piece of roof zinc was the burned wooden trunk with the charred pair of black-and-tan high-heeled pumps. And as I turned the corner toward the kitchen and away from the road, I could have sworn that I heard Nanna calling the chickens for their early-morning feeding.

"Coup, coup, coup!" she used to call. And the chickens would reply, "Cluck, cluck, cluck!"

And after a while, sounds and smells of my past slowly penetrated my senses, and it was their slowness that was to be my downfall—those soft tentacles that penetrated and sucked and squeezed my already-shattered soul. It was the putt-putting of my mother's hand-operated sewing machine; Nanna's chair rocking to and fro, fro and to, bruising the floorboards on the veranda; the cluck-clucking of the chickens in their coops; the laundry dancing double time on the clothesline in the brisk midmorning breeze. I smelled the strong coffee with the pinch of salt added, the callaloo cooked in coconut milk, the salted mackerel, the ackee and salt fish, and the crusty hard-dough bread baking in the Dutch pot. And when I heard Nanna's mattress rustling as she rose from it for morning devotion, I crouched in the remaining ashes in the backyard and wept.

Before I left Mill Yard that day, my body and clothes grimy and dirty from the ashes, I found the tin pan with the cut ends of Dove's blond hair, her red wig, and the handcuffs that I had hidden in the cubbyhole behind the back steps. The tin pan was unscathed.

Chapter 23

Life at Cocoa Walk became idyllic. Miss Priyanka found pleasure in educating me in the fineries of upper-class etiquette. Her best silver knives and forks were laid out for every Sunday dinner. I learned how to walk like a lady, to sit like a lady, to groom myself like a lady. I learned the proper way to iron a man's khaki trousers and how much rum to mix into a man's Christmas eggnog. She taught me the process of pressing unrefined cocoa butter from the cocoa seeds, and we spent hours sitting in the afternoon shade of the broadleaf tree smoothing the butter into our hair and our skin until we glistened. Miss Priyanka explained several times that all this grooming was a bridge to better things, not a goal.

She even schooled me in how to make living with Bro' Man easier. She told me never to tell him that I had a "great idea." I slipped up once and provoked nearly an hour-long lecture on the pitfalls of great ideas.

Bro' Man took us to see several silent movies at the movie house in Blue Bay, and I knew then that Barabbas had made up most of the dialogue of his Saturday morning stories.

The dreaded Sunday evening visits with Bro' Man's friends eventually turned to entertainment for me the first time we went to visit Mister Percy. The men began by raising their mugs, and Mister Percy made his usual toast: "From the womb to the tomb." Then in the middle of the somber conversation, a slow-rising stench invaded the veranda, and Mister Percy shooed his dog, Egbert, out of the house and apologized to us for Egbert's lifting his tail. I was never sure if Egbert or Mister Percy was to be blamed.

The discussions at these Sunday visits gained steam about the pending war in Europe.

One of the main topics was the MS *Saint Louis*—the German ocean liner that had left Hamburg, Germany, for Cuba, with 937 passengers, mostly Jewish refugees seeking asylum from Nazi persecution. Most of them had planned to relocate eventually to the United States and were on the waiting list for admission. But when the *Saint Louis* had reached the port of Havana, the Cuban officials had refused them entry to the usual docking areas, and the MS *Saint Louis* had had to drop anchor at the far end of the harbor, where the passengers would wait aboard for six days.

The six days on the harbor were agonizing for the passengers and crew. It was finally announced that only passengers who had official Cuban visas would be allowed entry. Only then were twenty-nine passengers allowed to disembark on Cuban shores, including one passenger who had attempted suicide and was taken to a hospital in Havana.

As the situation worsened, the German captain of the ship personally negotiated and schemed to find a safe place for his passengers. He, along with groups of academics and clergy, pleaded with the United States and Canada to take the passengers, but the officials of these two countries did not intervene.

After long negotiations, 908 passengers were forced to return to Europe. One died en route.

At first, to most of us on the island, the war was a faraway event that was reported in the newspaper and was something to discuss at gatherings to show how up to date some of the elders were with current events. Then, very soon, the first up-close vision of the world war would reach our island, as it did everywhere else, when the Royal Air Force established a base at the eastern end of our island, in Town, at a place called Sandy Gully. The American camp was established in the middle of the island, which meant that we at the western end of the island were sheltered away from most of these activities, except for two small lookout stations that were set up on the coast at the most westerly point.

In a few months, the worldwide war was like a vat of molten solution slowly coming to a boil on the island, with isolated early-warning bubbles popping up hither and thither and waiting to burst on the seemingly peaceful surface. Soon soldiers in full uniform and with gear and big tanks and guns were sighted being transported around the island in great trucks.

And then the war became more personal to us on the island, when the armed convoys at sea toppled the import-export structure, and regulation and restrictions were placed on the amount of food that could be bought from the shops. Then items such as rice, flour, cornmeal, soap, clothing, fabric, kerosene oil, and canned goods became scarce, and even when we could get these items, the shops would have no brown paper to wrap the loose items. We would take a tablecloth to carry the rice and flour home.

Shopkeepers exploited the situation by marrying merchandise that was least needed to another product that was in great demand—cornmeal was married to flour and salted mackerel to salt pork. The government had to establish a price-control system.

In Naggo Head most of the food we consumed, such as breadfruit, bananas, and yams, was harvested fresh from the fields—eggs from the chickens, fresh milk from the cows, and fruit from the trees—so we were scarcely affected by the shortage of tin goods.

One of Bro' Man's guests at Cocoa Walk enjoyed telling how times were so hard that at dinnertime the mothers wouldn't say, "Come and get it"; they would say, "Come and find it."

Before the war we would take a torch with us at night to see our way along the moonlit paths in Naggo Head, but during the war, there were blackout nights, when the only lights we were allowed were candles inside houses, with the windows closed. The children were no longer allowed to play outside after dark; they had to play inside.

Big headlines in the newspaper screamed that volunteers were being sought for overseas service as well as home guards for local defense. Many of the unemployed and the unemployable signed up for service.

A grand ceremony was held in Blue Bay to send the volunteers at the western end of the island off to Town to begin their overseas service. Bro' Man attended in an official position. Free whistles were handed out to all, and as the men and boys marched under banners to police band music, the crowd blew whistles and waved flags.

It was a quiet Tuesday morning that Bulla marched into Cocoa Walk. Funny that I would remember which day it was, but I remember the day because Tuesdays were wash days in Cocoa Walk, so Miss Priyanka and I were under the ackee tree up to our elbows in wash pans of soapy water and scrubbing boards. Miss Priyanka was complaining about the scarcity of soap. It was a very hot day, and our hair and our attire for washing clothes were soaking wet with the dirty, soapy water and from perspiration.

Bro' Man was at home, wearing soiled, old khaki pants and a sleeveless undershirt. He had just finished gathering a whole lot of old metal household objects, railings, old metal tools, and old pots and had placed them on the side of Naggo Road to be collected by the government to be shipped off to England to make ammunition. He had decided to kick his shoes off and was tinkering with the wireless on the veranda with a tall glass of lemonade beside him.

We heard the voice calling from the entrance of Cocoa Walk just off Naggo Head Road, but none of us recognized it. And then the caller came in sight, but it was not until he was standing across from us that we recognized him. The shirt of the khaki suit he wore was fitted perfectly across his shoulders and chest, and the crisp pants were pressed and creased sharply and ended exactly on top of the shoes that were polished to a high sheen. A soft cap was perched sideways on his closely cut hair. All this he carried on an upright, taut frame, the chest pushed out with responsibility and pride as he strode purposefully onward.

We stood watching him, shading our eyes from the sun with our hands.

He stopped a short distance from us, and with a finger and a thumb on the edge of one lens, he daintily adjusted the new wire-rimmed glasses on his nose. He gave a polite and slight salute to Bro' Man on the veranda, and as he took the last few steps toward Miss Priyanka and me, he removed the soft cap from his head.

"It's Bulla!" Miss Priyanka cried.

Bro' Man asked how he had traveled to Naggo Head, and he said a friend and his motorcar were waiting for him on Naggo Head Road. We sat on the shaded veranda, drank lemonade, and listened as he told us his story while the sweat spots at his armpits and at the back of his shirt dried.

He had seen an advertisement in the newspaper stating that "The Mother Country Needs You" and had volunteered for over-seas service and was shipping out in two weeks for England. Speaking with a new but slight British accent, he told us about his tests and preparations at the RAF base at Sandy Gully and about the people he had met at the rehabilitation camp established in Town for refugees, from Europe in general and from Gibraltar in particular. He was thinking of taking up photography after his service in the armed forces, so his mother and the preacher had bought him a camera as a going-away gift.

Perhaps still seeing myself as a child who should be seen but not heard, I sat and listened to Bulla's self-assured manners, his improved speech, his use of slang, and his knowledge of current and foreign affairs. Then I noticed that behind the lenses of the spectacles, he had good eyes—not kind but good.

Then I realized that all three were looking at me expectantly. I had missed something important. Bulla smiled a becoming smile and repeated it. He said that the government was providing allow-ances for wives of men who were going into military service for the war effort. And he had this brilliant idea that he would marry me so that I could collect that money while he was away, and that after he returned from overseas, I could do what I thought was best for me. At this point Miss Priyanka and Bro' Man excused themselves and left—she to continue washing, and he to watch her wash.

Bulla continued. He said that he loved me, and he knew that I didn't love him and that I had no family to look out for me, and I could use the money to continue my schooling so I could better myself. He asked me how old I was.

"Almos' eighteen," I said.

He said that I was almost grown up now and that I couldn't live with Miss Priyanka and depend on Bro' Man forever, and that it was time I started thinking of my future. He asked me not to be angry at him for speaking so frankly.

I didn't know what to say. I didn't know what to do. But he was right. Recently I had been thinking along those same lines in my bed at night, but I had to save face, so I quickly explained my situation to him.

"I wanted to go for further schooling," I explained, "but first we had the workers' strikes and unrest, and now the world war, and all that caused me to put off school."

He said that that was the exact excuse he'd given someone who spoke to him about straightening out his life. And that person told him that the real war was thousands of miles away across many oceans in Europe, and what we had here on an island in the West Indies was just the shadow that the war cast.

"What is going to become of you, Cherrimina?" he asked.

I sat in silence, looking down at my hands folded in my lap for a long time. I couldn't raise my eyes to look at him because

I knew exactly what he saw when he looked at me. He saw a girl who had behaved badly and caused the horrible death of her family and who was now an orphan on the cusp of adulthood and living off her kind neighbors and benefactors like a parasite. Even the dress I was wearing had once belonged to Miss Priyanka.

Then I looked up at him and saw the new Bulla, with a new maturity and putting effort into a slight British accent, who would be traveling overseas in a few weeks to save lives, the same Bulla who had once grown his mustache like Hitler's and on whom I had once had a mad crush—a mad crush of lust and energy.

A sudden sense of being left behind, of being outpaced, like an old bicycle that had to pull off the road to give way to a new-model car, a sense of loss and of sorrow, came over me, and I bowed under this weight. I threw my head back and opened my throat, and a wail escaped from deep in my stomach. Bulla jumped up from his chair and backed away, and Bro' Man and Miss Priyanka hurried up the steps onto the veranda.

Bro' Man assured the shocked Bulla not to worry, that he hadn't done anything wrong, and that it would be better if he wrote to me from overseas. I nodded a fervent consent at this suggestion, dried my tears, and apologized to him because I knew that I had truly scared him half to death. He accepted my apology and asked hesitantly if he could take our pictures. We posed for pictures under the midday sun, Bro' Man in his bare feet and old khaki pants, without his usual tailored vest and without his pocket watch, Miss Priyanka in her wash-day clothes and hair, and I with my tear-stained face.

I watched Bulla walking briskly away from Cocoa Walk, his new shoes creaking a lively tune, and I knew he would do well.

That half boy and half man would learn to camouflage a rifle—the shape of the tan color should be smaller than the shape of the olive drab green and dark brown. He would learn to camouflage his emotions—body held at rigid attention and whitewashed in politeness, courtesy, and respect. He might never know that his weapon had been made by the lowest bidder and that five-second fuses always burned in three seconds. He would smell of sweat and mildew; he would smell death, blood, and fear. He would learn to use his hands like armaments and armaments like they were his hands. Visions of mines and snipers and exploding mortars would dance in his head, right next to a woman. He would mend his own clothes, cook his own meals, and patch his own flesh. And he would return home. He would return home thinner in body, with thick calluses on his hands and feet. He would save lives. Yes, I was sure he would save lives.

I asked Bro' Man who was the Uncle Sam that Bulla kept mentioning, and he explained that Uncle Sam was a nickname for the United States of America.

Miss Priyanka went back to washing, and I, curious to see what Bulla had seen, went inside the house to look at myself in the mirror. My hair had grown almost down to the small of my back due to Miss Priyanka's weekly special oil treatments, but it was still wild and windswept when not tied with a ribbon. I had grown about two inches and was about five feet four and a half inches tall by now. My lips. The lips that would not stay buttoned a few years before were now closed a little too tightly in almost a straight line. The sprinkle of freckles on my nose had vanished because I was no longer out and about in the blazing sun every day. And there was something different about the eyes—they were narrower, not wide open or as clear as before, and quite shockingly, the longer I looked into the mirror, the more I saw glimpses of Nanna's eyes. Yes, my eyes were older. Of late I had wondered once or twice what was to become of me. Would I in a few years begin paying for my coffin in installments? Or would I begin wearing an apron like a uniform? Would the young, spritely boys and girls in the village on their way to Blue Bay begin stopping by to ask if they could purchase anything for me?

I did not see what most would think an orphan should look like. I did not look hungry or half-starved, abandoned, ragged, or abused. Bro' Man and Miss Priyanka were very good to me. I could not have asked for any better treatment. I made a promise to myself right then and there that I would never again allow myself to feel like an orphan. And it would be an easy promise to keep.

There were not many curfews at the western end of the island, but that night there was a curfew with a blackout, so we had to use candles or lamps placed underneath tables instead of on top of them, with the windows closed. And while the planes flew overhead and Bro' Man showed his cronies how to make a low-light lamp using a shoe-polish tin, coconut oil, a saucer, and bits of cotton, I went to Miss Priyanka's bedroom to apologize to her for my behavior earlier that day.

I told her about the sudden feelings I had had of loss, of being left behind, and of being an orphan, and she accepted my apology. Then she lowered her voice and asked me to close the bedroom door. She made me promise never to let Bro' Man know that she had said what she was about to say. I nodded without eagerness because her eyes were very serious—too serious. She made me raise one hand and repeat an oath of silence.

Then she told me that I was not an orphan, that she might know who my father was. She said that a long time ago, Bro' Man had heard someone mention that my father was a Syrian who operated a sewing machine and sewing supply shop in Blue Bay on Saint George Street. She said that he might not have known that he had fathered a child.

She went on to tell me a story of a fish and why Bro' Man would leave her if he knew that she had repeated this secret, and I sat quietly and listened and heard little to nothing. She finished the story, kissed me on my forehead, and I felt nothing. I walked to my bedroom but saw nothing.

I could be part Syrian? Even though Miss Priyanka had used the word *might*, in a matter of seconds I had gone from being an orphan to having a new word attaching itself to me, attaching itself to my identity. Who were the Syrians? Syrians to me at that point in my life were foreign male shop owners with dark, wavy hair and fair complexions, and Syria was a place mentioned in the Bible. But why did they come to our island? How did they arrive? When had they first arrived? These were the first thoughts that went through my head. Next were thoughts of my mother. Why hadn't she told me? Why could she not bring herself to tell any-one who my father was? Then thoughts of Nanna. Had Nanna known who my father was?

I went to bed that night feeling that my life going forward would be far different than it had been in the last three years.

Chapter 24

It was during lunch break when I entered the Naggo Head Primary School yard, my old school. In one corner groups of boys were marching around playing soldiers, with pieces of tree branches as guns.

I stood in line with two men, waiting to see the headmistress, Miss Vanhorn. The men were there for assistance with filling out their applications for farm-working jobs overseas. The shortage of farm laborers in the United States of America following its full involvement in the war allowed many unemployed West Indian men an opportunity to work overseas as farm workers in the "farm labor scheme." As the war progressed, the number of American men being drafted or enlisting in the US military grew, and since the defense plants were recruiting and offering high salaries, young farm men naturally navigated toward those jobs. The farm labor shortage quickly became severe, especially for fruit and vegetable producers, and so the farming industry had to rely on migratory farm laborers.

I sat in front of Miss Vanhorn and asked her permission to use the school library to do some research. A friend overseas was searching for her relatives, I lied, and because there was nothing on this topic overseas, she had asked me to research the history of the Syrians on our island.

This was my first time visiting the school since finishing, and Miss Vanhorn had aged tremendously. In ordinary times in villages such as Naggo Head, teachers were everything to their neighborhoods: letter writers, letter readers, parents, ministers, nurses, counselors, and bankers, among many other things; therefore, the war years must have been an extremely trying time for them.

She expressed her sympathy once again for my past misfortunes, and I thanked her, wondering if she had heard about my previous carrying-on and then suddenly feeling a strange joy that I had remained untouched by any man.

She told me I wouldn't find any books in the school library on that topic, but she had many newspapers, newspaper articles with photographs, and magazine clippings at home that she would lend to me if I came back the next day.

Out on the street, a motorcar with a megaphone on its roof crawled by in its usual round as the driver announced news of the war. The boys and girls all ran to the fences, pushing and shoving. A lifeboat full of English sailors had landed on the shores of a nearby island in the Caribbean Sea the day before.

Their ship had sunk off the coast of Africa, and all the surviving men had had to fit on the one lifeboat they had managed to save. Some men were inside the lifeboat, some were tied to the sides, and others were clinging to the sides. They had had no food and only rainwater to drink. They had been attacked by sharks, and having no weapons to protect themselves, they had had to kick and beat these man-eaters off with their boots. Luckily, they had come upon an old raft floating in the waters; they had succeeded in roping it in and had been able to get everyone safely out of the water. When they had landed on the island, their flesh had been ripped and bleeding from the shark bites, and their skin had been badly sunburned from the intense sunlight.

Of course I went back the next day, and I learned that the first set of Syrians, also called Lebanese, had arrived on our island in 1891. The main reason for their departure from their native lands—Lebanon, Damascus, and Bethlehem—had been religious persecution.

The interchangeable use of the terms *Syrian* and *Lebanese* confounded me at first, but I chose to ignore the terms and forged on.

I found two reasons why the Syrians had chosen to settle on our island. One popular view was that visitors to the Great Exhibition of 1891, held on our island at a school in Saint Ann's Town, had drawn over three hundred thousand visitors from around the world, including the Middle East, who took back home tales of a beautiful British colony, suggesting great prosperity and kindling interest in the island. America was still troubled with the trauma of its civil war, so Britain was seen as the country of freedom at the time, and they chose to seek the protection under the British flag.

Another view was that the first arrivals had disembarked for the island because they had not had a clear idea of exactly where they were going, and with the island being the first stop the ship made—and a colony of Britain—they decided to stay.

What they had seen when they landed at Saint Ann's Town harbor, at the eastern end of the island, was an energetic, thriving trading scene, with single and double horse-drawn traps and mule-drawn tramcars hustling around the harbor transporting finely attired businessmen. The islanders, the long-ago-arrived East Indians, Jews, Chinese, and women in their fineries, had intermingled, traded, and bargained over prices. Even though there had been open drains along some streets, there had also been electricity and a water system.

Many Syrians had started out as street-side or door-to-door peddlers. Then, as business improved, they had borrowed money from more prominent members of the Syrian community to add a horse and buggy or perhaps a motor vehicle and taken their goods out to other towns, out to the countryside and villages.

Their goods had often been sold on the basis of credit, which was very suitable to their customers. As time passed, and the peddler accumulated enough money, he would open a dry goods store in downtown Saint Ann's Town and then perhaps another. Some would venture into the banana industry. They had been careful with their money and worked hard and were known for their sharp business sense. They had played a significant role in the commercial and industrial development of the island.

The photographs were of Syrian businessmen standing in front of their dry goods stores in Saint Ann's Town on King Street, of family gatherings, of business meetings on West Street, and of new Syrians arriving at the harbor.

It was almost two months before I could bring myself to take a trip into Blue Bay, wearing one of Miss Priyanka's frocks and a pair of her sandals. I didn't have an umbrella, so I protected my face from the sun with her wide-brimmed straw hat.

Blue Bay had changed in the past three years. It was an extremely warm day without a breeze. Unable to bring myself to enter the store immediately, and hoping to cool off by the sea breeze, I walked down to the wharf and watched a mechanical contraption with an enormous magnet grab the metals that had been collected around the neighborhoods and load them onto boats—flat-bottomed boats, the wharf worker explained, because the wharf and its operations had changed and could no longer accommodate the bigger boats. I even recognized parts of Dadda Brooks's windmill that men in uniforms had blasted with dynamite from his back field near Sweet River a few weeks earlier.

On my way back up to the Syrian's store, someone called my name from across Great George Street. It was Barabbas. He had good news. He had been one of forty men accepted to the farm labor scheme, and he would be traveling to Florida to work on fruit orchards and vegetable farms. He knew a young boy over in Green Island who would take his place at the Fergusons' shop.

He had such great plans for the money he would earn. First he was going to work so hard and well in Florida that they would want to give him a second contract. Then he would open a bicycle shop right here in Blue Bay. He was good at fixing things, so he would sell refurbished bicycles as well as brand-new ones— not everyone would be able to afford the brand-new ones. He assured me that he knew all of the businessmen on Great George Street and had done favors for most of them, so they would support him.

The government would be paving all the local and gravel roads after the war, and that would mean more jobs and more money to spend on more bicycles to ride on these better roads. Soon donkey and carts would go out of style in the villages because folks like us in Naggo Head would be able to afford bicycles. We would be able to ride instead of walk. Then, with the profit from the shop, he would buy a motorcar that sighed like a woman. He would make so much money that life wouldn't be long enough to spend it.

Then his eyes widened with recollection, and he slapped his forehead with the base of his palm. He had forgotten to tell me about the spa he had heard several of the wealthy businessmen discussing. They had said that the water bubbling out of the earth at Sweet River's fountainhead had physical and spiritual healing powers. It was mineral water. They had said that way back in the olden days, certain tourists and the ailing from all over the world would travel to Naggo Head and pay big money to bathe at the head. That would mean building better and bigger piers, restaurants, and transportation, which would mean more jobs and money. Naggo Head would be famous.

"Progress, Cherrimina! Progress!" His excitement was contagious.

He asked me where I was going, and I turned and pointed to the sewing shop. I turned back to him, and his gaze had dropped to his feet. He shuffled his feet, and when he raised his gaze again, he put a hand to his forehead to shade his eyes from the sun and to avoid looking directly at my face. It was the first time that I had seen Barabbas so unsure, and I knew then that he had also heard the rumor about who my father might be.

I thanked him for all of the help he had given me. He wished me good luck in everything, and I wished him the same with his new job and with the bicycle shop. He walked away, and I wondered how the news about my mother and the Syrian could have gotten out. Could the culprit be Ponga, the East Indian sewing machine mechanic who fixed the sewing machines in the workroom at the side of the shop?

I held my head up and walked into the shop.

I had made no plans except to walk in at the time of day when the shop was busiest with customers and to look at the Syrian through older eyes, through the eyes of who the people of Naggo Head once thought I was—a tramp; through the eyes of who I was—a girl in the twilight of childhood, shifting into the dawn of womanhood; through the eyes of who I was on the way to becoming before I had been checked by the fire—the whore of Naggo Head.

The shop was busy indeed. The burnt-umber curtains were still separating the back room and were now faded but clean. And there he was, average height and a robust body. An average businessman. He did not have the look of a ladies' man or a man-about-town. I removed the straw hat from my head and fanned my face with it and, in so doing, unwittingly drew his attention to me. He gave a start, gave me a second glance, and quickly composed himself. He ran his hands through his jet-black wavy hair, brushing down the sides into place. He nodded politely as a tailor with a tape measure hanging around his neck and bits of thread on his apron pointed to and explained the problem with his tabletop sewing machine. Then they chatted a little about the tailor's ill father.

Another customer paid for the pair of scissors she had left to be sharpened and addressed him as Mr. Azan; it was the first time I was hearing his surname. I knew him as Edward. I considered shifting my place in line until I was the last customer in the shop but decided against it. I stood my ground.

The next customer ordered three spools of black thread. He waited patiently, the hairy arms protruding from under rolled-up white shirt-sleeves shoved into the pockets of his dark-gray pants, while she took a knotted handkerchief out of her bosom, untied the knot, took out her coins, and paid for her threads.

It was then that I decided that I could just make my purchase and leave. I did not have to do anything more. I had already looked at him through different and new eyes, so what more was there to do? Why should I expect or want more?

Then my turn came at the counter.

"Good morning, Mr. Azan," I said rather reservedly.

He looked at me directly in the eyes, returned my greeting, and waited with a small smile.

"May I have two of those size-ten white crochet threads? And do you have any size-seven steel hooks?" I asked, taking care to speak in a mature tone of voice.

He nodded and reached for containers on the shelves behind him. In silence he wrapped the items in brown paper and twisted the ends, and I paid him. He picked up the containers and moved to put them back on the shelves, and then he changed his mind and swung back around to face me.

"Was it your house that got burned down in Naggo Head around three years ago?" he asked me.

I nodded.

"I was very sorry to hear," he said.

I nodded again.

"I knew your...I knew Mary Mary."

I nodded again.

"Was Mary your...mother?"

"Yes, sir," I replied. "She was my mother."

"I am very sorry," he said, shaking his head gently.

We stood looking at one another in silence, him shaking his head and me turning Miss Priyanka's hat in my hands. Then I smiled. And just before I turned and walked away, I reached out my hand to him. He reached for it, and we shook hands. And we shook hands. And we shook hands.

What I did next was something I had learned over the past three years. What I did is instinctive to the wild dogs. Like a wild dog burying a bone, I dug a hole and buried that chapter of my life. Unlike the domesticated dog, who buries its bones for fun, the wild dog buries food because of a survival instinct deeply ingrained from its wild ancestors. When its food resources are too plentiful or too scant, the wild dog digs a hole and puts away some, for the time will come when it will have no other option available and will dig into its reserve.

In good times or bad, I have had to dig into my reserve and have found that the aging process can enhance the flavor of the bones, and the earth can camouflage the smell.

When I told Bro' Man about Barabbas's news, he said Barabbas was amplified protein. He said he was one of those people whose intellect needed to be constantly rebuilding, repairing, maintaining, and recycling. He said Barabbas used to run around at night stealing because of the challenge of it, the daring, but because of the adjustment to the shock of a new culture and dealing with the racial prejudice that he would experience overseas, he would no longer feel the urge to steal. He would be too busy meeting these challenges and gratifyingly and excellently overcoming them one by one.

CHAPTER 25

The war in Europe raged on, and life in Naggo Head crept on as we became more comfortable with the restrictions on the island.

Bulla had taken Bro' Man's suggestion and had been writing to me regularly, extolling his experiences overseas, and I welcomed his letters. I had never had a letter given to me at the post office addressed to me before. He and the rest of the volunteers had set sail from Saint Ann's Town for England on the SS *Cuba*, but the journey had not been an easy one. Due to warfare activities in the Atlantic Ocean, the ship had had to dock in Newport News, Virginia, where they had camped and waited to be escorted across the Atlantic. At the camp, one American soldier had differentiated the Caribbean men from the African Americans by referring to the men from the Caribbean as "King George's n——rs" and those from America as "Uncle Sam's n——rs."

When it had become apparent that it would be unsafe to set out to sea again from Virginia, they had been put on a train to New York. He wrote about seeing the tall buildings in New York for the first time and about the trains that ran through a tunnel underneath the ground.

But in New York, they had had further delays. There they had stayed in a camp, where he had washed dishes in the kitchen, collected dirty laundry, and issued supplies. Eventually the waiting was over, and they were included in a convoy of sixty-one ships, including tankers carrying millions of tons of oil and gasoline from the United States and the Caribbean to the war zones and to our allies, merchant ships from other nearby countries, destroyers, and other boats to be escorted safely across the Atlantic. He described how the merchant ships were set very low in the water because they were heavily laden.

The convoy had been about halfway across the Atlantic when a German submarine was sighted. Reports had come through that the convoy was being bombed, but luckily they would not be attacked. They had eventually arrived at Liverpool docks and been taken to Lime Street Station, where they had been greeted with cheers from the locals. One of his first impressions of England had been that the houses were factories because they had all had chimneys with smoke spiraling up out of them. By his next letter, he was driving milk lorries in Leominster, Herefordshire, collecting milk for the Cadbury's depot.

I kept his letters tied in a bundle on top of Dove's wig, her hair, and the handcuffs, in a carton box under my bed.

We were kept up to date about the war overseas via newspaper or by a motorcar with a megaphone on its roof, but we heard little or nothing about how it was affecting us on the island. That changed when the government began operating a public broadcasting station. It began regularly scheduled broadcasts once per week, lasting one hour, and they very soon began daily broadcasting.

Wireless receiving sets were distributed to over two hundred designated listening points throughout the island where people naturally gathered, such as restaurants, schools, police stations, and village shops. The grocery shop at Cross Road received a wireless, but none was designated to Naggo Head. However, Bro' Man brought home one.

By this time the Fergusons' grocery shop was doing little or no business due to the shortages, curfews, and blackouts, and the customers with the money had to buy from the bigger and better-stocked shop at Cross Road.

Since Bro' Man was the only resident of Naggo Head who had a wireless, and because the grocery shop had been closing earlier than usual, the folks naturally began gathering around the radio in Cocoa Walk, with some bringing their own stools and chairs. As the crowd got larger, Bro' Man and his friends set up an open-sided thatched-roof shack with wooden benches at the nearest edge of the cocoa orchard for the gatherers. The radio provided BBC news and a link to the arts and humanities; radio drama serials drew the biggest crowd.

A popular radio program with the Cocoa Walk crowd was a BBC series named *Hello Caribbean*. The program related stories of West Indians in England, from factory workers and war workers to military men, and their experiences in supporting the war effort—or just people saying quick hellos to their families in the West Indies. In his last letter, Bulla had shared that he might be appearing on the program soon, and I became a regular listener.

And so this night the neighbors gathered around the wireless, with the younger children huddling farthest away from the dark stretch of cocoa trees and closer to their parents because of the ghost stories some of the young men told.

"'I have loved the stars too fondly to be fearful of the night,'" said Bro' Man, quoting Oscar Wilde.

A popular calypso song about the war played on the wireless: "A banana a day will keep Hitler away," the singer sung. The song ended, and the broadcaster announced that it was time for *Hello Caribbean*. The crowd of men, women, and children sat and listened in awe. Bulla was the last one to speak.

"And up next," the broadcaster announcer, "is Mr. Claude McPherson!"

Then Bulla's voice saturated the shack. He spoke with a much more pronounced British accent than before he had gone overseas. A whispering went around the shack about the "British in his mout'." In the less than a minute he was allotted, he managed to say that he was happy to be in England doing his share in the war effort, for the friends he had made from all over the world, and for some of the trades he had learned in the training centers.

And at the end, when he said, "I would like to say hello to all my family and friends in Ballyholly and to Cherrimina in Naggo Head!" the crowd stood up and cheered and danced to the calypso music that ended the program.

Sometimes out of bad comes good, and that may not be the end because out of good can come better, and perhaps out of better will come best.

I received Dove's letter exactly three years, ten months, and three days after she had left Naggo Head. One minute I was wandering into the post office out of the afternoon sun, and the next minute I was walking home with a letter addressed in a large, sweeping cursive to "Miss Cherrimina Murrow" from "Miss Dove Diamond." I felt it burning holes in my fingers.

I had often thought of what I would do and say if I should see her again but had never once thought that I might receive a letter. It was a thin, pale-blue envelope with "via air mail" stamped in one corner. Turning it over back to front in disbelief, I walked all the way from Cross Road to Cocoa Walk before I opened it. And I opened it the way I had watched Nanna open hers and how I had been opening my letters: I ripped a narrow strip about one quarter inch wide from the top of one of the narrow ends. This time I extracted the page only to find that in my anxious state I had forgotten to shake the envelope first so that the page could settle toward the bottom—I had ripped the folded page in three pieces. I held the pieces together and read it. It was a half page long.

"My Dearest Mina," it began.

How are you? How is everyone doing? Say hello to Nanna, to Miss Mary Mary, and to Barabbas. Tell Miss Mary Mary that I miss her callaloo and salted fish. I'm doing very well, Mina. I had been singing in a gin mill in the Big Apple, but I just received word the day before that a big-time club wants me. What have you been up to? I don't want to write a long letter when you might not receive it. I will tell you all about myself and my new life in my next letter if you reply to this one.

Mina, not a day goes by that I don't think of you and Naggo Head. Write soon.

Lots of love,
Dove.

I reread the letter over a dozen times during the course of the day. That night I began a handwritten letter to her but then, deciding that a letter to her should be special, borrowed Bro' Man's typewriter, sat in front of it, and wrote an epistle, what Nanna would call a six-page letter. I had a lot to tell her. She had not mentioned the incident with the German, and neither did I.

By now my world largely revolved around the post office. I was literally restored to exuberance by wood fiber that was beaten to pulp, pressed, and dried and on which a story was told, and then folded, sealed with glue, whacked with stamps, and dispatched to eager fingers and minds. Stepping into the post office with a letter to Bulla or Dove and pushing it through the glass window slot toward the postmistress, releasing it from the grasp of sweaty fingers, hearing the final thud as she whacked it with the stamp, waiting with bated breath while she searched through the stack in the slot for my incoming letters, and then hearing the *swish* as she slid them through the slot toward me was a much-thought-about, exhilarating experience. It was sweet.

I did not need trips to Blue Bay, nor did I need money. All I needed was a white sheet of paper and a pencil—or even better, a typewriter. I was good at typing after practicing for years on the phantom typewriter in my head. I had sunshine outside and within. I had my own sunshine, and I basked in it. Sunshine for one. No more secondhand sunshine. I had a new song to sing, a new story to tell. I felt contentment. I was never sure if contentment made life simple, or if a simple life brought contentment.

It should be a truth universally acknowledged that contentment requires awesomeness in at least 50 percent of your life—an overwhelming feeling of reverence, admiration, and veneration for something or someone, whether it be for deity, man, vegetable, or mineral. But it is also said that time puts a halo on everything.

I began writing poems and short stories and giving them to Bro' Man to read. He was impressed. He critiqued them and gave me passages from books to read that illustrated his critiques. I scribbled on bits of papers all over the house.

I began sending these poems to Dove and Bulla. Dove wrote and suggested that I get my passport ready to take a trip to New York City when the war was over. Miss Priyanka thought it was a wonderful idea, and she assisted me with this passport venture.

She said that people should travel more, that there was so much to see and learn in other people, other places, and other cultures. Traveling, she said, gives us the chance to find out about our heritage. Traveling helps us to understand the causes and reasoning behind other people's politics. We get to enjoy different kinds of food, architectural buildings, and wonders of the world. One of the best ways to understand other cultures is through their music.

She said that staying in one place and knowing only one kind of people was not good because the only difference between a rut and a grave is the depth. Then she told me about an island in the middle of the Atlantic, named Tristan da Cunha, where everyone was descended from only fifteen ancestors—eight males and seven females—who had arrived on the island at various times between 1816 and 1908. The remote location of the islands made contact with the outside world difficult. While this isolation was good in many ways, it had its downside because the citizens married their close relations, causing the gene pool to become more concentrated, which resulted in instances of health problems, including asthma and glaucoma. And she predicted that in fifty years or so that island would have the worst incidence of health problems on the planet.

In the next letter from Bulla, he wrote that he was no longer serving in the Royal Navy as an ordinary seaman; he had been transferred to the marine section of the RAF. His unit located and rescued flight crews of any nationality shot down at sea. They sailed among lifeless and mutilated objects that had once been men, their bows striking corpses as they steamed forward to assist the remaining survivors.

He also laid flare paths for the flying boats to land or take off at night and transported aircrews and maintenance crews to planes. His other jobs included refueling, reloading bombs, and towing seaplanes to dry docks.

A few days after receiving Bulla's letter, his father received a visit from a government man. Bulla had been killed in action.

Clever fellow, death is. He has a way of killing many birds with one stone: the dead and those that are left behind. He strikes, and we are surprised; we make noises. The blood will dry, or the wind will stir the ashes. Then the conqueror nods off, keeping one eye open to watch as we clean up, wrap up, and tuck the package away under stone or in the brown beneath the green. Then we wander around under an indifferent sky among indifferent people, and before we know it, that episode has become just a slight interruption in life. The lucky dead are those that are taken while doing something they love.

Chapter 26

The blade of the letter opener I used to stab Bro' Man was only three and a half inches long, but it went in deep, and it went in easily, very easily. One inch from his spinal column and at his shoulder blade, they told me.

It had been raining all that night, and it was about five thirty in the morning when he fell to the floor unconscious, naked, and bleeding. In the backyard a rooster began crowing.

All this had begun when Miss Priyanka announced that she was going to visit relatives in Town who were from Trinidad. She planned on staying three to four days. Bro' Man had seemed fine with the idea until the day she left. They had never spent a day apart since their marriage. After a week he had received a telegram from her expressing that she would have to stay longer than she had planned. Then, about two weeks later, she had written that she would be coming home in a week's time, but would have to leave again soon after because her mother in India was ill and she would have to visit her.

He had begun drinking heavily then, as though there were a hole in the bottom of the glass. I had done my best to take care of him. I had cooked, washed, and cleaned as best I knew how, but there had been no consoling him. Then I had begun waking up at night when he would bump into the furniture in my room after sitting up drinking into the wee hours of the morning until he was falling-down drunk. His excuse would be that he had lost his sense of direction in the dark. I would usually have to drag his heavy body to his bedroom. There were no locks on any of the internal doors, and he was heavy and strong.

And so, with blood all over my clothes and hands, I ran down to the Fergusons' grocery shop, woke the shop boy, and asked him to bicycle out to Cross Road and ask Mr. Brown, one of the few car owners, to drive Bro' Man to the hospital in Blue Bay.

I went back to Cocoa Walk, and that was when I saw the tattoo of the eight-point stars on Bro' Man's left knee—and the one of Jesus on the sole of his right foot. They say a tattoo is often a symbol of a story waiting to be told.

By the time Mr. Brown arrived, I had slowed the bleeding with bandages, and Bro' Man was more decently dressed.

At the hospital, the doctor and nurses asked what had happened, and I told them I had stabbed him because he was heavy and I could not breathe. The police came, took me away, and locked me in jail. I could not sleep that night, nor could I eat. I spent the entire time wondering why I hadn't lied to the doctors and the police. Why was it that I could only think of lies after I had told the truth? Why did I find it so difficult to lie, when it came so easily to others? They gave me two meals, but I could not eat.

They unlocked the bars and let me out of jail late the next day. I was allowed to take a shower. They said that Bro' Man was in stable condition and was out of the hospital. He had stated that he had been intoxicated at the time, and someone could have broken into his house and stabbed him. The matter was considered closed, and not even the newspaper would report the stabbing. They gave me bus fare to get home to Naggo Head.

It was after the Blue Bay Primary School had let out for the day, and the streets were fairly quiet. I waited for a bus, and it was while I was waiting that a strong urge to visit the Syrian's shop came over me. I didn't stop to wonder why or to reason about it. Perhaps being a jailbird can upset one's reasoning. I simply turned and walked past the street vendors and the market hagglers and along the pier and up Great George Street to the shop.

Huge signs reading "Business Closed" were on white paper and pasted across the two street windows. I could not believe it. I went to the side shop, but Ponga, the sewing-machine mechanic, was not there. Instead, another sign reading "Business Closed" was pasted across that door.

The street vendors would be able to explain what happened; they knew everything that went on in Blue Bay. I rushed over to them. My voice was shaking in my chest. One woman removed the pipe from her lips and told me that the Syrian had gone back to Syria about six months before. Another one, wiping her child's nose, said that he had moved to Town to get married. A vendor selling oranges said the Syrian had moved to Town to open another business. And yet another said that she had heard that he was sick and at death's door.

And just like that, I was cut loose and felt as though I were blowing in the wind again, alone. He was dead. I was sure. My mind raced. I leaned against a wall. God was punishing me. Was there a place in this world that was free from God? One more blasphemy! I should try harder not to blaspheme, I told myself, with the little reasoning ability I possessed at that moment. Why curse him and nail him to a cross? It had already been done.

I think I may have called out but was unsure of it because I was cocooned in the same silence, the same stillness that I had experienced after the fire. It came back so strongly that I almost fainted. I was so visibly anguished that one vendor offered me her smelling salts.

"Here, chile," she said, "dis wi' steady yu. Take i' wit' yu." But even the ride on the bus up from Blue Bay was muzzled.

Perhaps he really was sick, I reasoned; men do tend to give off an illusion of healthfulness. And if he had gone to get married, I only wished him the best. And why should I care if his shop had closed? I hardly shopped there anyway. Why should I care if he was dead?

The bus rattled pass the Baptist church that I had not set foot in since the funeral, and a sudden desire to pray rose unbidden in my soul. Nanna would have prayed. For years I had honestly believed that I had suffered too much to believe that praying to God would help, and that I had blasphemed too shamefully for him to listen to my prayers.

So, instead of walking up to Naggo Head, I turned back toward the Baptist church, a psalm escaping from my lips aloud even as I walked across the bridge and into the church yard: "'In my distress I called upon the Lord, and cried unto my God: he heard my voice out of his temple, and my cry came before him, even into his ear. Then the earth shook and trembled; the foundations also of the hills moved and were shaken, because he was wroth...He bowed the heavens also, and came down, and darkness was under his feet. And he rode upon a cherub, and he did fly; yea, he did fly upon the wings of the wind...Let the words of my mouth, and the meditation of my heart, be acceptable in thy sight, O LORD, my strength, and my redeemer."

I walked through the unlocked door and fell to my knees in the cool tranquility of the church. When we need to find God, he cannot be found in noise and restlessness. God is the friend of silence. I had learned to pray by listening to Nanna in her daily devotions, and it came back quickly and easily. Some of the most powerful bodies in this world work in silence; the stars, the moon, and the sun, they move in silence.

The praying and the smelling salts refreshed me, and as I walked up Naggo Head Road, I wrapped up that episode neatly and put it away. That was just another bone to be buried.

I got home to Cocoa Walk in time to see Miss Priyanka in the kitchen cooking kidneys and green bananas for a late lunch. She had arrived earlier that morning while I was in jail. She hugged me and expressed how glad she was that I had not been hurt by the burglar. She wanted to know if my grandfather's cousin was feeling much better and how much she had missed me last night when she had arrived and Bro' Man had told her that I had gone to visit a sick relative.

I was hungry and ate the cow kidneys and green bananas and went back for seconds. Bro' Man was in bed. I didn't go to his room. My room was wiped clean of blood and the sheets had been changed. As far as I could tell, Miss Priyanka was in the dark about what had taken place two nights before.

The next day Miss Priyanka began packing for her trip to India to visit her ailing mother. Through the closed bedroom door, I could hear Bro' Man begging her not to go, not to leave him. Then the begging turned to weeping. I had only seen him once, when Miss Priyanka had asked me to take his dinner on a tray to his bedside. He had looked poorly and avoided looking at my face. Later, when she brought the tray out, he had not eaten the Scotch bonnet pepper.

That evening I went to the post office. The truth about the stabbing event had not been broadcast in Naggo Head, because the new postmistress expressed her sympathy for Bro' Man and an oath with a curse on the burglar and pushed a letter through the slot. It was rumored that this new postmistress had a nasty habit of steaming letters open, reading them, and then gluing them shut again.

The letter was from Dove. It had a Park Avenue return address. I read it on the way home. She had enclosed money for my boat fare to New York City.

April 1, 1945

Dear Mina

How are you? I hope well. It will be summer soon, and talk of the war ending and the hope that everything will be back to normal before the summer is on everyone's lips. I hope you have your passport ready as I had suggested. It is time for you to visit New York. My ship has finally come in, Mina. One week ago I signed a contract to headline in a cabaret act at the Tic Tac Club downtown. The show will be fantastic. They are writing that I am the toast of New York City. They will come from all over the world to see me.

I am enclosing money for the boat fare. Come as soon as possible. I am leaving instructions at a rooming house run by my friend, Yvonne, on Tenth Avenue to house you, feed you, and to take you shopping for a fabulous dress to wear to the Tic Tac Club. I will reserve a table for you. Write and let me know when you are setting sail. Please get here safe and soon!

Your Friend Forever,
Dove

On the fifth day after Miss Priyanka had come home, she was packed and ready to leave for Town the next morning. Bro' Man got out of bed and followed her around the house like an anxious, lovesick boy, and she did everything to soothe his anxiousness except breastfeed him.

Eventually, he allowed himself to be shooed from Miss Priyanka's shadow, and in an exhausted state he followed me out to the shack and sat beside me on one of the benches. He made several attempts to talk about the stabbing but ended up talking about the weather and his cocoa orchard. He finally apologized, and I accepted it. He said he had no idea how he ended up in my room, and the last thing he remembered was trying to find his way to his bedroom.

We sat in silence for a while. Where was the destruction and damage to my self-esteem and psyche that I was supposed to feel at what he had attempted, I wondered. Women in novels would have already started a downward spiral at such an attack, and with the imprisonment, why hadn't I? Why was I so different? I made several deliberate attempts to feel what was expected, but each time they ended up turning into pity for him.

I could see his lips trembling with unpronounced words while I worked up the courage to ask him about the tattoos. I felt I had to ask him about it because while sitting beside him and listening to him talk, I had images of his slack, loose, naked body and his tattoos dancing around in my head. But I lacked the courage.

"Miss Cherrimina, I have hurt you, disgraced myself and Miss Priyanka, and if she ever finds out, she would leave me, and I wouldn't be able to bear it. I am sorry, Miss Cherrimina. Please forgive my drunken behavior…I've always thought of myself as above that kind of behavior…"

"You were heavy, and I couldn't breathe," I said quickly.

"I had always thought I was above that kind of behavior. I looked down my nose at other men who indulged in such behavior. And all along I was unware that it was inside me, festering. Festering like a malignant growth. Why is it that youth is the only thing that can impress a man of my age? Isn't it ironic? Because men of my age look the most ridiculous standing alongside youth."

We sat in more silence.

"I have something to tell you; may I?" he asked in a low voice. The words fit funny on his teeth and tongue, and he ended in a whisper like a shy schoolgirl. I nodded uncertainly, wondering if I was capable of being his confidant.

"I don't want Miss Priyanka to go to India. Could you ask her not to go?"

I swung my head around and opened my mouth to protest, and he shushed me. I was stunned when I saw tears streaming from his large, baby-round eyes and down his face.

"She will listen to you," he assured me. "Tell her that I can't live without her. We have never been apart all these years, and I wouldn't know how to survive without her. I don't think another man has ever loved a woman the way I love her. I know it is self-ish of me asking her to stay when her mother is ill, but I can't help it. I've been a happy man in a…an open soul…She made me want to be better at everything…

"I've always believed that we should be careful about who we share our joys and sorrows with—it can cheapen them. Before I encountered her, I had always met feelings of superiority more than halfway and was always in charge of every step I took in life. I didn't know that someone else could make me want to do better or take better steps…It was all-consuming. I became more ambitious; I turned to the ground…close to the ground…I was hunter, trapper, and pioneer…We built this empire of cocoa pods…We planned…We made promises…We knew what the other was thinking ninety-five percent of the time…each other's likes and dislikes…I listened carefully to her words and body; I didn't want to miss anything, and her message has always been the same: 'I love you, Harry'…Yes, I will permit myself to embrace that one cliché. I met her on an ocean and brought her home to an enchanted island of sunshine and sand…I had never seen a more beautiful girl and still haven't…I loved the colorful clothes she wore; I didn't know that those colors existed…I didn't have to spend my life proving that I was not a rollicking rogue, as I have seen other men doing.

"I have always done my fighting standing up, and now, when I need to fight the hardest, I can't even stand up. I have seen the collapse of five of the last modern empires: Russia, Germany, China, Ottoman Turkey, and Austria-Hungary. I was digging alongside Hiram Bingham III when he rediscovered Machu Picchu in Peru. Before she became the rage of Paris, I chased Josephine Baker in New York City for an entire day and a half. There were footprints on the ceiling. She was the only woman I have ever met who made me feel that I was a lot more likely to get pregnant than she was."

After raving further about Josephine Baker's beauty and sensuality, he suddenly turned to me, gave a slight bow of his head, and simulated a tipping of a hat he was not wearing. "Miss Cherrimina," he said, "please forgive me for forgetting myself and speaking so plainly."

I nodded forgivingly, and he continued.

"I have danced the famous ritualistic Danza de los Voladores de Papantla dance in Mexico. I knew I had to try it the first time I saw it. Five men of the Totonac Indian tribe climbed to the top a pole approximately three hundred feet high. One played a flute and danced while the other four men dangled from ropes wrapped around the pole and tied to one of their feet. As the pole turned, the rope unwound, and the men were slowly lowered to earth. It was the most thrilling experience of my lifetime!

"I, Harry Stanford Waters," he said, beating his chest somewhat in a sudden attack of feeble manliness, "have seen the inside of the Black Dolphin Prison, the toughest Russian prison. The toughest prison in the world! Mark you, it was only for a few months because I was sent there in error, but I have seen it and survived it.

"I was a private entry in the grueling marathon event in the 1912 Summer Olympic Games in Stockholm, Sweden, running a few yards behind the Portuguese Francisco Lázaro when he collapsed and died from heat exhaustion and dehydration. It turned out he had covered most of his body with wax to prevent sunburn or to improve his performance by not sweating, and the wax had restricted his body's natural perspiration.

"Yet now, now that I need to fight the hardest fight of my life, I can't even stand up straight. At this moment, I am realizing that nothing from my past is of any importance. None of it has prepared me or can help me out of this present predicament. My past, despite how momentous I've always thought it was, is insignificant. How can that be?

"Cherrimina, what you see in front of you is a shell that was once called man. I am no good at fighting the heart…at fighting love."

It was an essay of pure love, a story charged with love, a two-fisted love that poured from his lips in anguished words. Bro' Man had heart. He could love under the best and worst conditions. It is a beautiful thing to have heart, despite its susceptibility to pain.

I took the handkerchief from his hand and dried his eyes and wiped his face. He thanked me as fresh tears welled up in his eyes and rolled down his cheeks again.

"Alexander the Great wept when he saw that he had no more lands left to conquer," he said weakly, in an attempt at humor.

"I have a great idea," I cried. "Why don't you go with her to India?"

After a drawn-out pause, he took a deep breath and said, "Always be careful of great ideas, Cherrimina. You must always think of the long-term effect of great ideas. Great ideas are never short term. Once upon a time, someone had a great idea to go to Africa and kidnap some strong, magnificent, sun-kissed people, put them in chains in the bottom of ships, and transport them across the oceans to work his cotton fields and sugar fields. But this man with this great idea didn't think of the long-term effect.

"Did it ever occur to him once that with multiplication and birth rate, these enslaved people might one day come to outnumber his own race? Perhaps if I had been that man and found brow sweating that distressing and worrying, I probably would have called it indentured servitude instead of chattel slavery, called them field hands and bucks instead of men, and spewed myths about brain over brawn. And perhaps, in my bid to compete with their virility, I too would have acted out my frustration by whipping them into submission until the ends of my cat-o'-nine-tails dripped red blood.

"The saddest part about all this is no one else besides those helpless people will know the full depth of their suffering. It's such a pity that they were unable to express and record on paper the level of pain and cruelty that was inflicted upon them. Until the story of the hunt is told by the lion, the tale of the hunt will always glorify the hunter.

"Here's a question I have asked myself time and again: Who is of the superior mentality, the man who has the need to hurl adolescent insults such as *spear chucker* toward another, or the one who chucks spears?

"Time and time again, I have asked myself, if this man had worked the fields himself, would it have meant that his claim to superiority—or his *need* to claim superiority—would not be questionable?

"What those strong, sun-kissed, magnificent humans did wrong—the only thing *we* did wrong—was to survive. I have tried to imagine many times what the world would have been like, financially and politically, if not even one of those fine people had survived the crossing."

I listened in polite silence because I had never heard of slavery except the few times that he talked about it, and I didn't know any real slaves. The only one who came close to being one was Barabbas.

And when, in exhaustion, he stopped to catch his breath, I repeated, "Why don't you go with Miss Priyanka to India?"

He shook his head. "It's different in India. She can't go back to India with a husband like me."

"Why not, sir?"

He drew a deep breath as if to begin a long story and then stopped. "It's complicated" was all he said. And as if an afterthought, he said, "Pride goes before fall."

I didn't understand, and I didn't ask him what he meant.

I lay in bed that night wondering why the memory of Nanna's face was fading faster than my mother's. While Nanna's face was becoming more blurred, her hands were becoming more in focus. The fingers, short and broad as though she had rubbed them off on the scrubbing board in soapy water, were either turning the pages of her Bible or clasped in prayer. The twin moles at the base of the left thumb were just as vivid.

I fell asleep with visions in my head of aged and fading faces and of ancient gods fading. It was after midnight when I felt the bedsheet pulled roughly off me. It was Miss Priyanka, and she had a lit oil lamp in one hand and a machete in the other. Her hair was wild, and so were her eyes.

"Come quick!" she panted. "Come help me, Cherrimina!"

She rushed out of the house into the night, barefoot, toward the shack at the edge of the orchard, her hair and white night-clothes billowing in the cool night breeze. I followed barefoot and closely behind her. The light from the lamp swung toward the ceiling of the shack and at the rope that hung from it. At the end of the rope was Bro' Man.

His sharply creased khaki pants, the white long-sleeved shirt rolled to the elbow, the vest, and the highly polished shoes were all neatly arranged on his body except for the collar of the shirt and the ascot, which the rope had crinkled and put askew. His walking stick had been carefully laid on a nearby table. But it is his eyes that I remember mostly. The large, dark, baby-round eyes were open and staring eerily peacefully off into space.

Together we held his body, and she cut the rope.

Some events can dim our universe, and Miss Priyanka's universe was dimmed that night—dimmed and punctuated with a question mark. She was inconsolable.

"Why? Why? Why, Harry?" she kept asking.

Bro' Man was always worrying about the endangered species of this or that animal, not realizing that he himself was an endangered species. Later, when the motorcar came to pick up Miss Priyanka and her luggage to take her to Town, it took Bro' Man to the hospital morgue in Blue Bay instead.

Chapter 27

Miss Priyanka and I spent the next thirty-six hours only seeing the sunlight between the police station, the hospital, and the funeral home. We walked out of the funeral home into the streets at last and up Great George Street, which was jammed with people jumping with jubilation. The war had ended, and we did not know. Victory had been declared. Excitement was in the air.

Men, women, and children were marching and singing "Rule, Britannia!" and "Hail to the Island of Spring." Truckloads of men drove up and down Great George Street, blowing whistles and beating drums. Schoolchildren walked home hugging bagsful of sweets that had been handed out at their schools. The wireless carried the latest updates, but Miss Priyanka and I could not get it to work properly, and Bro' Man was not there to set it right.

⋏

It was early morning several weeks after that fateful night that Miss Priyanka and I were sitting in the back seat of a navy-blue Vauxhall motorcar that was struggling to climb the steep and winding road at Spur Tree Hill on our way to Town, our luggage and trunks piled high and tied to the roof of the car. In our handbags were our passports and other important documents for traveling overseas. It was a four-hour drive from one end of the island to the other.

Miss Priyanka had worked tirelessly to finalize arrangements for the funeral and the management of the orchard. She had asked about cremating Bro' Man, but the court official would not give her permission because it was unclear if cremation was unlawful on the island.

In the end, Miss Priyanka told the funeral home owner to deliver the wrapped-up body like a package to conceal the contents down to the seaside, because she intended to take Bro' Man on a last trip around the island before burial. She bought an old raft from a fisherman in Blue Bay and paid him to move the raft with the package to a very isolated area of the coast, not far from Pidgin Cove. She paid another man to stockpile wood at the same area of the beach.

And so, far, far away from the Machu Picchu and the Black Dolphin Prison, on an isolated beach near the flaming-red setting sun that turned the Caribbean Sea to liquid gold, Bro' Man was no more.

We sat on the rocky beach in silence and watched the flames rise toward the coconut trees and the flying embers blown by the wind. I realized for the first time how exquisitely and slowly the sun does set.

After three hours, we buried the few remaining bone fragments a little farther inland and scattered the ashes along the rocky coastline. Dust to dust; ashes to ashes.

We walked home in the twilight, wrapped in silence. Eventually, Miss Priyanka spoke, and her words were turned inward, as if she spoke only to herself.

"Life went where Harry went," she said, again trying to rub the ashes from her hands, which were caked, dry, and black from the ashes. The seawater was not sufficient to wash them clean of the great man's burned bones. "Harry was life, and now that Harry is no more, we must find our own life."

We continued walking in silence, and then, in that same introspective tone, she said, "I need the strength and protection of my relatives and ancestors."

Then she was sleeping deeply and soundly beside me as the breeze from the open motorcar window blew her hair so that it tumbled over her face. She was truly a beautiful woman, and it was no wonder Bro' Man had thought he could not continue living without her. On the other hand, I thought, she would have no problem continuing without him. She had her relatives, culture, and tradition for support.

The motorcar stopped at a roadside food stand, and she woke up, slightly disoriented. She bought roasted yams, salted codfish, and lemonade breakfast for all three of us.

Rested and refreshed by the meal, we settled back in the motorcar for the remaining two-hour drive. We talked all the way. Even the driver had regained his energy. Due to the narrow, winding roads, we couldn't make time before, but now we could, he explained, as he sped on the smoother road.

I asked Miss Priyanka why Bro' Man had thought he could not go to India with her. Her face turned dark for a little bit, and then she made a great effort to clear the darkness.

"It is very complicated," she said, repeating Bro' Man's reply to the same question. "In India, we have a caste system—high and low caste. If you were born in the low caste, you stay there; you cannot move to the higher caste—you cannot upgrade. You are considered lowly and unclean; in some cases, water is not easily available to the lower caste. A person's caste can be determined by his facial features, skin color, his cleanliness, his accent. Caste is tied also to hereditary occupation. A weaver's son knows he will become a weaver and will marry in his caste. Even prostitutes, singers, and dancers are in a caste of their own, and their sons and daughters will train to be prostitutes, singers, and dancers.

"It is very complicated, and Bro' Man knew all about it. He would have been looked down upon as low caste in India. My family would not have been able to hold their heads up in our community if the nationality of my husband were broadcasted.

"Bro' Man and I made the decision not to have children because a person of mixed Indian ancestry cannot be as Indian as I am. In Guyana and Trinidad and Tobago, where you have a lot of Indian immigrants, our child would be called a *dougla*. He would be considered low caste. Why subject a child to that?

"This is distorted thinking, because the 'Indian' race is the result of the mixing of the Caucasoid race and an African race. We are the original mixed race. We are not a 'pure' race as Africans are. It is lectured also that the Japanese is another original mix from Caucasoid and Mongoloid. What I find interesting is how it is opined that most races are somehow linked to the Caucasoids—I wonder how that got started? Hmmm.

"Tears and blood flow from all human bodies, no matter our caste, skin color, eye color; we put sustenance in our bodies at the same place and secrete bile at the same place, so the real issues are power and greed, or perceptions of it. Anyway, this distorted hierarchical system is not only an Indian issue."

We rode in thoughtful silence for a while as the car rocked over a rough patch of road.

"I had always thought that I would name my first baby boy Shahrukh," she told me. "In the Urdu language, *Shahrukh* means 'the king's face.'"

I told her about my visits to the Syrian's shop. I poured my heart out in the retelling of my first visit and of the most recent. She listened intently and then asked me if Bro' Man knew about my visits. I had to reassure her several times that he didn't. Then she gave me some advice.

She said that I was going out into the world for the first time and would meet all kinds of people. I would associate happiness with some and unhappiness with others. But I should keep in mind that no one could be happy all the time because the mind measured happiness against the way things were before, especially the more recent times. If things were getting better, you felt happy. If things stayed the same for too long, no matter how good they were, I would eventually start to feel less happy because the mind would be comparing how it felt today to how it felt a week or a month before.

She said she wouldn't give me advice about money or men, but she was sure of one thing: one's greatest asset was a calm mind. She told me to learn to meditate, learn how to keep my mind from jumping and from making comparisons, and learn what would keep my mind satisfied, and keep feeding it that.

⋏

The car dropped her off at the pier. The size of the ship out of deep water was shocking and frightening. Did everything have its place and was therefore threatening when out of place? We said our goodbyes, trying to be brave and not to weep all over each another, and we succeeded. She climbed the ramp, and at the top she turned and waved. I waited until the ship sailed because I couldn't seem to disentangle myself from the last bit of connective thread to Naggo Head.

Oh, the things people will take with them and leave behind when they depart this earth or depart from your life. My mother left this earth taking with her the true identity of my biological father, leaving behind a mystery of my true roots. Miss Priyanka left our island for India with no knowledge whatsoever of Bro' Man's activities when she was away in Town, leaving behind a cruel heartbreak she had missed by a hair's breadth. In the suitcase that I gripped tightly in fear of the con men and thieves I had heard about, I was taking the jumbie-bead necklace, the handcuffs, the bunch of Dove's hair, her red wig, and the dusty-pink dress with the pale-yellow flowers. I was taking with me lessons learned. Lessons of love and loss, lust and desire, strengths and weaknesses. Lessons of soft pyramids. It was easier to hide our weaknesses than our strengths. Bro' Man had hidden his weaknesses well, but Barabbas could not hide his strengths. Was it possible that people we viewed as strong were just people who were better at hiding their weaknesses? As to what I was leaving behind, I started thinking about it, but my heart began aching, and I didn't dwell on it.

Miss Priyanka had arranged for me to spend the two days before my ship sailed in a rooming house on Orange Street. The room was clean, but I had only slept in two beds before, and I had a hard time sleeping. On the second evening, I decided to go for a walk; the exercise might help me to sleep. But it was the concrete sidewalk under my feet that I would remember most from those few days in Town. To walk without pebbles shifting underfoot, without skipping over mud puddles or clumps of grass, was a new feeling, a steady, firm assurance that I had never experienced in Naggo Head or Blue Bay. I was walking on the sunny side of King Street, looking in the windows of the haberdashery stores, when I heard someone calling my name from across the street. A man clad in a white shirt and black pants and standing in the entrance of a store was waving at me. The sun was in in my eyes, so I could not see clearly who it was, but I stopped and waited politely as he ran between the motorcars, moving dangerously fast down the street.

He got closer, and I saw it was the Syrian. It was such an exquisite surprise. He was not dead! Instead, he was out of breath and smiling widely.

"What are you doing here?" he asked, still out of breath.

"I can't believe it's you!" I replied.

We were both smiling widely and then uncertainly, as if we didn't know what to do next.

"Have you eaten yet?" he asked, and I shook my head.

Then he took my arm firmly and led me to a restaurant two doors down from where we stood. I went along easily with him.

I felt safe with him, like I used to feel when Nanna and my mother were taking care of me at Mill Yard. He pulled out my chair for me. He asked me if my chair was comfortable. He watched over me like a hawk.

"If the sun is in your eyes, we could ask to be moved to another table," he told me. He ordered from the menu for me. We had turtle soup followed by curried shrimp and rice. We talked.

He had moved his business to Town because he had gotten married and his wife did not want to live in the countryside. Also, he had wanted to expand his business. He was doing very well now, but it had been a struggle at first. He lived on the hill overlooking the cricket field.

As the sunlight faded and the sun began to set, electric lights were turned on, illuminating the restaurant's interior design and creating a different ambiance as the dinner crowd came in. It had begun to rain lightly, and outside the wet street glistened.

I told him about Bro' Man and Miss Priyanka, and he expressed his sympathy. And when I told him I was leaving by boat for the United States the next morning, his face fell. I explained my friendship with Dove, leaving out the gory details, and immediately he looked worried and began cautioning me about the pits and falls of going out into the world alone, but then he stopped short suddenly and dropped his gaze. I gently touched the back of his hand that rested on the table, and he smiled softly. I wrote the address that Dove had sent me on a piece of paper and gave it to him.

"Please, let's stay in touch," I said. He nodded and folded the paper carefully and placed it in his wallet. Then it was time to go. He walked me to the rooming house. We shook hands. By now

I'd had enough experience with saying goodbye, so this one was not as painful as I would have thought. Or perhaps it was because I was so happy at the reunion that it was impossible to be sad at the separation.

Chapter 28

did not expect anyone to see me off at the pier the next morning, so I had no reason to be standing on deck among the several waving, sobbing, cheering passengers as the ship pulled away. Then I saw him. The Syrian. He was standing at the far edge of the crowd, between a pile of wooden pallets and a group of women shading themselves from the morning sun with gaily colored umbrellas. His robust arms were shoved deep into his pants pockets. He knew I had seen him because a wide grin powered by joy broke on my face. He didn't wave, nor did I. We just watched each another. I didn't wave because I thought it would embarrass him. Waving goodbye was something men did not do very well. But as the ship got farther away from the pier and the general cheering tapered off, I waved tightly at him. He didn't wave back, and I didn't expect him to; he couldn't have seen me at that distance. And yet my eyes began to sting, and I fought it. Defied it.

The first day aboard the ship was uneventful. The first night was my downfall. Perhaps it was the jumbie-bead necklace, which had fallen out of my suitcase earlier that evening as I was dressing for dinner and clattered noisily to the floor, that started it,

or perhaps it was the constant rocking of the boat that had dis-
lodged my carefully buried bones. Or maybe it was the seafood
dish that I had had for dinner—the pink shrimps curled up like
the crayfish we caught in Sweet River and roasted on burning
coals. It might have been hearing the different accents of other
passengers all during dinner.

It was late night, and I had just walked out of the dining room
and made my way on deck for some fresh air when it happened.
The water was choppy, and the deck was empty of passengers.
The ship's orchestra was playing an updated version of the 1920s
song "I'll Be with You in Apple Blossom Time," which was Bro'
Man's and Miss Priyanka's favorite song. How they would waltz
lovingly whenever it came on the radio.

It began with a sense of having forgotten something, and
then that feeling turned to a sense of having misplaced something, and then to a feeling of losing something personal, like an
earring or a shoe, for which I must search urgently. Then slowly
it became clear. It was me who was missing—the old Cherrimina
that I had known for almost twenty years. This girl standing on
the deck of a ship sailing to a strange land to live among strange
people. Strange people with strange customs that she had only
read about in books and newspaper. But what did it matter where
this girl lived and with whom? She had no one of her own, no
home of her own, so everywhere and everyone would be strange.
But how would she manage away from her golden-in-the-sun
island, the land of sea and sand? What would this girl do without
the bright yellow sunshine? The sun would shine in that new
land too, but in certain seasons, it wouldn't warm the air, and it

wouldn't ripen anything—it would just leak. On her island, the sun splashed. It reigned and ruled. Would this girl, this motherless girl, be able to breathe living so far away from Nanna and her mother, even though they were now resting under the jumbie tree on the bank of the Sweet River? This last thought had extra weight, and it weakened my knees. And when the ship lurched, I tumbled to the floor. I crawled on my knees to a darker corner of the deck.

The sounds came at me slowly at first and then faster: the slow shifting of gravel on Naggo Head Road; the faraway rumble of Sweet River that I had been hearing every waking hour of my twenty years on earth; the roosters crowing, declaring it early dawn; the woodpeckers drumming on the trees because, unlike other birds, they had no songs; the carefree laughter of children singing ring-game songs; the resounding midmorning crack of the women of Naggo Head's sledgehammers breaking through rocks; the patois, yes, the patois, the deep, raw patois heard in the seaside market; the pitter-patter of raindrops on tin roofs before they were trampled over by the powerful huffing and puffing of hurricane winds; the Baptist church choir; my mother's sewing machine. And Nanna's voice. Nanna's first-morning voice, weak and cracked from lack of use, sneaking from her darkened room, singing a chorus at the beginning of morning devotion.

Then the smells came. That morning smell of steaming, strong coffee after the pinch of salt was added (and only after the salt); that intoxicating whiff of juicy, sweet star apples warmed by the midday sun just as the deep-purple peel was first ripped open by eager, sticky fingers; freshly made coconut patties with the pink dot on top of the pure-white grated coconut.

And then I had an overwhelming feeling that this would be my last chance to indulge in self-pity and sorrow, and I wallowed in it, folding tightly into a fetal position and letting the hot tears flow until there were literally no more. And right there in that dark corner on the deck, I began to pray. I prayed long and hard for guidance before getting up and walking to the cabin I shared with a lady from Barbados. She was asleep in her bunk in the old-clothes-in-a-bag position.

And when the sun rose the next morning and the ship rocked gently across the Atlantic Ocean, I had already buried another bone and had pushed all the others back into their rightful places.

CHAPTER 29

I did a lot of walking the first day that I landed in New York City. It was a Friday. My feet on concrete brought an assurance that pushed aside most of my fears. I walked gripping the handle of my suitcase in one hand and the letter with instructions from Dove in the other as I wove between the tall buildings, the vehicles, and the endless pedestrians that kept coming up out of and going down into holes in the ground. This was not the kind of place where I would see barking dogs, screaming children, weeping widows, and mothers breastfeeding babies.

I was hungry. A three-wheeled pushcart advertising "red-hot frankfurters" and "cold soft drinks" was nearby, and I purchased a frankfurter without knowing what it was. It was a pink tube of meat set in the middle of a long bun. I purchased a cold soft drink too. The vendor did not return any change from the dollar bill I handed him, and I was too timid to ask for it. I sat on my suitcase and ate. When finished, I didn't know what to do with the empty bottle, and I could find use for it—Nanna would have found use for it. I opened my suitcase very slightly and pushed it inside. I continued walking.

I found myself standing in front of a busy building named Pennsylvania Station, watching the passersby. Someone yelled, "Stand aside, colored girl!…Colored girl!" I looked around to see what a colored girl looked like until I was nearly knocked over by a pushcart full of hanging garments. "Lady with the baby!" the pushcart driver went on to yell at a lady pushing a baby buggy. "Baghdad on the Subway," I had once read in reference to New York City.

Two Asian men passing by were stopped by a third one exactly in front of me, and all three began conversing. They took turns bending slightly at the waist and taking quick looks down on the street and their shoes. As each one looked down, I looked down too, out of curiosity. Eventually they moved on, and I wondered what on earth were they looking for. Had one of them lost something?

I made my way to the Tenth Avenue address as Dove had instructed, with images of samurais, delicate, painted folding silk fans, teahouses, geisha girls, kimonos, and cherry blossoms in my head—the same images I had seen in one of Bro' Man's books. I wondered what it would be like to visit Asia.

Miss Yvonne welcomed me, eagerly looking me up and down, and then raised one pleased corner of her mouth. She was a large-breasted, curly-haired, sweet-faced woman who spoke as if she had fuzz on her tongue, called everyone "honey," and paid absolutely no attention to what anyone else said. The white buttoned-front shirt she wore had the sleeves rolled up and the front hem tied in a knot at the waist of the wide-legged, baggy pants. She introduced me to a few of the other roomers that she had met on the way to my room. One was a male dancer with long legs and a short chin and long fingernails manicured to clawlike points, which he carried around as if he had just dipped them in a finger bowl and was waiting for a towel with which to dry them. Another was a couple who shared a room. The only thing strange about that was I could not tell which gender they were, and Miss Yvonne did not explain, even after seeing my quizzical look. She gave the pretty young girl putting a key into a door a short nod and a long, dirty look. "She just got engaged last week," she said to me inside her mouth, "and I don't have the heart to tell her that the ring she's been flaunting looks more like a diamond chip than a diamond."

She wondered if I was hungry, and I said no, since I was secretly still burping the red-hot frankfurter and cold soft drink. She said Dove had changed a few of the instructions and had bought a dress for me to wear instead of having me choose one. She tried to show me the dress, but it was in a garment bag, and I couldn't see it properly—the room was dark—but it looked like it was a dusty-pink color, with matching shoes. It smelled like dog—the last roomer must have had a dog. It was afternoon when she finally left the room, and I fell facedown on the bed in exhaustion, wondering if the dog had lifted its tail, like Mr. Percy's dog did, in such a small room.

It was dawn the next day when I woke up to a lot of banging and clanging. I later found that they were the garbagemen, milkmen, and newspapermen. I fidgeted around in my room, alternating between trepidation and anticipation, because tonight was when I would get dressed in a new gown, get in a car, and be transported to the club where I would see Dove for the first time in six years. I looked at the dress, and no, it was a soft amber, with matching-color shoes. The stole and elbow-length gloves were antique white. I tried on the shoes and the dress, and they were the perfect fit.

I found the bathroom and knocked on the door, and Miss Yvonne opened it, wet and stark naked, with a towel in her hand, drying herself. She greeted me nonchalantly, lifted a fleshy right breast, and passed the towel under it. She lifted the left breast, and underneath were a bunch of soapsuds. She passed the towel under it. After a breakfast of cornflakes and cold milk, Miss Yvonne took me on my first subway ride, to Harlem, to have my hair washed and ironed by a woman named Naomi, who operated a beauty shop and who was to send me back to Tenth Avenue with her taxi-driver friend. Miss Naomi was a quiet, elegant lady, with eyes that flickered often between sadness and kindness and who was quite in contrast to the colorful atmosphere of the exciting beauty shop and its larger-than-life male and female customers. But it was the way she handled money that struck me most. She would unfold the bills, caress the creases out of them, and then slowly and carefully turn over each one to face the same direction before she laid them lovingly in the till. The coins were stacked in rows of similar sizes, without them making a clinking sound.

Her shop was full of contraptions and processes that I had never heard of before. A slogan ran across one front window and read, "Where the Kinks Go Straight." The poster of a beautiful woman on the far wall was of Josephine Baker, the actress and singer, Miss Naomi explained.

She wanted to paint my nails red, but I begged her to just buff them to a sheen instead, as another customer had requested.

She showed me how to apply lipstick, and I bought a tube. She showed me how to stuff powder puffs in my bra, and I wondered who was the genius who had thought of this first. She plucked my eyebrows and reshaped them, shaved my armpits, and showed me how to wear an elbow-length glove and a stole and carry a purse at the same time while walking in high-heeled shoes. Miss Priyanka had taught me the proper way to eat, to sit down, get up, and walk, but neither of us had thought that one day I would need further tutelage for a finer lifestyle.

I arrived back at Tenth Avenue plucked, pressed, polished, and painted. All that had stuck out when I walked in the beauty shop, such as my hair, was now flat and sleek, and all that was flat, such as my bosom, was now sticking out.

Miss Yvonne said Dove Diamond had called to see how things were going with me and to say she would see me later. I fell asleep again, but this time on my back—I didn't want to ruin the made-up face.

When I woke up, I had missed dinner. I nibbled at a cold plate of Miss Yvonne's "carryout dinner" of something she called spaghetti. Then it was time to get ready to see Dove, and as I dressed, the excitement inside me built. I took a few minutes to calm myself, and by the time I walked out into the cool night air, down the stoop, through the admiring lineup of the roomers, and into the waiting luxury car, I was composed.

The car pulled out ever so smoothly into traffic, and without meaning to I lifted one gloved hand and waved to the roomers. They waved back—*enthusiastically* would be the word. The car sailed down the broad streets and amid the majestic structures and twinkling lights, and I felt like I was in a dream, a wild, sparkling, colorful, heady dream. There was not a single star in the sky—it seemed as if the whirling buildings, shop signs, and lampposts had reached up with magnets, snatched all the stars from the heavens, and put them along the streets, shining them directly at me, as if the heavens had opened and spilled their baubles of happiness all over New York City and staining me with it.

Then the car lurched a few times and came to a stop. Other motorcars settled in the same manner around us.

"Hot damn! One of dose geezer gasbag is having a cabbage-raising event over on dis side of town tonight," the driver explained. We waited. I fussed with my hair. I removed my gloves. I put them back on. We waited. We crawled. The driver hit the side of the car with his free arm and yelled, "C'mon! Get a wiggle on!" I wound the window down, hoping that swallowing gulps of fresh air would keep the bile down that always threatened to rise when I was late—even when late for school.

"Will we be late?" I eventually asked the driver.

"We ain't gonna be on time," he replied.

I wanted to ask how late but decided against it.

"About fifteen, twenty minutes late," he volunteered. Then he pulled off onto a side street, made several left turns, and hurtled and twisted onto other streets until finally the car pulled up to the curb of the club behind a limousine.

The marquee read, "An Evening with Dove Diamond." And there really was a red carpet running from the sidewalk to the entrance.

I thanked the driver.

"Ahgk!" he exclaimed. "It was a cinch!"

The door of the luxury car in front of us opened, and a man exited. I watched as a woman sidled out behind him, carelessly flung a fur stole over her bare shoulders, picked up the front of her gown slightly with one gloved hand, expertly swung the heavy fabric behind her, and then swiveled up the red carpet and into the entrance.

I copied the same exit and entrance.

I gave my name at the window as Dove had instructed, and an usher led the way. An act had just finished before we entered, and the applause was dying down. I kept up with him all the way between tables to one front and center of the stage. He removed the "Reserved" card and pulled out my chair. A small vase of calla lilies graced the center of the table. A murmur went up among the surrounding patrons, and it was then that I realized that a spotlight had been trained on me.

I leaned forward and smelled the calla lilies. Oh, divine! I took another whiff. Calla lilies became my favorite flower.

A man at a table of a rowdy group behind me gave a waiter his order above the chatter. "Bourbon," he said to the waiter; "no glass, no ice." He was so pleased with himself for slurring his words that he guffawed and slapped one of his friends sitting next to him.

A few seconds later, another waiter came to my table. He bent from the waist and politely asked me what I wanted to drink.

"Bourbon; no glass, no ice, sir" was my reply to the question that I had never heard before, never been asked before, or even considered before. This caused the waiter to hastily straighten his back to a ramrod-like position. He quickly composed himself, but I had already seen the shocked expression on his face.

"Moo juice?" I asked, and his expression changed from shock to something that I did not recognize.

Minutes later, he placed a white, frothy drink with a cherry on top in front of me.

"Here's your white cow, ma'am," he said.

I sucked the thick concoction through the straw. It was sweet and milky, and I liked it.

From offstage a voice introduced the act: "Ladies and gentlemen…" That was all I heard, because I heard the sound of drums and realized it was my heart beating in my throat.

Then a spotlight hit the darkened stage and landed on Dove. I drew in a quick breath as one would if hit by a thunderbolt. There was no curve-hugging, steel-blue, floor-length gown weighted down with eight hundred beads from top to bottom, no neckline plunging to the waist in the back, no dyed-to-match steel-blue shoes, no long black gloves that gave way above the elbows, no low, sleek chignon, and no diamond earrings glistening at her ears.

Instead, there was a tuxedo suit with a gray pin-striped vest, a bow tie, cuff links, and a white carnation in the lapel. Her blond hair was trimmed low, with a part on the left, and brushed back from her face. On her feet were highly polished oxfords.

There was a piano and a piano player. He played, and she began to sing. It was a ballad, slow and low. Then, out of the darkest end of the stage, a wall of voices merged with hers in the chorus. A band from out of nowhere joined in. Spotlights lit up the stage near the ceiling behind her, revealing just the outline of a choir of African American singers in church robes. The tune was that of Nanna's favorite church chorus; the lyrics were different, though. It gave me chills. It was thrilling. At the end the applause was thunderous. She bowed. She smiled, and she smiled.

"That was quite an unusual way to begin my show," she said breathlessly into the microphone, "but a special friend of mine is here tonight, and that song was inspired by her grandmother." Then she lifted a hand and shaded her eyes from the spotlight and looked out into the audience. The spotlight followed her gaze. My heart began to race. It was not so much the racing heart of someone scared or frightened but perhaps the racing heart of someone being born, being pulled into a new world.

At intermission, when the lights went up, a man wearing an eyepatch and a tuxedo took my elbow and led me backstage to Dove's dressing room. She was sitting at the dressing table. A few visitors lingered in the background.

"You won't get anything out of me, Sebastian," Dove was saying to one.

"That's what Samson said the night before he woke with his hair trimmed," Sebastian replied. The visitors laughed happily.

"Mina, my friend!" she greeted me, jumping up out of her chair, grabbing both my hands and holding them tightly in hers, drawing me slightly toward her, and bending slightly to kiss both my cheeks. Her cologne was light, but it still invaded my senses.

"You were late," she said with one eyebrow raised, pulling me forward as she moved backward to sit back in her chair. "I thought that you had gone back to Naggo Head."

I couldn't breathe. But I had to say something, and fast, so I took a deep breath.

"Hot damn!" I began. "A geezer gasbag is having a cabbage-raising event over on that side of town, and the driver couldn't get a wiggle on, and…" I ran out of air and couldn't finish. I felt lightheaded.

Dove laughed. She rose from the chair again, bent forward, and whispered in my ear. "Did Naomi show you her powder-puff trick?"

With that remark the knot that was tying my insides up released, and in the outflow came laughter. I threw back my head, and the laughter rippled out in peals and chimes. Dove joined me. The others joined us.

I listened to talk of things I cannot remember. I heard laughter, and I laughed along beside it. Then Dove removed the white carnation from her lapel and put it behind my ear.

"I told you that you would be gorgeous one day, Mina," she said as I was escorted out of the room. I got back to my table just as the lights dimmed.

As I sat there that night amid the celebration of music and voice, the applause, and the jabs of delight and jolts of pleasure, I centered myself—because isn't there more gravitational pull at the edges of a spinning carousel? What was all this? Was all this for me? Who was this girl? What was this glory, and who was this glorified one?

And when the lights went up at the end of the show, they spilled shadows around the room. Mingling along the edges of the glitz and the glamour, diamonds and pearls, champagne and tuxedos, I saw a shadow of the girl with the unbuttoned lips that I used to be, another of the girl I had almost become in the dusty-pink dress with pale-yellow flowers, and one of the woman I was to become. And I wasn't afraid. Nanna would have been glad to know that I wasn't afraid of my shadows. I realized then that I couldn't run from my shadow, but I could dance with it. And dance I did.

Chapter 30

Twenty-two years after I sailed away from my island home to New York, I went back. I had always known that I would go back home someday, that I would *have* to go back; it just took longer than I thought it would. But throughout all those twenty-two years, not a single day went by that I did not think of Nanna. This was due mostly to the fact that I associated most of the events and situations that had happened in my life with the brilliant island proverbs and sayings that Nanna had repeated daily.

Dove and I had been living in Paris, France, for the previous nineteen years. After my four-year college degree, which Dove had insisted on, and which I finished in three years, we moved to France.

The day we arrived in Paris, it had been raining, and it was said that Paris smelled its sweetest when it rained. Again, I had been aware of a new sensation when my feet had hit new concrete. We moved around a lot at first, mostly because boozing and drunken brawls were not among our prioritized pleasures. This was at the height of a time when the ability to fit in was considered a success. We visited the salons on the Rue de Fleurus and Rue Jacob, where Dove prodded me to come out of my shell and to express myself. I began to write, and with my published novels came the glamour and the glory. And with the island proverb "Fire deh a mus-mus tail, him tink ah cool breeze" always in mind, I kept a level head and an opened eye for a disaster around the bend. But none ever came.

We began traveling to the best places and mingling among the elites: James Baldwin on the Left Bank; Gertrude Stein and Alice B. Toklas; William Burroughs before he was implicated in the possible importation of narcotics into France; the gorgeous Josephine Baker just after she had returned from Cuba for a five-week residency at the American Theater, having been denied lodging at the prestigious Hotel Nacional due to the color of her skin; Maya Angelou performing in *Porgy and Bess* in Paris. I would be present in a theater in Morocco when Maya Angelou brought the entire Moroccan audience shouting and applauding to their feet after she sang a spiritual song.

Our family of two had grown to a family of three after we secretly adopted a two-year-old baby girl and named her Kaya. That was three years ago. We had spoken fluent French when in public and English and French when at home. Dove and I had been inseparable. If this were a love story, I would tell you about our love, but all I will say is that our love for each other was steadfast and enduring. We had turned toward each other the way flowers turned toward the sun. It is said that the sunflower, forever yearning for the light, turned its face toward the east in the dark so it would be ready to catch the first rays the moment morning broke. No, this is not a love story. It is a story about an island in the sun, its people coming of autumnal age, and the sophistries of summer days. It is a story of regrets and unforgivers and redemption. No, and no again, this is not a love story.

Dove and I were one, even though we had different personalities. I liked the modern fashion of miniskirts, shifts, boots, and hot pants, and I aimed for the Bardot and Jane Fonda look; Dove never changed from her short haircut and her linen or broadcloth Nehru-collar jackets and pants for daytime and brocade or silk shantung Nehru-collar jackets and pants for nighttime. We were never happier. I was living a life that I sometimes found unbelievable.

The year that we decided to take a vacation back home, Ronald Reagan, the movie actor, was inaugurated as the new governor of California. The Doors' "Light My Fire" seemed to play nonstop on our record player. The Green Bay Packers defeated the Kansas City Chiefs 35–10 in the first AFL-NFL World Championship game at the Los Angeles Memorial Coliseum.

Clint Eastwood starred in the newly released *A Fistful of Dollars*, and Dove and I found ourselves constantly in intense debate over who was the most handsome man on the planet, Clint Eastwood or Alain Delon. The launching of the first French nuclear submarine, *Le Redoutable*, made the television news.

Elvis Presley and Priscilla Beaulieu got married in Las Vegas, and that was where the idea of going home on vacation took root. Dove's idea of home was New York, and mine was the little island in the sun. In the end, we decided that all three of us would travel to New York, and then Kaya and I, after an overnight stay, would travel on to my island. Dove would join us a week later.

Kaya and I disembarked at the only airport on the island in Saint Ann's Town, and the first moment the sparkling rhythmic patois of my people hit my ear, it vibrated and reverberated sweetly in my head. It was a Thursday.

The distance from Town to the western end of the island by hired car was still a three-hour drive, so I hired a boat instead. It was an hour's travel by boat. Kaya slept all the way. I watched the boat parting the cool, turquoise Caribbean waters. The closer the boat got to the Blue Bay harbor, the faster my heartbeat raced, alternating between apprehension and delight. It was early evening when we docked, and delight became pictorial.

What used to be just a beach of sea, sand, sun, and mosquitoes was now a gloriously developing seaside resort. Streetlights lined the smoothly paved roads that ran along the coastline of the blue and turquoise Caribbean water. Suntanned tourists dressed in swimsuits and shorts and with towels in hand trailed across the road from the beach toward the cottages. Some hovered on the sidewalks among the stalls of straw baskets, straw hats, straw handheld fans, and decorated seashells. Groups of schoolgirls in colorful uniforms and hair ribbons and boys in khakis and neckties frolicked at bus stops.

Pushcart vendors hawked their roasted corn and peanuts, and through the open car windows came the sounds of the sea breeze thrashing though the palm trees' branches, the waves crashing on the sand, and the familiar "Roas' kaahn, lady? Buy yu peeeeanuuut!"

I removed my sunglasses and breathed in the native air. I breathed in my culture, my past, my heritage.

When the taxi finally pulled up at the cottages about fifteen minutes outside downtown Blue Bay, the dying sun was blazing vivid red in the sea.

Under a cottonwood tree just below the main entrance, a small group of locals had gathered with a mento band. They scraped a metal grater with a fork, beat drums, slapped banjo, and sang:

Dis langtime gal mi never see yu,
Come mek mi hole yu han'
Dis langtime gal mi never see yu,
Come mek mi hole yu han'
Mek we wheel an' tun
Till we tumble dung
Mek mi hole yu han', gal…

"Mama, Mama!" Kaya cried out to me, her teeth chattering with excitement. "*Ils chantent votre chanson!* They're singing your song, Mama!" She had recognized the folk song that I would sing and dance to at home.

I took her hands in mine, and under the cottonwood tree, with the sun setting on the horizon, my daughter and I twirled and wheeled and giggled until our perspiration ran like rivulets down our faces.

Even the dysfunctional phone lines that kept us from making an overseas phone call to Dove later that night did little to quell the excitement of our first night on the island.

After Kaya and I had feasted on roasted breadfruit, johnny-cakes, ackee, salted codfish, and cocoa tea the next morning, we made appointments to have our hair braided later that evening, and then we ran down to the beach for our anxiously awaited first dip in the cool water. The telephone lines were still not yet back in service, so I could not call Dove.

We had just gotten back from having our hair braided when a messenger told us that we had a visitor in the main lobby. Who could it be if not Dove, the missing member of our family? With our heartbeats in chaos, Kaya and I rushed over to the main cottage, the beads in our braided hair clinking happily as we ran.

The man stood in a darkened area of the lobby, with his hands shoved deep into his pockets, his back to the door. He turned at the sound of the running footsteps, snatched the old-fashioned newsboy-type hat from his head, and proceeded to wring it tightly in his fists. I stopped and stood rooted to the floor at the entrance of the lobby. The sluggish ceiling fan suddenly developed a thumping sound in its rotation. Or maybe it was my heartbeat thumping.

"Barabbas!" I shrieked at last. I let go of Kaya's hand and catapulted across the room. And I tripped.

"Miss Cherrimina!" he cried, dropping his hat to catch me as I tripped and pitched forward into him. He steadied me on my feet, and we both doubled over with hearty, healthy laughter. Unable to take his eyes off me, he searched blindly for his cap on the floor. His hair was still cropped low, only now the sides had a sprinkling of gray. His khaki pants and navy-blue shirt were well worn and were still about a size too small but clean and nicely creased.

"How did you know I was here?" I gasped when I was able speak.

"Miss Cherimina, mi have fi come see yu wid mi own eye."

We laughed heartily and in unison.

I stunned him when I introduced him to Kaya. He bent, took her tiny hand in his, and pumped it reverently. And before we could finish the walk to a bench under a coconut tree, he was Kaya's new best friend.

"How did you know I was here?" I quizzed him again.

The boat that I had hired from Town belonged to Squid, he explained, but was operated by one of his employees. Squid had noticed my unusual name on the receipts and remembered he had heard Barabbas talk a few times about Nanna and Cherrimina from Naggo Head, so he had sent word to Barabbas, who had then found the driver of the taxi that had taken Kaya and I to the cottages.

"Everybahdy in Blue Bay know mi," he boasted.

He lived on Darling Street, a side street off Saint George Street, not far from the seaside market. He no longer worked in the fields; he now repaired bicycles in his backyard. He had been going on the farm work program every year since it had begun, and it had helped to keep him out of the field, but somehow his big dreams were always just out of reach, though he had come close many times. He didn't even see them as dreams, he confided in me; he saw them as possibilities. He had gone back to night school for a time but stopped when he had had to work nights to provide for his family: his wife, Sweetie, who was a very nice lady from Pidgin Cove, and his three children—two boys and a girl. His family was the best thing that had happened to him. All along he had known that something vital, something dynamic, was missing from his life, and he had thought it was money. But it was not money; it was family. He was nothing without his family; they depended on him, and he protected them. He was a good father and husband because he was all they had. No child deserved to be left alone in this cold world, he told me.

He said his next big plan was to manage, if not own, a small beachfront resort. The beaches around Blue Bay were the fastest developing and the most popular places on the island. There was a two-acre beachfront property near the mouth of the Sweet River and away from the hustle and bustle about four miles up from the cottage in which I was staying. The beach was a little raggedy, and there were sediments and mangroves at the river mouth, but the water was warm, crystal clear, and shallow for a long way out.

Then a worker cutting the hibiscus hedges two cottages over stopped to pull his handkerchief from his back pocket and wipe the perspiration from his face. He looked over at us and called out, "Oye! Alpha!"

"Who's Alpha?" I asked, looking around.

"Oye, Ma'as Jahnny!" Barabbas yelled, and waved his hat at him.

"Everyt'ing ahright?" Ma'as Jahnny asked.

"Everyt'ing OK," Barabbas assured him. "No problem, man."

"He called you Alpha?" I asked him.

"Yes, Miss Cherrimina. Everybahdy in Blue Bay call mi Alpha. Alphanso is mi real name," he said without batting an eye, and continued telling me his plan as he paced back and forth like a professor in a lecture hall.

He told me that he would start with ten cottages with verandas, set not more than one hundred feet in from the beach. Thatched roofs. Colorful beach chairs. Flourishing green gardens. Coconut trees. The guests could swim, snorkel, hunt sea glass, watch the sunset, and catch crabs under the mangroves.

Bike riding and canoeing. And for those who were more adventurous, they could hike up the Sweet River bank, through hanging vines and lush forest, to jump off the rocks at the Blue Batty Hole. He and his buddies often went diving from the eighty-foot-high banks. Also, he continued, he and his buddies had found a very interesting cave not far from the river mouth along the coastline. It could be developed into a tourist attraction.

It was midafternoon when he sped off grinning and waving from his sputtering, faded, red-and-cream Honda motorbike, promising that he would come back the next evening to take me up to Naggo Head.

Later that night Dove and I spoke for the first time since I arrived on the island. We spoke for about five minutes before she hesitatingly made a confession.

"Mina," she said, "I can't come there."

"What do you mean?" I asked.

"I mean I can't come back to the island. Too many bad memories. I thought I could do it, but I can't."

I was shocked speechless.

"But…"

"I just can't do it, Mina."

"But there's nothing here to be afraid of now," I protested.

"I know that, Mina. It's the nightmarish memory of what happened there."

"I was hoping that we could spend some time together here." My voice sounded small in my ears, and with that smallness my island accent had returned. I knew that would be a catalyst for her guilt and resentment.

"For God's sake, Mina, I killed a man there! Your island is not a good place for me. It's bad luck for me."

Following a long silence, and with disappointment hidden carefully beneath my tongue, I changed the subject. "Barabbas stopped by to see me today," I said. "He heard I'm on the island."

I told her all that Barabbas and I had spoken about, and she was genuinely glad that he had a family and was living a regular life. She also thought that his idea of a resort was a brilliant one. We hung up, promising to talk again the next day.

I dreaded telling Kaya that Dove would not be joining us on the island. I explained as I tucked her into bed that night. As a five-year-old in an exciting place, she would soon move on to something new, I knew, and this time there was the excitement of wading at the edge of the cool, turquoise ocean. She chattered excessively about the baby goat she had seen in the bushes behind one of the cottages, oblivious of how her brown skin had gotten much darker in such a short time. Her skin was now a gorgeous shade of golden bronze.

Dove and I spoke sooner than I had expected. She called the next morning early. The producers of one the biggest shows on Broadway wanted her to guest star in a show.

"Mina, I know this is sudden, but it's only for a week. I can't turn it down," she gushed. "It's such a great opportunity! Wish me luck!" But she hung up the receiver before I could reply.

I did not get to wish her luck, nor to tell her that I missed her. Neither did Kaya get to say hello to her. I wanted to ask her who would help her memorize her lines. I did not get to tell that I loved her very much. I wanted to hear more about the role she was to play, to hear about the showbiz people she had met, to ask if she was sticking to her diet—her stomach had gotten delicate over the years, and it was best for her to eat bland food.

Chapter 31

They told me that the beach was almost empty when Kaya's baby-sitter ran frantically down the footpath toward it. They said it happened about forty-five minutes after I had ridden off on the back of Barabbas's motorbike, waving goodbye to a giggling, swimsuit-clad Kaya.

Because of the improved roadway, the four-mile drive up to Naggo Head on the back of Barabbas's motorbike went surprisingly faster than it had been when I used to ride the transport to and from Blue Bay. Cross Road was just setting up for the Saturday evening gathering. Naggo Head Road was still not paved, but the gravel and pebbles were more embedded into the road, making it a much smoother ride. The pink house on Pill Hill still stood strong. It had a new occupant, Barabbas said—an overseer at the sugarcane factory. The houses looked smaller, and the road looked so much narrower than I had remembered all these years, especially at the Congo Bridge. An overgrowth of vegetation, twisted vines, and foliage reigned triumphantly over Mill Yard, causing it to be completely invisible from the street. The grocery shop was now operated by the Fergusons' grandniece and her husband, and it looked smaller in size and stock. Now a standpipe and cistern built near the left side of the shop provided water to the public. Several young adults stood in queue with buckets and pails. I could still hear Sweet River crashing along beyond the bushes behind the shop.

Barabbas had just greeted those in the shop, picked up an elderly woman whom I did not recognize, swung her around, and steadied her on her feet as her body was wracked with girlish giggles when he cocked his head to one side and listened intently. A motorbike was grinding up Naggo Head Road at an unusually high speed. Barabbas stiffened and walked out of the shop toward the road. Others, on full alert, followed him.

"Dat noh soun' like ah Monkey Spanner?" Son Son asked.

"Yes, ah him dat, Son Son," someone else replied.

Monkey Spanner and his motorbike finally slammed to a stop in a cloud of dust in front of the shop.

"Alpha," he panted as though he had just sprinted up Naggo Head Road, "come quick wit' de fahreign lady. Dey can't fin' her likkle gurl. Dey t'ink she drownded!"

The two motorbikes sped down Naggo Head Road, kicking up dust and rocks.

⅄

By the time the swollen sun had set large and purple into the Caribbean Sea that evening, Kaya was no longer in this world.

The doctors said she had had a congenital heart disease. No, I heard myself replying to their question, I didn't know that she had suffered from that. She was adopted. I don't know her parents. She had never been diagnosed.

The four doctors standing around her bed were of different ages, heights, and coloring, yet they all seemed to have the same voice and the same look in their eyes. It was an expectant look, a look of hope. They were hoping to hear something from me that would shed light on the sudden heart attack of a seemingly healthy five-year-old girl. But I had nothing to tell them. I knew nothing about Kaya's background, history, or roots.

⅄

After I returned to the cottage later that night, I called Dove's hotel and left a message with the front desk.

"Please tell her to call me as soon as she gets this message," I told the operator. "It's urgent."

When I did not receive a call the next day, I left another message: "Please tell her that I'm calling about Kaya," I said.

When the return call finally came, it was swift, loud, and vicious.

"There's something strange and deadly about your island," Dove spat within a split second after I had told her why Kaya had passed.

I found out then that blame can be lightweight and can be very satisfying to those who need to throw it, and they usually throw it well.

The words came out of the earpiece in spikes and jerks and lodged themselves into my dull, mummified brain as she continued. The worst thing was, deep inside, I had a feeling that she could be right.

"I knew it. I knew something bad would happen there. Your island with its eternal sunshine, its smiling faces, its sea, sand, and sun. Well, what about the nights, the dark nights, Mina?

Your island is just natural lighting—that's all it is. Your island is just a sophistry of summer days."

"But…" I tried to speak, but my tongue felt like lead.

"I almost lost my life there, Mina, and now it took Kaya," she sobbed into the receiver.

"But…you almost lost your life…in…America too," I finally said.

"Yes! But I didn't have to kill anyone in America! You have no idea what it's like to live with that. I should not be saying these things over the phone…Bring her home, Mina. Bring Kaya home to me. I don't want her to stay another night in that evil place…your evil island!"

The receiver clicked on a heartrending sob.

I made two decisions, or oaths, that night. The first was to bury Kaya next to Nanna on the bank of the Sweet River. The second was to never speak to Dove again until she apologized for calling my island evil.

On the night of Kaya's funeral, I made a third decision: to build a dream vacation spot in Blue Bay. I had learned over the years that I coped best with crises when I planned projects, when I coaxed a dream into reality. In fact, it wasn't even a dream; it was a possibility.

Alpha looked in on me later that night. The timid tapping on my door led me to believe it was a female at my door. He read the surprised look on my face incorrectly, and he stuttered an apology. I managed to convince him that I was truly glad to see him.

We sat in silence on the steps of the small veranda in the moonlight, with the waves crashing on the beach beyond us. For once, Alpha seemed lost for words.

"I think I'm being punished," I eventually said to him, looking down on the sliver of moonbeam that had tiptoed through the palm tree fronds to sit on my hands clasped in my lap. The hands did not look familiar; they looked deeply veined and gnarled in the moonlight. Alpha reached out and placed an even more gnarled hand on top of those hands, and my fingers relaxed.

"Nanna would be ashamed of me, of my lifestyle," I said to him.

"No, Cherrimina," he cried. "Nanna would want yu to be yuself an' be happy."

"How do you know that?" I wondered.

He said that it had been a Saturday morning after breakfast. My mother was already polishing the veranda floor, the palm of her right hand bright red from the logwood dye. He was helping Nanna haul her mattress from her bedroom to hang it over the veranda rail in the sun. I was holding a piece of beeswax over a burning piece of firewood and wiping it on the coconut-husk floor brush when the wax was soft enough. Then suddenly the piece of wax had flown up in the air and fallen on the firewood, causing sparks to shoot everywhere, and my mother had yelled, "Button yu lip, chile!"

I confessed all my faults and sins to Alpha that night. This is not something I would recommend anyone do because of the head-gripped-in-a-vice, embarrassed feeling I got the next day that I saw him. My story was not sweet and harmonious like those told to a rosy-cheeked family dressed in pajamas around a fireplace and holding mugs of hot cocoa.

CHAPTER 32

It was in the second year after Kaya's funeral that I finally got the Blue Bay dream vacation project finished. Alpha was there beside me all the way. There were days that began before sunrise and ended after sunset. There were days when I hoped that he would not say anything nice to me because I might burst into tears. Days when I could not find a prayer in the Bible. Days when I was so lonely that even death seemed like a friend. Days when I envisioned my bank account sitting under a duck. Days when I believed that my people had nothing but senses and only two of them. Days when I got knee-walking drunk on grief because I held onto the belief that my grief was mine only and no one should have it. Days when I spoke not a word because I believed that heartache had its own language. Days when I looked into Alpha's eyes like someone who is still living but not alive. Days when it was exhilarating to say the words *fuck you* the way other people say *bingo*.

And there was the day when I tried to slap Alpha's face because my subconscious mind made mistakes and tried to convince me that I was a mink coat, not a bungalow apron. I can't remember what started the disagreement, but isn't it frustrating how fast an insignificant situation can escalate into the most regrettable of your life? He grabbed my wrist just before it made contact, twisted it away from his face, and said with clenched teeth, "Don't yu *ever* disrespec' mi like dis again!" He sped off in a cloud of dust on his Honda motorbike, and I quickly followed in a taxi to beat and scratch at his front door on Darling Street and to beg forgiveness.

Then there were the nights. Nights when I had so much stored-up energy that I would tramp through the bushes to climb up to the Blue Batty Hole and dive naked and nonstop for what seemed like hours. Alpha always managed to show up before dawn to wrap me in a towel or a robe, and with his arms around my shoulders, he would steer me home through the bushes.

The overproof white rum chased with cow's milk that I began sipping at bedtime soon cured my nocturnal diving. The warm and gentle embrace that the first mouthful placed at the back of my neck would spread slowly out toward the base of my ears and massage them, leaving my neck and spine loose and lubricated, perhaps in the same way Ma'as Charlie's fresh sugarcane juice slackened my rigid spine. The sensation was like a well-lubricated and highly polished luxurious automobile rolling and purring along some quiet lanes in an affluent neighborhood on a Sunday morning drive. I told myself that it was OK to have a crutch now since I had never needed one before. After all, everyone needed a crutch at one point or another in his or her lifetime. I began believing that God created alcohol to prevent women from ruling the world. Its strong spirit fortified the guts, lowered boundaries, and gave one delusions of grandeur.

In a bid to live naturally among the clinging, snug-fitting nature on the island, I cut my nails short and stopped painting them. To make matters worse, I had taken to wearing pants, button-down shirts, and boots. This began only for ease and comfort during the construction of the vacation spot. The straw hat was a gift from Alpha after I had mentioned once that my freckles were reappearing one by one due to the sun.

"To keep de sun off yu face," he had said to me. "Put it on!" I had put the hat on, and the image I had seen in the mirror had been frightfully reminiscent of Pootus.

I heard whispers of "de madwoman" and "de devil ah ride har" among the workers, beachcombers, and acquaintances. And with no one to whom I could say "Please help me," I truly believed that I was headed for hell. So several times I turned to God and spent those Saturday nights anxiously awaiting Sunday mornings, when I could weep and pray at the altar of the Baptist church on the riverbank as I begged forgiveness for my sins and to secure a place in the heaven I had been taught to chase.

For the first time, Miss Priyanka's advice had failed me. "One's greatest asset is a calm mind," she had said that day on our way to Saint Ann's Town in a taxi. "Learn to meditate; learn how to keep your mind from jumping and from making comparisons," she had said; "learn what will keep your mind calm and satisfied, and keep feeding it that." Almost daily, I resisted the temptation of believing that Dove was right after all, that my island was evil. I fought against blaming my oddness on the island, on the sun—because how odd was it that I was not considered odd in France? Gradually and painfully, like a carbuncle on the buttocks, this thought had developed and festered in my psyche. Unknowingly, I had been in conflict with myself. Then, like all carbuncles, the pustulant drainage began, and grief, malevolence, and melancholia miraculously and slowly turned to memory.

This was years ago, you understand? Years when Alpha worked tirelessly while I lagged, was enthused when I was low in spirit and positive when I had days' long negativity and self-doubt. I even had days when I could consider nothing except what I would reply if asked why I had no man in my life—I would reply, with a mysterious smile dancing on my lips, "How could I have settled for less when I grew up among men like Alpha?"

By that time, I told the time of day by the crowing of roosters, the length of shadows, and by the sun extinguishing itself in the sea. Alpha and I had a bond that went beyond constantly quoting Nanna. She was wisdom without a face, and he was the face of wisdom. By then, he had endowed me with the name Sister.

Then a day came that, while I was teaching him the French language (he insisted I teach him, since the majority of our clients were from France), I looked at him struggling with pronouncing *une* and noticed the new gray hair at his temples and new crow's-feet at the corners of his eyes, and I realized that he, too, might have noticed the passing years leaving footprints on my face. It was then that I was once again reminded that I could not afford to lose him. He had worked hard most of his life while waiting for his turn in the spotlight, while waiting for his ship to come in. His life was mostly made up of long, hard days and short but lucid dreams. He had looked out for me. He deserved a turn in the spotlight. I became sure that it was time for me to start taking care of him. I made him a legal partner in the business.

He wept as we walked out of the attorney's office into the boiling midday sun. Tears ran down his face, and he tried hard to pretend that he was wiping perspiration, not tears, with his ever-present crumpled handkerchief. He wept even harder and wiped even more perspiration when I revealed our new company car, with our logo emblazoned on the front doors. His hand shook when he reached for the keys that I held out to him. I clung to his shaking body, and his cap fell off. He righted the cap and promptly began telling me how he thought that the huge rock that jutted out into and overlooked the sea at the bottom of Blue Bay would be the perfect place on which to build a classy nightclub and casino.

"De touris' dem ask about dat kind ah entahtainment *all* de time, Sistah!" He declared, grinning from ear to ear. The Castle Rock Casino would be a good name, he thought.

And I have never loved him more preciously than I did at that moment. I loved him not just for the man he had become but for the boy I had known. The boy who had carried me slung over his shoulder to safety from Nanna's burning house; the boy who had helped Dove escape from the island to Cuba on a fishing boat. He was the only person who had known me as a girl in a dusty-rose dress with tiny yellow flowers and who had almost taken the wrong path in life—the only one to whom I could talk about Nanna before the fire and about Nanna after the fire. The only one who knew about my father.

In those two years, I had made two three-day trips to France to settle publishing business and to consult with architects, but neither of these trips included visits to Dove. I had made no attempt to see her. For over two years, I had stuck with my oath: I would only speak with her if she apologized for calling my island evil.

Then one night she walked in out of the moonlight.

I had just looked in on the night front-desk clerk to make sure that all was well. The foyer lights were dimmed; everyone was accounted for except for Monsieur Roux, who liked to stay out all night at a dance hall in Blue Bay. Many nights Alpha would take it upon himself to go looking for him in the dance halls and drive him home drunk and minus his wallet and his shirt. Treasure, the desk clerk, was practicing crocheting. The week before she had been sketching Snow White. I said good night to her and turned to walk out the back door toward my cabin.

"Mina?" a cool voice from the darkened foyer said, like someone asking a question to which she already knew the answer. The feelings I had were so unexpected, so strange, that I could not speak; neither could I look directly at this shadow. I hung my head instead, with my heart beating in my throat. I knew the voice but could not see her face clearly, and something about that made me think that it was OK to continue walking out the back door toward the beachfront. I carried joyless and wilting feelings gingerly and uneasily slung over my shoulders, because from my experience, the nighttime was for leaving, not arriving. She followed me, as if she knew fully and well that I was not simply running away. I wanted to be an adult, be respectful, and turn and face her, but I continued walking slowly and somehow steadily away from the rum bar and the entertainment on the beach. We left the footpath and crossed the street toward the isolated area overgrown with seagrape trees.

"How are you, Mina?" this faceless voice behind me asked after the squeals of the limbo-dancing tourists and the music from the calypso band had faded slightly behind us. There was a new strain in her voice, and I turned to see that she had stooped down to remove her shoes. She straightened up, saw me watching her, sank her toes farther in the sand, and smiled.

Suddenly, I realized that the oath that I had taken and the malice that I thought I had purged over the years were still buried deep inside me. They reared up, and I began to think that a smile from her so soon without uttering a word of an apology was inappropriate, so while trying to keep the bitterness out of my voice, I said, "You called my island evil."

Those were the first words I had spoken to her since the night after Kaya left this world. I had waited over two years to say those words to her, and through the veil of moonlight between us, I watched her face keenly to make sure that the cut I intended to make was deep enough. Her face remained unchanged, but she wrapped her arms at her waist in an attempt to make herself small. Or perhaps it was only to hug herself.

"You took Kaya from me," she replied. "You didn't give me a chance to say goodbye to her."

But unlike others I had known over the years, I was never good at playing God while standing face to face with my opponents, because that would bring about an immediate awareness that the devil had to be nearby—as in Bulla's case, it was well known on the island that the devil always got the preachers' kids by the shirttail. So I wavered in the middle of my malice. She saw my hesitation and continued.

"I'm no longer the old Dove," she said. "For almost a year now, I've been asking myself, what if I were just a girl? How can I be a boy if there was no girl? Perhaps I am just a girl. So I grew my hair and bought new clothes. Now, I'm just a girl on an island, standing in the moonlight in front of an island girl, telling her I'm sorry. I spoke unkindly about your homeland, and I was very wrong."

The hair that hung about her face was just below shoulder length and gave her a wraithlike look, just like that look she had had the day that I first saw her lying on the bank of the Sweet River. A slight breeze blew wisps of it across her face, and she lifted a hand and softly and slowly pulled the flirting strands behind her ear.

It was our apologies, of course, but perhaps it was also the wisps of hair, the moonlight, the glossy waves cresting like clumps of silver on the beach, but peace fell over us, at first in sprinkles and then in a shower.

I did not question her ability to change her personality, her nature, multiple times. You will ask yourself why not. The simple answer is because I loved her for whomever she was at any given moment. In fact, I understood this change since I, too, had been through similar changes, although unintentionally.

I will forever remember fondly the rest of that night as an easing of tensions, a peeling away of masks and baring of souls, of looking back fondly and fearlessly, of accusations, and of forgiveness.

I removed my sandals, and we waded out into the water, giggling, splashing, and diving until we crawled out weary and drenched but happy. We sat baptized and healing and unattached from the physical world under a coconut tree, each of us bracing our back on its trunk. We could still hear strains of the calypso band in the distance. We wrote messages in the sand with our fingers. We chatted into the night, and then we sat with sweet, comfortable silence between us, with the waves chanting, the crickets, the breeze in the coconut-tree fronds, and the stars twinkling.

While Dove dozed off lightly and easily, I pondered my life. Besides feeling safe, I felt strong—at least, strong enough to understand and appreciate that despite the turn of events that night, some things would remain constant. When the sun rose tomorrow, eager fishermen would row out on the Caribbean Sea in their canoes and cast their nets hopefully into schools of fish, lobsters, and shrimps. The farmers in water boots balancing with one hand a machete, hoe, and field fork steadily on one shoulder and a lunch pail in the other hand would trample the dew on the vegetation as they made their way deep into the greenery to work the fields. Or they would rock contentedly on top of donkeys taking languid steps with bulging hampers at their sides. Dozens of milk trucks around the island would clang and shudder to a stop at crossroads to collect fresh, frothy milk. Mothers would feed the chickens and goats, purse their lips, and blow on dim coals until they burst into red flames under pots on the fireside. They would fry johnnycakes and pour rich, sweet cocoa tea into tin mugs. Primary school students in colorful uniforms and gay hair ribbons and grasping for dear life their one and only slate and slate pencil would sprint in rowdy groups over rivers and through fields on the way to school. The sugar factory would blast its siren for the morning shift as men with lunch pails dangling from the handlebars of their bicycles furiously pedaled through its flung-open gates.

The yellow sun would heat up quickly, injecting color into the vivid crimson hibiscuses and fragrance in the naseberries on the trees. And women would lift wash pans of dirty laundry from their heads, place them carefully on rocks in the roaring Sweet River where it shallowed and widened near Cross Road, and, with water swirling around their knees, they would loop their skirts between their legs, beat soapy clothes on these rocks, and volley bits of gossip between them while their kids turned over smaller rocks and grabbed at flitting crayfishes. Lean and sun-drenched sugarcane cutters with wiry muscles glistening with sweat would wield glistening, treacherous machetes over their heads and slice through the sweet stalks and hurl them into mounting piles. The tourists in sunglasses, gaily colored tops, and shorts would sip iced drinks, get suntanned on the beach, and shop straw hats, straw fans, and straw baskets at the craft markets. The Caribbean Sea, cool and turquoise, would pound and beat a merry melody at the coastline to show ownership, entitlement. Way up in the mountains, extroverted woodpeckers, enthusiastic parakeets, and yellow-billed parrots would lead an impromptu symphony that would soar across the clear blue skies and under the lush flora in the gullies, where croaking toads and lizards would rehearse a chorus of their own.

Alpha would arrive early at the resort, bound up in crisply starched and sharply creased khakis and limitless energy. He would greet everyone with assured spirit and delight and quickly get things going in order and on time. He would have already heard of Dove's arrival. He would greet me, search my face, and read my mood in a split second. I would look into his eyes and grab onto the strength he had placed there just for me. He would know that I was not greedy and wouldn't take all this strength, only what I needed. And he would understand that soon I wouldn't need to supplement my strength with his. He would understand that the broken wing had healed and could once again sustain flight. And he would rejoice in this.

Yes, I felt strong enough and at home. Yes, it would be a great day in the morning. Yes, I was at home.

O isle of unbounded summers! O green island in the Caribbean Sea! O homeland glorious and free! My strength, my heart, and my loyalty I pledge to you.

O my island in the sun!

AUTHOR BIOGRAPHY

Jenny Lofters's work explores the triumph of the human spirit over the hardships and obstacles of life. Her love of the West Indies and its history, culture, and superstitions informs her writing. Lofters is the author of both short stories and novels, and her work has been awarded an Honorable Mention in the Ernest Hemingway Short Story Contest. Jenny studied fashion design, an industry in which she worked for many years. Born and raised on a Caribbean island, she now lives in New Jersey, where she embraces a holistic lifestyle, including natural food and skin-care products.